COLLECTED STORIES,
VOLUME I

SHASHI DESHPANDE

PENGUIN BOOKS

An imprint of Penguin Random House

PENGUIN BOOKS

USA | Canada | UK | Ireland | Australia
New Zealand | India | South Africa | China | Singapore

Penguin Books is part of the Penguin Random House group of companies
whose addresses can be found at global.penguinrandomhouse.com

Published by Penguin Random House India Pvt. Ltd
4th Floor, Capital Tower 1, MG Road,
Gurugram 122 002, Haryana, India

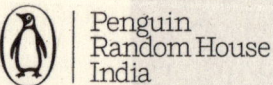

First published by Penguin Books India 2003

12 11 10 9 8 7 6 5

This is a work of fiction. Names, characters, places and incidents are either the
product of the author's imagination or are used fictitiously, and any resemblance to
actual person, living or dead, events or locales is entirely coincidental.

ISBN 9780143029526

For sale in the Indian Subcontinent, UK and the Commonwealth, except Canada

Typeset in Aldine401 BT by InoSoft Systems, Noida

Printed at Manipal Technologies Limited, India

This is a legitimate digitally printed version of the book and therefore might not
have certain extra finishing on the cover.

Contents

Copyright Acknowledgements

These stories have appeared earlier in the *Onlooker*, *Femina*, *J.S.*, *Eve's Weekly*, the *Deccan Herald*, the *Book Review*, the *Illustrated Weekly*, the *Telegraph* and the *Statesman Festival* issues.

A shorter version of 'Independence Day' was read out on BBC World Service during the fiftieth anniversary of India's Independence programmes and later appeared in this form in *Persimmon*.

Some of the stories have also appeared in collections brought out earlier by Writer's Workshop.

Foreword

Shashi Deshpande, in a writing career of thirty-one years, which includes nine novels, four books for children, innumerable short stories and more recently, translations of her illustrious father Shriranga's works into English, has consistently rejected attempts to label and define her works. She has stated an aversion to descriptions and the plethora of titles which inevitably attach themselves to writers and their writing today—essentialist and reductive definitions so integral to academic theories and bookshop shelves. Her works are 'not', she says, 'not Indian, not Indo-English, not woman, not feminist, not third world'. The list goes on—'not Asian writer, Indo-English, Indian writer in English, third world writer, postcolonial writer and so on' ('Of Concerns, Of Anxieties', *Indian Literature: Women's Writing in English, New Voices*, 1996).

Be that as it may, Deshpande makes gender central to her writings. Her works deal not only with ordinary women in ordinary, urban situations but stem from a firm belief that our lives are to a great extent governed by gender. Women, she feels, have not participated in the process of word-making; the stories, myths and legends in our Puranas, epics and *kathas* have been written by men. Moreover, women have been conditioned to a great extent by myth: 'To be as pure as Sita, as loyal as Draupadi, as beautiful as Laxmi, as bountiful a provider as Annapoorna, as dogged in devotion as Savitri, as strong as Durga—these are ultimately the role models we cannot entirely dismiss'('The Indian Woman—Myths, Stereotypes and the Reality', 1977, private papers). Deshpande feels that women never start with a picture of themselves on a clean slate, their self-image honed by the hegemonic influences of myths, movies and current-day soap operas. She sees herself as a writer whose writing comes out of, she says,

> my own intense and long suppressed feelings about what it is to be a woman in our society, it comes out of the experience of the difficulty of playing the different roles enjoined on me by society, it comes out of the knowledge that I am something more and something different from the sum total of these roles. My writing comes out of a consciousness of the conflict between my idea of myself as a human being and the idea that society has of me as a woman ('Of Concerns, Of Anxieties').

Deshpande, however, expresses her unhappiness at the consistent ghettoization of 'women writers', at their marginalization or categorization usually tinged with a note of apology.

> I call myself just 'novelist and short story writer'. Truth is, I am a story-teller. I'm deeply interested in human beings, in the human condition. Through the stories I tell I am probing into this condition. I am asking those questions most of us ask ourselves some time or the other—about life, about death, about our relationships with one another, with society and our moral values ('Where Do We Belong: Regional, National, or International', 2002, unpublished paper).

Deshpande's stories in this collection give a perspective on women in their complex and real relationships. They are about mothers and daughters, grandmothers and wives, women working outside the home, negotiating a balance between tradition and modernity, women analysing or just expressing their insecurities and fears and desires. As Deshpande says about the protagonist of *The Dark Holds No Terrors*, 'What we

want to reach at finally is the telling, the breaking of silence'
(in an interview with Romita Choudhury, *World Literature
Written in English*, 1995).

Some of the stories in this collection depict poignantly the
mother-daughter relationship seen from the perspective of a
mother trying to reach across a barrier to her daughter. 'Why
a Robin', 'It Was Dark' and 'My Beloved Charioteer' are first-
person narratives of a woman's real concern at her inability to
be an ideal mother, the epitome of succour and comfort, and
her difficulty in communication. Deshpande examines the
problematic of the mother-daughter relationship, 'warts and
all', in several of the stories, and while commenting that this
relationship is rarely dealt with in traditional stories and legends,
she feels that her portrayal of the uncompromising relationship,
at times, 'makes some readers uneasy'. She asks, 'Isn't it because
we have this stereotypical image of what a loving mother is
like that we find any variation to be lacking in motherly feelings?
It seems to me we need to get rid of these images to be able to
release ourselves from guilt . . . We had to wait for women to
write to bring out the truth of this relationship' ('The Indian
Woman—Myths, Stereotypes and the Reality').

Corresponding to the mothers' narratives are the daughters'
portrayal of their mothers in 'A Liberated Woman' and 'The
Awakening', and their attempts to contend with the ghosts of
the past and the complexity of their present. Memory and the
counter-pointing of the past and the present are devices
effectively used by Deshpande both in her novels and short
stories. 'Memories are not records: they refuse to stay enclosed
within covers. They choose their time and spring out at you,'
she says in 'Independence Day', a story ironically celebrating
Bharat Mata's victory, even as the horrors of Partition decimate
the country. Deshpande the 'storyteller' uses almost similar
narrative techniques in her short stories and novels despite the
fact, as Lakshmi Holmström says in her introduction to *The
Inner Courtyard; Stories By Indian Women* (1990), that 'the short

story imposes certain restrictions, intensity, concentration, suggestiveness, surprise.'

Deshpande incorporates all these elements in a first-person narration by one of the 'stone women', in 'The Inner Rooms'. Iravati Karve's *Yuganta* inspired Deshpande to retell Amba's story from the Mahabharata, or rather to let Amba tell her own story, to express her anger, her disgust and despair at becoming a pawn in the hands of Bhishma. 'The Stone Women', in fact, is almost emblematic of this collection of short stories, for Deshpande goes beyond and behind the facade—the beautiful sculptures created by men which she saw in the Channakeshava temple in Belur—and the myth of the ideal woman, to explore the inner self of women. 'Yes, women writers are now exploring the myths and stereotypes, a phenomenon which has been partly influenced by the growing strength of feminist thinking. This has made it possible for us to ask a great many questions, questions which had never been asked before' ('The Indian Woman—Myths, Stereotypes and the Reality'). Deshpande states categorically, 'What we are now doing is retelling our own tales' (Ibid). These are not stories of victims, but of thinking women able to analyse their situation, as in 'The Intrusion' or 'The First Lady', while other stories such as 'The Homecoming' and 'Can You Hear Silence?' celebrate the triumph of resilience of the girl child.

Deshpande feels that now 'women writers are saying the kind of things nobody has said until now. They are showing you the world which the men have not known' (In Conversation: Sue Dickman with Indian Women Writers', the *Book Review*, 1995). This was not always so. Though women have traditionally been storytellers, according to Holmström, the short story written by women writers is a phenomenon of the twentieth century. In fact, when Deshpande started writing, she felt this sense of isolation, of writing in a vacuum, since she did not feel a sense of literary kinship with writers or a literary tradition. She speaks of a physical isolation as well. She had no room of her own and wrote, when her husband left for the hospital, either at the dining or kitchen table, in between meals or when her boys were in school. She started writing short stories which were published by *Femina* and *Eve's Weekly* and remembers receiving the princely sum of Rs 75 with which she bought the boys a scooter to play with.

Born in 1938, Deshpande grew up in a house which had a harmonious mixture of languages. Her father taught Sanskrit in a college and wrote in Kannada, but opted to send his daughters to study in an English-medium convent school. Deshpande recalls a childhood reciting poems about 'strange' things like tuffets and muffins and daffodils and daisies and, at home, learning the *Amarkosa* by heart. She read Jane Austen, the Brontes, Dickens, George Eliot and Hardy, but Kalidasa, Bhavabhuti, Shivram Karanth and Masti Venkatesh Iyengar were also as familiar to her as Ibsen and Shaw. There was no conflict when she decided to write—'I write in English because it is the only language I can express myself in'('Of Concerns, Of Anxieties'). Deshpande started writing late in her life, but could never identify with the kind of writing in English that she read. She did not write with a specific reader in mind, nor were her works slanted to an international marketplace. Her writing is not laboured and there is an ease and a lack of self-consciousness because her intent is not to 'present' India or Indians. She writes about people and the reality of their lives. 'What you are really speaking of goes beyond these facts to a complex and large picture that is closer to the truth of human reality than these mere facts are' ('Where Do We Belong: Regional, National, or International').

For all these reasons, Deshpande's stories hold an appeal for every reader. Refreshing in their simplicity, intense and concentrated, yet suggestive of deeper and myriad emotions in the lives of ordinary people, they are imbued with the moral vision of the 'storyteller'.

NEW DELHI, JANUARY 2003

AMRITA BHALLA
DEPARTMENT OF ENGLISH
JESUS AND MARY COLLEGE

Preface

xvi   *Preface*

Quite early on in my writing career, my father, a writer himself, advised me to have a collection of my stories published as soon as I could. 'If you don't do that,' he warned me, 'they will be lost.'

Putting together my stories written over three decades, I now understand what he meant. While many early stories were voluntarily abandoned (for fortunately the critic is born along with the writer) and others lost, even those that appeared in magazines exist either in scraps of typescripts or in the tattered pages of old magazines. Going through these to find the dates and the source has been a harrowing experience. Yet it has been a pleasant trip into nostalgia as well, because each story has its associations, each carries memories of a particular point in my life. Memories of places, too: Belur, Konarak, Goa, Mahabalipuram, a beach near Mumbai and so on. Some stories remain clear and vivid in my mind for other and varied reasons. 'The Intrusion', for example, the first story which made me feel—yes this is it, this is what I want to say, this is how I want to say it. 'My Beloved Charioteer' poured out of me in a satisfactory gush, whereas 'The Stone Women' took me over a decade to write. There is 'A Liberated Woman', dissatisfaction with which drove me into writing a novel, *The Dark Holds No Terrors*, and 'An Antidote to Boredom', which, to my delight, appeared in a special issue of *Eve's Weekly* along with the stories of such stalwarts as Anita Desai, Nayantara Sehgal and Amrita

Pritam. 'The Duel', when I read it after years startled me and I wondered, 'Now, where did this come from?' And 'The Legacy' my first published story—or so I think—which I wrote when a colleague in the *Onlooker*, where I was working, asked me to write a story for their annual. I have no idea why she asked me, I was no writer then, but she did and I wrote it in the next few days. And felt for the first time—yes, I can write, yes, I want to go on writing.

'The Legacy' was written in 1972 and 'Independence Day' in 1997—a quarter century separates these two stories in this collection. Yet both were written to order. It has been a surprise to me to see how many stories there are here which have been written to order; I always thought I was a writer who could not write that way. And yet, apart from 'The Legacy' and 'Independence Day', there is 'The First Lady' written after the editor of *Femina* asked me, 'Can you write me a story for our Independence Day issue? Within a week?' And I did. And 'Waste Lands' and 'The Day Bapu Died' for Puja-special issues. In retrospect, I know that the commissioning was only the nudge I needed to write stories which were already there, stories of people who were waiting inside me. It was like the unseen force that prodded me into beginning writing at the age of nearly thirty, stories pouring out of me for the next decade and a half. A very early story of mine is about two people who meet for a few moments, connect instantly with a miraculous ease and then part. Amateurish and awkwardly sentimental though the story is, it set me on the path I was to follow—exploring people's minds, trying to understand human relationships. Beware of anger, Virginia Woolf warned. Anger distorts. To me the danger is to begin with a theme. To do this is to create flawed writing. Everything begins with people; themes, situations flow out of people, out of who and what they are, out of their relationships. In a short story it is often just one situation. One moment of time brilliantly illuminated, a moment in a relationship put under a microscope. Always a catalytic moment.

One of the curious facts about English writing in India is the paucity of significant short-story writers, specially in recent years. This seems all the more remarkable when we compare it to the vitality of the form in the languages. It was not always like that; when I began writing, short-story writers were many. And for me it was the genre that suited me best. So many people thronging my mind, so many diverse stories they wanted me to tell, ten novels could not have contained them. There was too, something all women know and understand, the time constraint. With two small children and a home to care for, I could never dream of the luxury of having a long stretch of time to work in. And, equally important, there were many avenues of publication available for the short story then. I myself had stories published in *Femina*, *Eve's Weekly*, *Illustrated Weekly*, *Deccan Herald*, *J.S.*, *Mirror* and many others whose names I have forgotten. Over the years, political news and accounts of celebrities have elbowed the short story out of the pages of magazines and the Sunday papers. Which is a pity. Perhaps this accounts for the fewer number of short-story writers in English; I know that this is one of the reasons why I stopped writing stories, except when I was commissioned. This, and also because I found myself wanting to know my characters in a little more detail, to spend a longer period with them, travel with them for a little longer way. And so I moved on to the novel, taking to it with such fervour, that it almost eclipsed the short-story writer in me.

This collection has brought back memories of the pleasure I had in writing short stories, the challenges each one posed. And, to be honest, I hope the collection will remind others as well that I am a short-story writer as well as a novelist.

BANGALORE, JANUARY 2003 SHASHI DESHPANDE

The Legacy

HE HAD BEEN a hefty man with a vigorous voice and commanding presence when he had been stricken down. Now, as he lay in bed, he looked like a watered-down version of what he had been. The white stubble on his face gave him a peculiarly fragile, unearthly look.

'A doctor in bed looks a ridiculous sight, don't you think?' he asked me as I entered the hospital room. He used to fill any room with his personality. This time it was the cold, white room which seemed to be dominating him.

'You've bullied enough patients out of bed,' I bantered. 'Now it's our turn to do that to you.'

He turned his huge bulk in the bed so that he lay on his side. 'Not much that anyone can do for me now,' he said. 'If I were my own patient I'd have said . . . the next one and he's finished.'

The words were bold and the smile was broad, but his eyes were frightened. I could see the dark shadow of the hereafter lurking in them.

I did not stay long. Not more than ten minutes, they had told me. He was still not out of danger. And he was restless. He did not seem to find ease in any position. As I was leaving, he asked, 'How long have we known each other?'

I ruminated, 'Twenty years I think. Yes, that's right. Twenty years.'

'Twenty years!' He seemed surprised. 'You know, these past few days I've been thinking of all these years of mine . . . struggling with sickness, disease, death, stupidity, ignorance, poverty. And I've been asking myself, "What has it all been about?" '

I felt sad for him. He, more than anyone else, should have thought his life a fruitful and useful one.

'You should have had a family,' I said. 'A wife and half a dozen kids would have stopped you from thinking.'

At that he suddenly chuckled . . . a rich, fruity sound. He fished under his pillow. 'That's just what I was going to talk to you about,' he said. 'Where's that . . . ?' Then he brought out a piece of paper with a satisfied grunt and handed it to me. There was a name and address on it . . . nothing more.

'What's this?' I asked.

'My son.' He seemed delighted by my discomfiture.

'I never knew . . . ,' I said.

'I'd almost forgotten it myself . . . till last year.' His eyes held a disconcerting twinkle in them. 'Then I took the trouble of finding out this address.'

'Would you like me to send for him?'

He chuckled again, an odd throaty noise. 'Have you noticed the name?'

I looked at the paper again. Not his name. I was flabbergasted. He had always seemed to be above any human weakness.

'No,' he told me, 'not my illegitimate son. My real son.'

With that cryptic remark he closed his eyes. He looked tired, but there was an enigmatic smile on his lips. He was obviously enjoying the shocks he was giving me.

I got up to leave. As I was tiptoeing out, he suddenly opened his eyes. 'I can't bear living at half-speed,' he said seriously, his face entirely sober now, 'I hope I go soon.'

And he did. It was the day after his death that I received the letter, with his handwriting on it. It gave me an eerie feeling to see it. I had been very shaken by his death. He had been much more than a family doctor; a good friend and an adviser as well. I had had a heavy sense of loss on me since he died. I opened the letter with unsteady fingers.

'You remember what I spoke to you about in the hospital that day,' it began without preamble. 'Here's the real story. I have been writing it these past few days, hiding it from those blasted, officious nurses. Apart from this, there is something else. I would like the boy to have everything of mine. I seem to have collected quite a bit of money, these past years. Can you arrange it? Discreetly, of course. I think I can depend on you for this, because I don't really trust lawyers, as you know.'

The last line made me smile.

'The boy and his mother (if you read the rambling nonsense I'm sending along with this, you will understand) are not too well off, I have heard. The boy is . . . a satisfying coincidence . . . in the medical profession and I'm sure the money will come in handy. I had always thought that I would leave all my money to charities; but with death facing me, I seem to be reverting to type, and the old Hindu in me is clamouring for my own flesh and blood. So do this for me, will you?'

I looked at the rest of it. Two pages of closely written matter in his small hand which was so much at variance with his size. I was surprised at how vividly he seemed to have remembered some of the details. Perhaps, as he lay in bed, facing the thought of no tomorrow, the past, specially this episode, had become more real to him.

He had been young then. Just starting his practice and getting along as well as a youngster possibly could. Sometimes despondent, sometimes optimistic. It was a small place he had settled in . . . the usual district headquarters type of place with a few government officers and teachers forming the crust of society. The rest of it was made up of hide-bound, middle-class, orthodox people who considered paying a doctor a foolish luxury. One day, he hoped, his luck would change. And when he received the note he had thought . . . this is it. He recognized the name on the note . . . the big name in that town, the first family there. Real aristocrats. He had seen the house from outside often, a gracious old house, large and rambling, with a meticulously well-kept garden. And the man, when he met him, impressed him with the strange way he seemed to resemble the house. He was gracious but remote, his razor-sharp features and thin, spare figure expressing total and cold indifference to all the world but his bit of it.

To his disappointment it turned out to be a social visit. 'I don't think you will need that,' the man had said, pointing to his bag with a thin, faint smile which made the young man feel even more ridiculously young. He chafed as he thought of how he had packed it with pleasantly palpitating sensations. The invitation was repeated. There seemed to be no earthly reason for his hobnobbing with a struggling young doctor, but he could feel a gentle probing behind all the social inanities. As though I am on approval, he thought.

The third time, he was invited to dinner. For the first time he met the mistress of the house. She was as pleasantly rounded as her husband was sharp-edged. She seemed curiously shy of the young man and refused to meet his eyes. As her husband began to talk, he understood why. The wall was covered with portraits of his ancestors. They looked down benignly on the fantastic proposal the man was making to him. I wonder they don't turn their faces to the wall in shame, the young man had thought wildly. And he could not believe his ears. No, he said, no. The two looked back in dumb appeal, astonished by his vehement refusal. He suddenly realized that there was in them both the same something that gave them an odd similarity of looks despite the great disparity in features. Was it a kind of innocence? Ignorance of anything but their own little world? But it was her look which had really moved him.

'And, if I refuse?' he had asked the man, recovering his wits at last.

The man had looked down for a moment before replying.

'Then, I'm afraid, I'll have to approach someone else.' He had hesitated. What fantastic nonsense was this, he had thought, and what had he to do with this odd couple who seemed to belong to a different age? He looked at the woman again and thought of that 'someone else'. Something stirred in him which might have been called 'chivalry' in earlier days. And then too, he was young. And high-spirited. The feeling stole over him that this was surely something bizarre. Not ordinary dull life. A kind of adventure!

'But,' I now read on, 'it was not an adventure. It was an idyll. I looked up the meaning of the word the other day. Picturesque scene or episode, they say. And poetic. By God, it was all that. Here I am, past fifty, waiting for the next attack to finish me off. And yet, as I think of those days, I feel young again. I am twenty-six and tasting for the first time the sweetness of a woman. It was as intense and sharp as the taste of a green, sour mango. There was no yesterday, and no tomorrow. There was no one else in the world but us. We were the primeval Adam and Eve in Paradise. There was no talk of love. No futile promises. The few days we spent together were so complete in themselves they stand out like a splash of colour on the grey palette of my life. I have never met anyone who laughed so easily as she did. Days of laughter!'

I shook my head bemused. Did such things really exist? Could such things really happen? For this was what the husband had asked him to do for them . . . father a child for him. They were childless.

'It is my fault, I believe,' the husband had said in his precise way, a look of displeasure flitting over his face. And there was the family name, that house, their family traditions which were to him terribly important. Disproportionately so, the young man had thought, looking at the woman. They had chosen him as he was strong, healthy, personable and fairly intelligent. They had inquired too into his family background. He would have to spend a few days with the woman and then . . . disappear! From the town, from their lives. He was never to inquire about the child, if there was one.

'What do I get out of it?' the doctor had asked, feeling an insane desire to burst out laughing.

The man had shrugged his shoulders, looking surprised. Apparently, he had not thought about it from that point of view at all. Then he had looked at the woman. She had blushed, richly, deeply as she met his eyes fully for the first time. The young man had felt the hot blood creeping over his face too as he looked back. And the husband stared at them impassively, only the twitching of his lips showing his emotions.

'It seems strange to me now that, after the initial shock, I took the whole thing so calmly. I never thought of morality and conventions. Perhaps because the two of them had decided to disregard such things. Or, because of her maybe. She had an odd, endearing innocence about her which made the whole episode entirely natural and even beautiful.'

When they parted, they did so with no regrets. She had only asked him one question with a strange anxiety.

'You will keep your promise?' she had asked.

To stay out of their lives . . . 'Yes,' he had replied.

'I have kept it till now,' I read.

Surprisingly, it was she who had broken it. He had received a letter with a newspaper cutting enclosed in it. About the birth of a boy. That was all.

Somehow, that had rounded off the episode for him and he had relegated it to the background of his life. Then last year he had read of the man's death. That had spurred him on to make some inquiries. By devious channels he had learnt that the widow and son were left badly off financially, and that they had had to sell the house. He had laughed at that. It was for the house that the man had done it all!

I felt it my duty to carry out my friend's wishes. It was done as discreetly as possible. The woman and her son were told that it was a 'distant relation' who had remembered them in his will and that he had preferred to be anonymous. The legacy was thankfully accepted. And my job was done.

But the last time I went to Bombay I had a sudden desire to meet them. I wrote to her explaining that I was the lawyer who had handled their recent legacy, and could I meet her? I got an immediate reply. I was always welcome.

I was disappointed when I met her. It was inevitable. I had read of her from my friend's rapturous narrative, written when he was seeing the past through a hazy roseate glow. She was, frankly, old now. Her talk was frequently punctuated by the words 'my son'. He was not at home. But there was a photograph on the table. I thought I could see in him a faint resemblance to what my friend had once been.

A home like thousands of middle-class homes in Bombay. A woman like thousands of middle-aged women. I could not associate that strange story with such an exotic flavour with her middle-class mediocrity. And who did she think of, I wondered, when she saw her son? Did she remember the man who had fathered him? I felt vaguely dissatisfied on my friend's behalf. On an impulse I decided to tell her who it was that had made them that welcome legacy. I asked her the question as I rose to go. Did she know who it was?

'No,' she said. 'I just could not guess. All that I know is that it was a God-sent boon.'

I told her the truth. It gave me a shock that she did not remember him at first. The name apparently meant nothing to her. Then suddenly, she remembered. She flushed like a young girl and I saw her as she must have been then, at that time. There was a tender, amused smile on her lips as she said, 'Oh, him!' And then, immediately, 'Do you know about it?'

I nodded. He had told me just before he died, I said.

Then she smiled again. 'Oh, but you don't know everything,' she said. 'This is not that child . . . my son, I mean my first son, died in early infancy. This is my second child.'

I don't know what I said or did. I know only one thing. If I wanted to leave with my dignity intact, it was time for me to get up. As I left I imagined a ghostly chuckle following me. How he would have enjoyed the joke against himself!

The First Lady

SHE WAS ALL ready. 'You look very nice,' the servant said, with a kind of respectful admiration, as she moved off towards the bathroom, a pile of crumpled clothes in her arms. Toadies! Nice! Why don't they tell me frankly that I am old and ugly and fat, she thought bitterly. Ugly . . . the word gave her a pang even as she thought of it. But then, she consoled herself, what can you expect when you're nearly seventy?

She moved heavily towards the dressing table and sat before it, staring anxiously at her reflection. My pearls, she thought wistfully, they're the only nice things about me. And even they can't do anything for me now. What a pity I got them forty years too late! She tried to visualize her own face and figure at the age of thirty, but failed. I must look up those old albums tomorrow. She continued to stare unseeingly into the mirror, until he came in and said, 'Aren't you ready? We have to go.'

'I'm ready,' she replied and got up, smoothing down her heavy silk sari. Life is a circle, she thought. One always goes back to one's beginnings—if one lives long enough, that is. As a young girl, she had been used to wearing heavy silks in her father's home. Later, in the austere atmosphere of her husband's home, she had worn only white khadi saris. How often she had groaned at their weight, specially when she had to wash them herself. And now, back to silks again!

She kept pace with him walking through the large, silent rooms. But as they neared the big hall where the reception was being held, she suddenly felt tired. I don't want to go there, she thought with a touch of petulance. I don't want to smile and fold my hands and mouth inanities to people I don't care for. And who care nothing for me, either. Only for what I am. I wish I was sitting in my own room, with my feet tucked under me, and my bra, that is constricting me so, off, my petticoat strings loosened, my false teeth out. She remembered her grandmother at meals, champing her toothless gums together in unashamed gusto, oblivious of the saliva dribbling down her trembling chin. And how she used to embarrass them all by her uninhibited behaviour, belching loudly, even breaking wind sometimes, so that they were all ashamed of her. At least, she thought complacently, my grandchildren are not ashamed of me. Unless, her mind suddenly took alarm, they too have learnt sycophancy from the people around us.

As the large doors were obsequiously flung open for them, she arranged her sari over her shoulder and put on her public look. 'The first lady' the magazines called her. Even, sometimes, 'our gracious and dignified first lady'. God! If only they knew what an effort it was to keep up the pose all the time! She responded mechanically to the respectful smiles, the polite masks, the soft murmurs and looked admiringly at her husband who smiled and spoke with the right mixture of dignity and condescension. I can do it too. What is it, after all, but a performance that we go through? All that we need are the correct gestures . . . a smile, a faint inclination of the head, folded hands, the right word for the right person. We've been doing it these six years now and God knows how many years more!

There had been, some time back, a rumour that her husband had displeased those who mattered, that he would be put on the shelf when his term ended. He had been panic-stricken. 'My God, what shall I do?' he had exclaimed. But, seasoned politician that he was, he had known what to do and the powers had relented. 'I've gone to jail twelve times,' he said, when he heard that. As if that mattered! Whatever the reason, they had charitably allowed him to continue to hold on to his position— all splendid trappings and no power. Pompously he had put out a statement that he was ready to serve the people as long as he could, to the best of his ability. Why can't you be frank, she had thought irritably and unreasonably, knowing it was impossible, and say that you enjoy this kowtowing, this feeling of being important, and that you intend to cling on to it as long as you possibly can? But she had some compunctions about destroying his illusions about himself, especially the one that he was indispensable and powerful. She had said nothing.

In the meantime, the reception went on. Faces came close to her, smirked, said a few polite words and moved away to make room for more faces behaving in the same way. And then yet more. So many receptions, so many occasions, so many banquets. Her mind moved along a long vista of such formal, dull functions. Cold and correct. And meaningless; as meaningless as a word becomes by constant repetition. What was this reception for? She suddenly found she couldn't remember.

'What's this for?' she asked the guest who stood before her. The face stared, blank, astonished, with goggling eyes. 'What's this reception for?' she repeated doggedly, knowing she was making a fool of herself.

The young man whose job it was to hover behind her (as if, she thought testily, I'm a lunatic and he's my keeper) now moved forward and with a scarcely perceptible gesture, waved the guest away. But the face turned for a curious backward look and, becoming a human being for the first time, said loudly, 'Independence Day.'

Independence Day? Her mind jolted with a jerk from the present and she was happily unaware that the young man behind her was struggling to keep up a stolid front, trying not to exchange mocking smiles with someone else. Independence Day? And I didn't know. I didn't remember. And all these people—how many of them know? Or care? What does it matter to them what day it is? It's enough for them to be here, a chance to show others how important they are. That they belong. All that they care about is a job, a contract, a position, profits. And then she realized how much she despised them— these people, her husband too, and yes, even herself. Suddenly, standing there in the midst of the reception, all solemnity and no spontaneity, the memory of the first Independence Day came back to her vividly.

It had rained that day. God, how it had rained! Like water spouting from an elephant's trunk, as her grandmother used to say. She had been in a tonga with the children, trying to reach the place where her husband was to hoist the flag at midnight. The rain had pelted down furiously and in a minute they had been drenched. The driver had ineffectually wielded his whip on the poor frightened horse, who had reared up, whinnying frantically. The children had screamed and clutched at her in fear. But she had not been frightened, only desperate that she would not get there in time. 'Hurry up, hurry up,' she had urged the man breathlessly. And he, knowing who she was, had done his best, so that they had reached there in time, though only just. The children and she had huddled in their wet clothes on the fringe of the large crowd that had watched, in pin-drop silence, the tricolour flutter up. And then, there had issued from the throats of that vast crowd an indescribable sound—an aaaaah of absolute rapture.

Later, after the people had quietened down, her husband had given a speech. Brief, dry and simple. 'I'm a plain, matter-of-fact man,' he always boasted. He could never have thought of phrases like 'our tryst with destiny', she had thought wistfully after she had heard that speech. But for the crowd, his little speech had been enough. A kind of joyous madness had seized them. They had discovered her and the children there at the back. 'What are you doing here?' they had yelled. And in a light-hearted frenzy she had been passed on from hand to hand, until she had reached the dais. Someone had given her a hand and she had clambered up. And standing there, watching all those ecstatic faces wet with rain and tears, she had thought— this . . . this is the beginning of glory.

Only, she thought now, looking sadly at the faces in the room, it had not been the beginning but the end of glory. And life has lost its meaning because it relates to nothing but one's own petty concerns.

She had tried to say this to her husband once. 'What's wrong with the present?' he had asked her crossly. 'You live too much in the past.'

'Well, there's a lot of it,' she had retorted with spirit. He had snorted irritably; he hated any reference to his age. But she had persisted. 'Don't you find all this . . .' she had gestured vaguely around their splendid room, 'don't you find all this futile and meaningless?'

He had put down his glasses and stared at her in amazement. 'What's wrong with you?' And then, after a pause, as if trying to justify himself, 'One can't go on struggling forever. What's wrong with being comfortable?'

Perhaps, she thought, we had been too exalted, too uplifted for too long a time. So that we had to come down to earth from that rarefied atmosphere with a vengeance. And that's why 'want' and 'have' have become the keywords instead of 'sacrifice' and 'self-denial'. And 'I' is the invariable prefix.

'What's wrong with being comfortable?' he had repeated aggressively.

'Nothing.'

I love my comforts too. I wouldn't like to go back to being just any housewife, struggling to make ends meet, to get the ration and the milk, to run after buses. I enjoy being served by bustling, efficient servants, I enjoy the good food, the good living. After all, she often thought wryly, remembering the fragrance of the expensive cigars her father had smoked, I'm my father's daughter. Yes, I love my comforts. But the whole price has not yet been paid. For me, this is part of the payment for those comforts, these public functions that I'm finding more and more irksome.

Gracious and dignified! No, I'm only a tired, old woman, whose feet swell up to grotesque proportions after an evening like this. And then the doctors come and look concerned and murmur comfortingly about exertion and strain, about medicines and rest. When they know, and I know, that the real trouble is I'm too fat. And I'm fat because I eat too much. And I eat too much because I'm bored. And I'm bored because there's no truth in anything we do or say.

Her mind had wandered and she was distraught. People were looking at her curiously. She didn't notice them, but she saw the look of displeasure he shot at her. She struggled to get back to the present. What a pity, she thought, looking at him, smiling and suave, I can't do this as well as you do. You do it as if you were born to it. And perhaps you were. Who knows?

She remembered how reluctant her father had been to agree to their marriage. 'They believe in all the Gandhian stuff,' he had warned her. 'How will you adjust to that kind of life?' He himself had been a well-to-do man, fond of the good things of life. But she had seen the young man at a public meeting, she had heard him talk and had been unable to get him out of her head after that. His white khadi clothes and his burning patriotism had given him a romantic halo. And so she had brushed away her father's fears.

And she had been right. Adjustment had not been difficult for her. She had given up all her rich saris without a pang. Perhaps, she thought wryly at times, it has been easy because simplicity had been the fashion then, and any woman likes to be in fashion. The only thing she had missed had been tea. How she had longed for a cup of tea, especially during her pregnancies! But even to talk of tea in her husband's home would have been blasphemy.

Luckily, there had been very little time for regrets. After her wedding, she had immediately been swept into the whirlwind of the Independence Movement. There had been no time even to think. Certainly no time for love. But then—it had taken her a long time to realize the truth—the passionate and dedicated face she had fallen in love with was incapable of loving another human being. By the time she found out, they already had three children and it didn't seem to matter so much. There had been too many things to do. She felt nostalgic when she remembered the quality of excitement that had filled their lives then. Her husband more often in jail than out of it, the whole burden of the household on her shoulders, all kinds of people in the house all the time. And, of course, the police. But how alive we were. Not half-dead like these people. We were taken out of ourselves, carried away by an immense emotion and our lives were never dull, never petty. No, I regret nothing. Except . . .

It was after the birth of their third child. He, her husband, had come to her and unusually nervous and awkward, had told her something that had shocked her. Celibacy? Why? Recovering his composure, he had quoted to her all his Master's principles. He had almost harangued her. The purpose of sex is procreation. And since we don't intend to have any more children . . .

She had agreed. There had been, in those days, a kind of perverse satisfaction in denying oneself pleasure, a kind of hysterical urge for self-denial, to which she herself had succumbed long back. It made matters simple. But perhaps it was her deprivation that had made her sensitive to the young man's admiration, so that she had sensed it, perhaps even before he had been aware of it himself. At first she had felt only the pleasurable thrill any woman feels when she knows she's admired. But it had not stayed that way for long. She had found herself longing for something more than just surreptitious looks and nebulous signs. She had wanted him to touch her, to hold her, to have her. It had shamed her terribly. She, a mother of three!

But she had shown him nothing of this. She had kept aloof, and his privileged position in their house had been due to her husband's fondness for him, his most devoted disciple. And one day, he had come to them with a distraught face, saying, 'I'm going.' She had listened silently, while her husband had tried to battle with his resolution. She had known why he was going, she had known that one word from her would have held him back. And she hadn't said it. But now, when she could no longer remember how he looked, could no longer recall even his name, she often sighed that she had sent him away. And then laughed at herself, an old woman, for lusting, even in retrospect, after the body of a young man who had been dead for so many years. For he had died soon after, in a police firing. And now he lived on in her mind, eternally young, eternally loving and admiring her. And how glad I am, she often thought, that he is dead and can't see me as I am now. It's not that I am old and fat; it's what I have become, what we have all become. He, I. All of us. We've betrayed all those who died.

Time for them to leave. She could see her husband signalling to her. The gorgeously dressed flunkeys opened the doors for them with a flourish. She adjusted her sari over her shoulder and walked out. Thank God that's over. Another boring function done with. And what does it matter that it's Independence Day? The words left her cold. No, nothing matters now except to go to my room, take off all my finery, my false teeth, to eat my food, loosen my petticoat strings and go to bed. To sleep and not to dream. That is happiness enough now.

Your old men shall dream dreams, your young men shall see visions. Wasn't that in the Bible? Well, the old don't want to dream now and the young men see no visions. And suddenly, as they walked through the rooms that always seemed empty in spite of being impeccably furnished . . . suddenly she remembered the face and the name that had eluded her for so many years. The young man who would never grow old, never stop loving her. She said the name aloud so that it should not escape her again.

'What?' he asked her disinterestedly, and she knew the name meant nothing to him.

'Nothing,' she said. Thinking, how lucky he is that he is dead. He has never known the disenchantment of success.

'We've lived too long,' she said loudly and clearly as they reached their rooms. 'We've lived too long.'

But he had removed his hearing aid and didn't hear her.

Anatomy of a Murder

IT WAS NOT, for a connoisseur of crime, an interesting case. Not unusual, either. An impecunious young man had murdered a middle-aged woman in her flat. A painfully common story. But there were two intriguing facts. The man had been found sitting by the body nearly an hour after her death. He had made absolutely no attempt to escape. And then, there seemed to be no motive. Neither robbery nor rape had been attempted. (The woman was past forty, anyway.) And, in fact, there was no link between the two. So it seemed that there was a large WHY looming behind the obvious fact of the murder. But then, who cares? The law had its evidence and the man was found guilty, convicted and forgotten. It was much later that I found out the truth. It was a fascinating story. So fantastic that no one would have believed it had it been told.

He was a most ordinary young man. His father, who had died of TB, had been a mill hand. He lived in a chawl many people would have called a slum, though to him it was an enviable home with a radio, a fan and other whatnots. Like countless young men he spent his holidays on the streets or in the movie theatres, dressed in gaudy shirts and floppy-bottomed trousers, long hair slicked to a point, huge belts . . . desperately aping some film star or the other. In fact, many times after seeing a movie he felt himself a movie hero, overpowering girls and villains with his charm, virility and strength. These fantasies inevitably tapered off into confused, erotic dreams that had no relation to his real life. But while they lasted they were, to him, the only reality.

Real life was dull enough. He worked as an assistant in a groceries' shop. A job of endless, mindless drudgeries. Not that he saw it that way. It was, to him, just a means of getting money for food, for clothes, for movies, perhaps a meal at a hotel. So long as he had these he did not mind anything. He was, in fact, almost an animal in his unthinking awareness of anything but his own pleasures. A man as unselfconscious as an animal. When such an animal wakes up, it becomes dangerous.

It was one of those days when there was no time to breathe. Customer piled upon customer in that little shop and the world seemed to be composed of humans asking in shrill, peevish voices for something. It was May, steaming hot, and the animal smell of sweat was pervading the room. The assistants were snarling at one another, the customers were snarling back at them. He was working mechanically, thinking of nothing, not even the time when he would finish and get out. New faces replaced old ones, all equally a blur. He never saw any of them. Coffee, he thought, wiping his face with a rag. Where is it? Not here. Have to get it from inside. He came back, his arms full of tins, to find his way blocked by a customer. A woman.

'Move aside,' he growled, too tired to be polite. She turned around too sharply, her elbow hitting the tins. They fell from his hands. With dull booms they bounced off the floor, rolling in all directions. He made an indescribable sound compounded of rage, exhaustion and impatience. He began accumulating filthy curses in his mouth for his own satisfaction, knowing he couldn't say them aloud. Not to a customer. No doubt, she'd start storming at him herself, saying the tins had hurt her.

'Why can't you be careful? Have you no eyes?' he said offensively, to forestall her. To his surprise, he saw that she was kneeling on the grubby floor, picking the tins from between the feet of the customers who didn't even bother to move. She stood up, neatly piled the ones she'd picked on the counter and smiled at him. 'I'm sorry,' she said in English. 'I'm sorry about that.'

It was strange. He at once felt that he was seeing a new angle, a novel peephole. So that it looked completely different. In his world there was no such word as 'sorry'. One pushed and shoved and jostled, and if someone got hurt in the process . . . well, it was just their hard luck! One had to look after oneself. It was simple. Now he felt as if someone had opened a new door. Someone hurts you and you say 'sorry'. He felt as if he had plucked a stringed instrument and the vibrations had released some music he couldn't understand.

He worked the rest of the evening in a kind of stupor, an intent faraway look on his face as if he was trying to listen to something. When they closed up, he stood outside the shop staring stupidly at the crowds, feeling alienated from them. But he had to go home. He pushed through the people and hawkers on the pavements, scarcely seeing them, still hearing the words 'I'm sorry'. He knew how little those words meant. They said them all the time, meaning nothing. But this woman . . . she'd said them not so much with her lips, as with her eyes. Do you say sorry to the person who shoves you on the back and hurts you? It was crazy, stupid.

He remembered her face. She was thin, with the bones standing out sharp and clear in her face. Her eyes were exaggeratedly fluid and soft in that angular face. And her skin . . . thin, like paper. Made you feel it would tear if you touched it. Something clean and transparent about her, like rainwater collected in a clean vessel.

All at once, he was angry. What right had a woman like that to come into a crowded shop? Someone was bound to hurt her. And she would go around saying 'sorry'. Perhaps, he thought, it was easy to do that when life gives you everything with both hands. And with her white face and expensive sari, it was obvious she was one of those.

As he walked home, emotions were churning inside him with a violence which made him sick and dizzy. Something had happened that made himself and all his life seem tawdry and cheap.

As he entered his chawl, it was as if he was seeing it for the first time. The filth, the squalor . . . had it all been there before? He was sickened by the noise, the smell, the naked children playing in the dingy common passage. The stink of urine from the communal toilets, combined with the smell of cooking, nauseated him.

When he entered their room, his mother was squatting in front of the kerosene stove . . . grunting like a pig, he thought dispassionately. Suddenly, he realized that that woman must have been as old as his mother. He looked at her with a new awareness. She got up and walked to the bed. Her large hips jiggled as she walked. She raised her arm and scratched her head. Perspiration had soaked her armpits and he could clearly see the dark shadow inside. He looked away.

'Don't you want to eat? Your food is ready,' she called out loudly. The smell of onions and garlic. And dried fish. For a minute he could almost smell the fragrance that had wafted to him from the woman as she had stood there, piling the tins. It had been delicate, elusive. He buried his face in the pillow with a sudden violent gesture, feeling a pain within him agonizing to be born.

'I said food is ready. Don't you want to eat?'

'No.'

'Why? What's the matter? Too high and mighty to reply? Too great to eat home food? What shall I do with your share? Throw it in the dustbin? Money grows on trees, I suppose? Who stands in the ration queue for hours? Throw it out?

God, what children! And that sister of yours. Not home yet. The bitch . . . '

He closed his ears. 'I'm sorry.' What a soft voice! He'd never have heard it if he hadn't been so close. And that smile! What foolishness to smile at a stranger! He never did it. You had to be cautious of people you didn't know.

As the days passed, his restlessness increased. He couldn't understand what had happened. Life had lost its savour. Nothing was the same any more. He couldn't get that woman out of his mind. He was obsessed with her. He was surprised. If she had been young, he'd have called it love. He knew all about *that* from seeing so many movies. It meant young, plump, giggling girls, coy glances, sly touching, sighs. And there was the other thing, never mentioned in movies, but which he often experienced himself. A violent fury within him when he mentally undressed every female he met and performed orgies of erotic acts in his mind. But what was this?

It didn't fit in anywhere. A woman with grey streaks in her hair. Where did she fit in? He was bewildered, grappling with emotions he couldn't understand, longing for something he didn't know. He became slow and stupid at work, surly and quarrelsome at home. And then, one day she came back to the shop. He was aware of her presence with a sudden impact. There was a boy of fourteen or fifteen with her. Her son obviously, from the resemblance between them. She rested her hand lightly, unselfconsciously on his shoulder. He felt a wrench within him as he stared. The boy said something to her. She bent down and listened, a small smile on her face. He did not know he had the same smile as he watched, though it was like a distorted reflection of hers. For, while his lips framed the same, light, joyful smile, his eyes were blank. He was remembering his own mother. Could a mother smile at her son like that? His fuddled mind groped with the idea and even when she stopped smiling, it seemed to him that her smile lingered in the air, like her perfume, her very being, which had tantalized him all these days even when she wasn't there.

That evening he did not go home at once. He tramped around for a long time in a kind of daze. He returned home still feeling queer. He felt as if he was boiling inside and memories came frothing up to the surface like bubbles. He remembered his father. He had been a long time dying. It was not his fault; he was the most innocuous person alive, but for some reason his presence had enraged his wife who had abused him without restraint; while the man, with a meek, apologetic smile plastered to his face, had coughed himself to death. Now he thought, perhaps the old man had been, in some way, apologizing to them for his pain and suffering as he lay dying, though he had never said the word 'sorry'.

He was unexpectedly gentle with his mother that evening. Refused to let his sister's idiotic friend disturb his equanimity either. After dinner, he lay on the bed, forgetting all of them. He remembered how she had smiled at the boy, put her hand on his shoulder. He smiled to himself as he thought of it, and if he could have seen himself, he would have known that this time, his smile was a perfect replica of the woman's smile. If only she would smile at him like that . . . he would . . . what?

She never came to the shop again. His whole being was in a constant state of waiting, but she never came. He found it difficult to go back to what he had been when he had first seen her. It was painful, like wearing a pair of shoes that were too small for him. A kind of hopelessness seemed to creep over him, and he could have wept with angry rage like a child cheated of a treat it had been promised.

He had given up all hopes when one day he was sent to deliver provisions at a home. Normally he would have enjoyed the change of routine, but today, as he cycled, he was blank. He had no feelings, no thoughts. No premonitions, either.

Nevertheless, when he rang the bell and she opened the door, he felt no surprise. It seemed natural, inevitable.

'The provisions?' she asked in Marathi, opening the door wider. 'Bring them in.'

The same smile, the same perfume. But a little vague, a little distant. Still held by the same enchantment that had clutched him since he had seen her, he tugged the heavy bag in. He put it down, gave her the list and stared dumbly at her. There was a happy flutter inside him. It was as if all his life, he had been waiting for this moment. This was fulfilment. She scribbled a signature on the list and gave it back to him. 'You can go,' she said briefly. But he could not have moved to save his life. The finality of the moment had not yet pierced him. For him, it was still the precursor to something. Why doesn't she smile at me, he thought vaguely. But her eyes were indifferent and she turned away from him, picking up the book she had put down on his entry. The flat, he now noticed, was completely quiet. Not even the tick-tock of a clock disturbed it. He had never heard such a silence in his whole life. His life seemed to have been passed in the midst of a long, meaningless, discordant shriek. This silence is where she belongs. I too could belong. If she would let me. If she would take me in.

But still she didn't look at him. 'Close the door after you,' she said in an indifferent voice.

And now, for the first time, he realized that he did not exist for her. That while he had been obsessed with thoughts of her, he did not exist in her world at all. No, not even on the fringe of her consciousness. He had a strange feeling of dwindling, disappearing, dematerializing. And now he was captured by a stronger emotion than any he had felt all his life. He had to enter her world. He had to smash his way into the centre of her consciousness. He stood stock still, painfully working his way to this conclusion when, for the first time, she really looked at him. She took in his presence, his stare, and her eyes became twin points of alarm, of apprehension. It enraged him. He had to make her smile at him. Last time he had entered her world by hurting her. He could do that again. He moved forwards, hands held apart, fingers clenching and unclenching themselves. Why was she backing away? And why was she smiling like that? Like his father? No, not that way. Smile at me. Smile at me, he went on saying as he moved towards her. A vein was fluttering under her thin skin, at her temple. Her features had hardened into a propitiatory smile, while her eyes were those of a terrified animal.

Smile at me, smile at me, he went on muttering while he sank his fingers into her throat. For some time, she struggled, made convulsive movements. Then she was quiet, completely still. He took his hands away from her throat and stared down into her distorted, grotesque face. All that his dim mind could comprehend was that she had ceased to exist. Even the silence in the flat had a different quality, now that she was no more a part of it. He could never enter the world again. The door was barred to him forever. Conscious of a huge, inconsolable grief, he sat by her side, as still and motionless as her, until they came and found them both.

Can You Hear Silence?

WE'VE BEEN SITTING here watching the road since the morning. When I woke up, I knew, even without opening my eyes, that it was not like every day. The noises were different. Splashing sounds on the road. A car starting, sputtering and dying away. A funny lap-lap sound as if the sea had come close to us. And, above all this, a loud drumming sound. I opened my eyes and it seemed dark. And there was Papa reading the newspaper instead of rushing about getting ready. Then I knew what it was.

'Is it raining, Papa? Is the road flooded?'

'Go and have a look,' he said, his eyes still on his paper.

It was flooded. You couldn't see even the tops of the drums they put round the new trees to protect them. I rushed back in.

'Rashmi, hey Rashmi,' I shook her. 'It's flooded, no school today.'

'Good,' she said and promptly went back to sleep.

It is still raining, but not as heavily as it was in the morning. The water on the road has gone down. At the edge of the pavement, there is a crooked line of rubbish left by it. All kinds of trash, even—ugh!—a dead rat. A crow is pecking at it daintily, as if choosing the tastiest bits. Rashmi shudders when I say that and makes a vomiting sound and face.

'Lunch,' Mummy announces.

'Mummy, you're not going to work!' Chhaya says accusingly, seeing Mummy dressed to go out.

'I have to. But after you've had your lunch.'

'You promised you wouldn't,' Chhaya says, half-angry, half-crying.

'No, I didn't. I said if it kept on raining and if the roads were still flooded, I wouldn't go. I don't have any leave, Chhayu,' Mummy says coaxingly.

But Chhaya doesn't relent, she picks at her lunch. I can't eat much, either. I think of the crow and the rat.

As soon as we've finished eating, we rush back to watch the road. The door bangs. Mummy has left. She waves to us from the pavement. She looks very small from up here. In a moment, she's lost among all the umbrellas.

With Mummy out of sight, I'm suddenly bored with looking at the road. 'Come, let's go out and play,' I say to Rashmi.

'No, we can't. We have to wait until Tarabai finishes the clothes.'

Tarabai came late today and in a worse mood than usual. It was almost like the band we hear in the park sometimes, the way she clanged the pots and pans. Mummy hates it, but she doesn't say a word. She's a bit scared of Tarabai, we guess. Now Tarabai is banging away at the clothes. Thwack, thwack—the sounds come from the bathroom. In a while, she comes out muttering angrily to herself and begins pulling yesterday's clothes off the line. She throws them at us. 'Here, do something about them,' she says. They're still damp. Rashmi and I look at them helplessly. Where do we put them? Tarabai is draping the wet clothes everywhere, wherever she gets some place, shoving us rudely out of her way as she walks about.

'Tarabai, what about these?' we ask.

'Hang them round your necks,' she says rudely.

I want to retort angrily, but Rashmi stops me. And I remember Mummy's, 'Now, don't fight with her, girls. I need her.'

'Tarabai, why are you so angry?' Chhaya asks.

'What do you want me to do? Sing and dance?' she retorts, but not so angrily. She's fond of Chhaya. They have long conversations and Chhaya knows all Tarabai's problems—her drunken husband, her son who's with the 'daru-walas' as she says, her daughter who goes sneaking out with boys . . .

'Can you really sing and dance?' Chhaya asks curiously, while Tarabai goes on mumbling, 'No sleep the whole night, the rain kept pouring in, and I have to start making the chapattis at four . . .' She goes on and on, while we chivvy her, asking her to hurry up, for we want to go out and play.

When she has gone, the room looks most peculiar. The curtain which divides the room into two has been pushed aside; instead, there is a curtain made of towels, petticoats and pyjamas. The fan flaps them into strange, exciting shapes. I would like to watch them, but Chhaya says, 'Oooh, I'm feeling cold,' and Rashmi hustles us out.

It's like a Sunday with the corridor full of playing children. Games are already in full swing. Once or twice the dustbin lid falls off with a loud clang; as one of us runs round the corner at full speed and bangs into a dustbin. If you don't put the lid back, you get a terrible stink, a mixture of stinks really—rotting vegetables, fish and all kinds of queer things. In a while, heads pop out of doors, calling children home for tea. Sometimes Panna's mother calls us in and asks us to have tea with Panna. We always refuse, but I feel left out when the others go in. Not for the food, really, though, to be honest, sometimes it's also the food. Like the days they were frying onion bhajias in Vidya's house. I almost died.

Now we go in, have our milk and biscuits—they're so soggy Chhaya refuses to eat them, the spoilt baby—and then go back to play. We're playing hide-and-seek when Mummy comes home. I'm sitting on the floor, my eyes tightly closed, my back against the wall, counting in tens, when I hear Chhaya scream 'Mummy'. I open my eyes—I'll have to start counting all over again now—and there she is looking angry and sad. But she only says, 'Why are you sitting in that filth, Megha? Come on, get up.'

'Auntie, she's the den. Megha, you're cheating, you opened your eyes. Count again.'

'No, that's enough of games. Come in now.'

As soon as she opens the door, she sees the clothes flapping. 'Oh God!' she says. And then, 'Who hung them up?'

'Tarabai . . .'

'Did she expect you to stay in this?'

'No, Mummy we went out to play as soon as she went.'

She looks at her watch, tightens her lips and says, 'Five hours?'

In a rush, she takes off her slippers, flings her bag away, washes her feet and begins rearranging the clothes. Chhaya gets excited and makes a game of it, hiding behind something and saying babyishly, 'Where am I?' Her hands are grimy and she leaves a dirty mark on Papa's pyjamas. Mummy sees it and gives Chhaya a slap. A little one really. She can't slap properly, like Papa does. Sometimes. For, of course, Papa is rarely home long enough to punish any of us. There are days when Chhaya doesn't even see him. He goes to work before she wakes up and she's asleep by the time he returns.

There was a time when he used to come home much earlier. But then he had a job. 'Now it's my own business,' he told Rashmi and me once. 'And I have to work very hard for a few years. Once I get going, I'll be able to spend more time with you children.'

'By which time,' Mummy had said with a smile that was not really a smile, 'the girls will wonder who you are when they meet you.' Strangely, soon after this, we met Papa on the road and Chhaya didn't recognize him. 'There's Papa,' Rashmi had said. 'Where?' Chhaya asked. 'On the other side of the road, you silly.' But Chhaya kept saying, 'Where?' until he came right up to us.

We laughed at her and told Mummy about it. But she didn't laugh. That night, I heard her speaking angrily to Papa and Papa saying, 'But it's for them. We've got to struggle for some time.' And I heard Mummy say, 'How long? My God, how long?'

Now Chhaya cries until Mummy babies her and soothes her. Finally they both lie in Mummy's bed, Chhaya with her thumb in her mouth. Mummy pulls it out—it comes out with a pop—but in it goes again. I look about for Mummy's plastic-netted bag, the one she carries in her handbag when she goes to work. She always brings home something in it—vegetables, of course, but also biscuits, samosas maybe, or some cakes. Today it's empty.

'Mummy, I'm hungry.' It seems hours since we drank our milk.

'Didn't you get anything for us?' Rashmi asks accusingly.

Mummy opens her eyes slowly, as if she's too tired even to do that. 'I forgot,' she says. We stare silently at her. 'I was too tired,' she adds. We stand glum. Suddenly she smiles—and when she smiles she looks like Chhaya does when she knows she's done wrong and is trying to mollify you—and says, 'Why don't you go to the corner shop and get something for yourselves? Take some money from my purse.'

Rashmi points out some cakes to the boy—she's so bossy, she never gives me a chance to choose—and a man waiting for his change smiles at me. The huge man behind the counter pushes some coins and notes across the glass top. The man pushes back a note and says, 'A bar of chocolate.' The boy brings our cakes and goes for the chocolate. I stand on tiptoe and watch the squiggly figures as the man makes our bill. The boy brings the chocolate for the man and Rashmi carefully counts out the money. 'Here, baby, for you,' the man says to me. I'm too surprised to do anything but take the chocolate from him. But Rashmi, picking up our change, turns round instantly, snatches the chocolate from my hand, plonks it on the counter and drags me out of the shop. She walks fast, without a word, until we reach the crossing. As we wait to cross, I look back. The man is going in the other direction.

'He's gone,' I say.

Rashmi relaxes her hold on me. The lights turn green. When we're across, she says angrily, 'Why did you take chocolates from him? Don't you know better than that?'

I do. Mummy has told us long back—don't talk to strangers, don't take anything from them, don't go anywhere with them.

'I didn't take it,' I say defensively. 'I was just going to give it back when you . . .'

'Taking things from a man!' Rashmi hisses at me. 'Don't you know what men do to girls?'

'Of course I do,' I say with dignity. 'I know everything.'

I know the word, anyway. And I also know it's the most dreadful thing that can happen to a girl.

Rashmi speaks in a more friendly tone now. 'Now, don't go and tell Mummy about it. You know how she fusses. She won't ever let us go anywhere alone.'

I promise. But somehow I blurt it out, after all. We've eaten our cakes and sorted out our books for tomorrow. Mummy has put the cooker on for our dinner and sits with us for our usual chat. Then I tell her about the man. She says nothing, only pats Rashmi approvingly. But I know she's going to talk it over with Papa when he comes home. She's waiting for him now; we all are. It's time for him to be home.

But he doesn't come. He's very late today. It's funny how, when you're waiting for someone, the tick-tock of the clock becomes louder than usual. That, and the sounds of other people's footsteps. Each time we hear footsteps outside the door, Mummy sits up and listens intently. But the footsteps go on and she droops again. At last she says, 'Let's talk of something.'

'Mummy, tell us about when you were a girl,' Rashmi and I coax her.

We love to hear stories of her school, her friends and her teachers. But today she talks of her home.

'I had a beautiful home,' she says and looks at us with that 'oh, you poor children' expression on her face. 'It had a tiled roof. Do you know how friendly the rain sounds when it falls on a tiled roof? And how gently it slides off from it on to the ground? It's a steady drip that can put you to sleep. Once, I remember, a bird came in, sheltering from the rain. It sat in the rafters the whole night. Once or twice I heard it ruffling its feathers. Otherwise it was absolutely silent. And outside, when it rained, the waters ran whoosh-whoosh in the gutters. We used to wade in them. The water was never dirty—nothing in it but twigs, leaves and mud.

'Sometimes, in summer, we slept in the courtyard. We could lie in the dark and watch the stars come out. And everything was so quiet that when we spoke the words came out soft, as if we were afraid of hurting the silence. The only sounds were the sounds of birds going to bed, or those insects that go on tik-tik all night. Sometimes, after it rained, we could hear the frogs croaking. You can't imagine how—how soothing that sound is. Otherwise . . .' she pauses as a bus screeches angrily to a stop, starts with a roar and goes on, '. . . there was just silence. I wonder whether I'll ever hear silence again,' she says sadly.

'Hear silence? How can you hear silence?' Rashmi challenges.

'You'll know some day—if you ever get out of this place.'

'Sounds silly to me, hearing silence,' Rashmi says scornfully. Rashmi has to be rude to Mummy these days. And if Papa says, 'Now, Rashmi, that's not the way to talk to your mother,' she bursts out with, 'You hate me, you're all against me,' and stamps out. And Papa says with a sigh, 'Growing pains.' And Mummy says, 'It pains me too.' And Papa laughs.

But it's true. Rashmi is growing. She won't let Mummy help her wash her hair, she acts funny with Ravi next door. And she's either sulking or in a temper. Except with her friends, of course. With them she's—oh, so jolly!

'You don't even know what silence is, do you?' Mummy says pityingly to her. And I think of how our friends yell for us—RASHMI—MEGHA. And we yell back—COMING.

All this while, we've been listening to the footsteps, hoping to hear Papa's among them. There are fewer now. Chhaya is almost asleep. Mummy suddenly rouses herself and says, 'Have your dinner, girls. Chhaya, wake up.'

We finish our dinner but still no Papa. Chhaya goes to bed. Rashmi and I argue about whose turn it is to sleep on the 'camel'. That's Papa's word for the hard, slippery sofa on which we have to sleep on alternate nights. It's my turn today. Rashmi goes off to her place near Chhaya, grumbling about how much space she's taken up. I try to make myself comfortable on the 'camel', but the pillow keeps slipping away from my head. I can't sleep, anyway. Why is Papa so late? I can see Mummy is worried. She snaps at Rashmi who's still grumbling. Rashmi pulls her blanket over herself and turns her back on Mummy; even her back looks angry. But Mummy doesn't notice.

Why is Papa so late? I am now sure he has had some accident. Suppose he's dead? I imagine all of it and what we'll do and how sorry everyone will be for us. My tummy feels funny as if I have to go to the toilet. I envy Rashmi and Chhaya for being so peacefully asleep. I wish I could go to sleep too and wake up in the morning to find Papa shaving at the small mirror propped in the corner of the window.

Finally, when I've given up all hope, I hear his key in the lock. Mummy gets up instantly. I hear Mummy asking him something as he takes off his shoes and puts away his umbrella. He replies softly as if he's afraid of waking us, but when Mummy goes on, his voice gets louder. I close my eyes tight, I feel cold. Don't make him angry, Mummy, I plead. It's terrible when he is angry. He doesn't see us, he doesn't look at us, he goes about as if we're all ghosts. And Mummy does look like a ghost—an angry ghost, that is. As the angry words go on, I pray—let it be the kind of quarrel that doesn't last. Sometimes, it doesn't. I wake up in the morning after a quarrel and for a moment there's nothing; then there's me and the day, and I'm happy. Then I remember the quarrel and the happy feeling goes away.

But when I get out of bed, it's peaceful. There's Papa shaving, squinting at himself in the mirror, whistling when he finishes and going off to wash his shaving things. And Mummy's in the kitchen, looking young in her nightdress, her hair in two plaits. She's rushing about, but I can see that it's a kind of happy rushing about, not an angry, holding herself in kind of thing. But some days it goes on and on and I feel as if the house is too small. I want to run away.

Now their voices are like small, hurting stones. I put my fingers in my ears to keep out the sounds. My wrists and fingers start paining and I remove my fingers. There's silence. But the silence seems even more terrible than the angry voices. Maybe, it's better than those whispers, though. The whispers that I sometimes hear from the other side of the curtain. When I hear them, I think of what Suchitra in our class had once told me, her eyes gleaming, her face excited in a nasty sort of way. And then I had hated Suchitra and myself and my parents and everyone and I wished I had a room of my very own.

Does Rashmi feel this way too? Is that why one day she said, 'I'm going to sleep in the gallery from today.'

'Can you sleep standing up?' Papa had teased her. The gallery has room only for brooms, brushes, old tins and other junk. But Rashmi had kept on and on and Papa had said, 'Maybe one day, when we get out of here, you can have your own room . . .'

And Mummy had asked, in the funny voice I don't like, 'Will we?' And that night I had heard them arguing once again, with Mummy saying, 'No, no.'

I wake up with a start to find that my pillow has fallen down and my neck is feeling stiff. I grope for the pillow and lie down on it, wondering—is it time to wake up? Then I hear the sounds of running water and I know it's still night. We get water in the taps only at night and Mummy and Papa have to store it up then. They work in silence. Only occasionally I hear them say something in a husky, middle-of-the-night voice.

Soon the sounds cease. The lights are switched off. And there is silence.

But only inside our house. Outside I can hear the trucks rumbling past. From a distance comes the hoot of a train. Soon the milk vans will start. The tramp-tramp of factory workers going to work. People going for milk. The screech of buses. These sounds don't trouble me, though. I'm used to them. They tell me I'm at home, in my own bed. And it feels good and comfortable even if I'm on the 'camel', with a stiff neck because my pillow keeps falling down.

But just as I'm drifting back into sleep, I see a picture before my closed eyes. A house with a tiled roof. The rain falling on it with a soft patter. A bird sitting silent and still, huddled up because it's cold. And I think of Mummy's words and wonder, like Rashmi had done—can you hear silence? Will I hear it one day?

A Liberated Woman

'CAN I COME and see you?'

I felt a mild surprise when I recognized her voice. We'd met only last week. My parting words had been, 'Let's meet some time.' She had replied, equally casually, 'Yes, let's.' And now this.

Even while I was hesitating, she spoke again, a little impatiently now. 'Can I come now?'

Surely her voice sounded—I balked at the word, but no other would do—desperate? I tried to keep my own light.

'Sure. But my wife has just gone . . .'

'Are you alone?'

'Yes.'

'Can I come then? Right away?'

No mistaking the urgency now.

'You're welcome,' I said.

As I put down the phone, I felt a flicker of apprehension within me. What was it? There had been nothing in our last meeting . . . except, perhaps, I now suddenly remembered, those strange words of her just before we parted.

'Do you remember,' she had asked me abruptly, 'comparing us to the Shelleys when we finally decided to take the plunge?'

'Did I?' I had grinned.

'Yes. And at that time I didn't even know who that was. Didn't even know Shelley was a poet. I found out all about him and about the marriage later. A romantic, runaway marriage.'

A romantic runaway marriage—if it is possible to convey inverted commas verbally, she had done it then. Put them around those words.

'But you never told me that Harriet ended up as a bloated corpse in a river!'

A totally irrelevant remark, I'd thought. Now, I wondered. Well, anyway, there was no question of carrying any messages to her parents now.

'She's dead,' she had told me bluntly about her mother. 'Died cursing me to the last. I can admire her . . . now! For a mother to be so unforgiving!'

No, her visit to me had nothing to do with her parents. What then? I studied her covertly when she came. She'd changed. She looked very smart, almost chic. But I had an impression that her look of composed elegance was a carefully cultivated one. That it was brittle and could shatter at a touch. Her eyes, I thought, looked like cracks in the glaze of her poise. Her hands, too, with their jerky movements belied her apparent composure. Drugs? I wondered. But why would she do that?

I lit a cigarette to tide over the awkward silence that fell between us after the initial greetings.

'How I wish I could smoke!' she said suddenly.

'You? Why? I'm old-fashioned enough to hate the sight of a woman smoking.'

'So am I actually. But you know what they called me . . . ?'

'Who?'

'Oh, a women's magazine which interviewed me. *The essence of modernity*, they called me.'

For the first time she smiled, a smile with little mirth in it.

'Well, aren't you?'

'Modern? In what way am I modern? Just because I dress the part?' She gestured vaguely towards herself. 'All this is just because I don't have the courage not to conform.'

I could see that she was obviously on the brink of some revelation. But, I felt, her compulsion to reveal was yet so fragile that a wrong word from me would break the link between us. I hesitated. Finally I decided to be direct.

'Tell me,' I said brusquely. 'What's wrong?'

'Wrong? Is it so obvious?'

'Yes.'

'Everything's wrong. I don't know why I've come to you, actually. Meeting you last week after so many years suddenly made all my wretchedness come to the top. How many years since we met? Twelve, isn't it? Yes, twelve years since my marriage. That was the beginning. And now . . . it's nearing the end . . .'

'The end? The end of what?'

'My marriage.'

I stared dumbly at her. What had I expected? Not this, anyway. She gave me a lopsided grin as though my bewilderment amused her. It was a brief animation, however, and she lapsed into a sombre gravity again.

'Do you believe in curses? Sometimes I do. You remember how my mother cursed me when I got married?'

Yes, I did. Actually, I was the one to have carried all those terrible messages back to her. I had been a friend of the family and a colleague, though much older, of course, of his. I had, I must confess, in a way encouraged them too. It had seemed to me an absurdity that two people so much in love should be kept apart because of something so trivial as caste. I can still remember trying to say this to her mother, a stolid, grim woman, frightening somehow in her refusal to understand.

'You know, sometimes when I remember the way I left home, I'm . . . I'm . . . astounded by myself. I had no doubts, no regrets, no qualms at all.' She flashed me a smile, sly and humourless. 'Well, all those things have returned to plague me now. Descended on me like locusts. Nice phrase, isn't it?'

I was silent. Let her talk. And she went on.

'And then there was the dreadful time we went through after marriage.'

She had walked out of her parents' home absolutely empty-handed. Taken nothing, not even her books or her clothes. I had often wondered what her parents had done with all those medical books later. Sold them?

'We had no home, scarcely any money—you know what his lecturer's salary was—and a year more of my college. God, it was terrible. But still, it was heaven. I was so fulfilled in every way, if you know what I mean.'

For the first time her face softened and I saw the girl I had known.

'Why don't you tell me,' I prompted her, 'what's wrong?'

She had picked up a magazine. Now she gave it a sudden almost vicious wrench.

'You tell me,' she said, startling me, her voice rising from a monotone to an alarming fierceness. 'You tell me what to say about a marriage where love-making has become an exercise in sadism.'

My mind didn't register the words for a few seconds. I stared at her blankly, understanding eluding me even when I realized what she'd said. She put her hand gently, pityingly almost, on mine.

'Have I shocked you? I'm sorry.'

Her palm was wet. I slid my hand away from under hers. She went on, speaking fast as though afraid to stop.

'It was all right for some time. Until our second kid was born. Since then we've been getting on. I've built a very good practice. I earn a good sum. I've earned a good reputation, too. Patients are now coming to me from far. In a few years, I've no doubt I'll be at the top.'

She said all this in a detached remote voice, as if she was speaking of someone else.

'But he—he's still teaching in that second-rate college. Earning not much more than what he did when we met. We were so sure he'd succeed with his writing, give up teaching . . .'

'Yes, I've wondered about that. What happened?'

It was a relief to talk of this, to forget those dreadful words—*an exercise in sadism*.

'Nothing. It just petered out. I think, perhaps he never had it in him to be anything more. He's mediocre. Shelley! Oh, my God!' She laughed, not a very pleasant sound. 'And now he can't forgive me for succeeding when he's failed.'

Failed? I thought of him—one of my most brilliant students. What had they done to each other, these two?

Her eyes were bleak as she spoke. 'Listen, have you seen really old-fashioned couples walking together? Have you noticed that the wife always walks a few steps behind her husband? I think that's symbolic, you know. The ideal Hindu wife always walks a few steps behind her husband. If he earns 500, she earns 400. If he earns 1000, she earns 999—or less. If he . . .'

'I get your point,' I said to stop her from going on and on.

'And it isn't only money. It's other things too. Never overtake your husband in anything. This is the only thing I should have told the girls in your college that day, instead of talking on "Medicine as a career for Women"!'

I wish I could convey the enormous scorn in her voice as she said this. The magazine in her hands was a wreck now. 'Tell me,' I had said. I hadn't bargained for this.

'You forget,' I said. 'I know him. I can't believe . . .'

She didn't let me finish. 'A sadist—that's what I have for a husband,' she said with a bitter emphasis, throwing me an impatient, angry look as she spoke.

I winced as if she had struck me. For the first time, I seemed to take in what she was trying to tell me. And, watching her brooding, distorted face, I knew it was true.

'When did all this . . . I mean, when did it begin?'

'The beginning? Oh my God. Yes, the beginning—I remember it only too well. It was the day that girl came to interview me. I'd liked her. Just a kid, I'd thought, with a lively, comical face—asking questions, really wanting to know. Then she had asked him—how does it feel when your wife provides not only the butter, but most of the bread as well? That night it happened.' She gave me a reflective look. 'I'm not embarrassing you, am I?'

Why not, I thought? Thirty years or more between us, but still, you're a woman and I'm a man. That won't stop you, anyway. And so I said nothing.

'You see, till then—to close the bedroom door, to shut out the world had been such a joy—no, not that. Bliss. And that next morning when I woke up, all bruised and sore and aching, my first thought was that it was a nightmare I'd dreamt too vividly. But there were the bruises—all over me.'

Spare me all this, I wanted to say. Instead, I repeated dully, 'Bruises.'

'So it couldn't have been a nightmare, could it? And then I waited for him to say something. Anything. Apologize. Explain. But he said nothing. Not a word. And I couldn't speak, either. It was too ghastly. It was shameful. Humiliating . . .'

The silence seemed to be filled with the echoes of all the dreadful things she was trying not to say.

'Why do you stand it?' I asked sharply. Anything to break the silence.

'Why? I deserve it, don't I?' She sounded so hopeless, my mouth dropped open. 'You can't understand that? Why? I don't know, really. And I can understand him, in a way, can't you? It's his way, the only way, perhaps, of taking revenge on me for what I've done to him. To his ego. Oh yes, I can reason it out coldly, logically enough in the daytime. But at night I become just a terrified animal. I can't scream, because the kids in the next room may hear. I can't cry, the kids may hear. I can't fight back, either, he's too strong for me.'

The composed way in which she said all this chilled me.

'And so I just endure.'

'Endure' she said, I noticed. Not suffer. Throughout I had the feeling that she had been trying to minimize the whole thing. As if it was the only way of keeping a tight control over herself.

'Suppose you give up working . . . ?' I suggested.

'I did try once.' She screwed up her face.

'And?'

' "Have you gone crazy?" he asked me. "Do you know how much I earn? How do you suppose we will live on that?" And he's right, you know. We can't go back. Not now. And again and again he kept asking me—"Why? Why?" '

'You should have told him.' I was bewildered.

'Oh! Impatiently she pushed my bewilderment away. 'I know how it sounds. But we've built up a wall of silence between us. And as long as it isn't broken I can pretend that the thing that happens between us at night hasn't happened. Or that it won't happen again.'

'But it does?'

She gave me a frosty smile. 'Yes, it does. Again and again and again. I know now what triggers him off. Sometimes I have a respite for days. Or even blessedly longer intervals. And we're a normal couple. A happy family. Then someone says something. Or something happens. And at night he attacks me like an animal. Then the next morning we wake up and he's the same. Absolutely the same.'

A long silence hung between us. I wiped my forehead.

'What are you going to do?'

'What is there to be done?'

I stared at her aghast. Even as I was clearing my throat to speak, she hurriedly put in, 'I know what you're going to say. Why don't you divorce him? Isn't that it?'

I nodded.

'No.' A determined negative. 'No. Let the kids know what's wrong?'

'They'll find out one day.'

'No. I don't believe in exhibiting my sores in public, anyway.'

'You should consult a psychiatrist.'

Her mouth twitched in amusement. 'Should I?'

'I mean, you should induce him to. He needs help.'

'I can't.' She sounded like a frightened child.

'Why not, for God's sake?'

'I can't talk to him. Not about this.'

'Shall I try?'

Isn't this what you've been working up to all this time, I thought wryly. But her eyes flashed to mine in genuine surprise.

'And?' she asked.

I shrugged my shoulders. She stared at me for almost a full minute. Then her face suddenly crumpled. It lost its studied calm look. Her hands released the tortured magazine at last.

'Well, OK.'

She rose to go and an awkwardness came between us as we tried to descend to the level of usual commonplaces. Then she abruptly broke in my farewell, saying, 'You know, I don't think he knows . . .'

'Knows what?'

'What he does. I think he sort of blacks out at that time, if you know what I mean. The other day he said to me, "Good God, look at that bruise! When did you hurt yourself?" And he sounded truly surprised. I can swear he wasn't pretending.'

I was grappling with that bizarre idea when she left. I decided I would not go and see him. If what she said was true, if his cruelty to her was something he did unconsciously, at a different level of his living, there was little I could do. Besides, how can I talk to him of such things? I belong to a generation that believes in reticence about certain matters. No, I can't talk to him.

And there's more—why did she come to me? Obviously she felt that in some way I was responsible for her tragedy. Because I had helped them to come together. But I reject the thought. I refuse to bear the burden of guilt for something for which I'm not really responsible. You can't, as they say, pass the buck that way. No, I will not interfere.

But what really astonishes me is her feebleness, her attitude of despairing indifference. Surely she, an educated, earning competent woman, has no right to behave this way—to plug all her escape routes herself and act like a rat in a trap.

All this was months ago. Since then I've tried to forget her. The other day, however, by an odd chance I came across the magazine in which she had been interviewed. I was idly turning over the pages and suddenly, there she was, her cool, poised face staring back at me, almost arrogantly. It gave me a little shock. I got a bigger one, though, when I saw the title of the piece. It was 'A Liberated Woman'.

Well!

Why a Robin?

'TELL ME SOMETHING about it,' she says. 'About a robin.'

'But why a robin?'

'I don't know,' she says carelessly. Then, firmly, 'Teacher said so. Teacher said a robin.'

Foolishly I ignore the finality of her words and blunder on. 'Why not a bird we know something about? A sparrow, or a . . . a . . . a . . . myna, or even . . . a peacock?'

'No. Not those. I want a robin,' she says with childish petulance. Her lower lip is thrust forward, her forehead is furrowed, her eyes are angry. But I am amazed at her beauty. How did I, so plain, so common, get a daughter like her? Her beauty always gives me a physical wrench. And saddens me. It puts distances between us. Can one envy one's own daughter? I think I do. She gets so much out of life, effortlessly, gracefully. While I . . . ?

'Tell me something about the robin.'

This is almost the first time my daughter is appealing to me for help. And I cannot help her. I frown in my turn, perplexed and worried. What shall I say?

'I don't know,' I say at last. 'I know nothing about it. Except that it's a pretty bird. With a red breast . . . ? And it comes in winter . . . ? Children feed it bread crumbs . . . ?'

The words come out haltingly, hesitantly; I feel like I did when I was a child, answering questions I was not very sure of. Her expectant look unnerves me even more. She is looking at me, head held on one side, almost like a bird herself. But not one that will let me ruffle its feathers. Not one that will come and peck from my hands.

As I stop, she bursts out, 'Oh! Is that all! What's the use of that? I'm supposed to do a two-page composition on the robin and you tell me two words. You can't help me, you're no use at all.' I'm conscious that I've failed her, I try to make amends. 'Why don't you write about a peacock? That's a beautiful bird.'

'Teacher said no ex-o-tic birds.' She pronounces the new word carefully and with pride.

'But a peacock isn't exotic. It belongs here. In some places it's quite common.'

'You don't understand,' she says scornfully, looking down at me. Already at twelve, she seems taller than me. Already at her age, she knows more than I do. There is no awkwardness in her; she holds herself with a grace and poise I have never achieved. 'We can't choose the subject ourselves. You don't understand. You don't know anything.'

I look at her terrified. She has already judged me and found me wanting. There is nothing more I can say.

'I'll ask Papa. He's sure to know, he'll help me.'

She begins to gather her books. For some reason, I don't want her to go. I want to hold on to the moment, to her.

'A peacock,' I say helplessly, feebly. 'I'll tell you about a peacock.'

'I said a robin.' She bites off her words sharply, irritated and impatient with my obtuseness. She is sharp, almost like a blade. When I was a girl, a friend told me to use a blade to keep my legs smooth and clean. I was clumsy and the sharp blade gave me little nicks, cuts that bled profusely, briefly, then healed fast. Now my daughter's words, her glances, lacerate me that way. Sometimes I feel I have bleeding nicks all over me, cuts that bleed profusely and heal fast.

'Why a robin?' I ask again, and this time I'm talking to myself. She isn't there any more. Why a robin?

How often have I wanted to ask my husband—why me? But I know he would walk out on me the way the child has, irritated, impatient, but not angry. He is rarely moved to anger. But his silences, more eloquent than any anger, freeze me. And I don't really need to ask the question—why me? Because I know. It was because of the speeding truck which rammed into a car on the highway. And a girl who died. Anyone, he is supposed to have said, my husband, just anyone. But why was it me?

As I sit thinking about this, she comes back into the room and I am filled with hope and eagerness. I half-rise from my chair. 'I have a peacock's feather, let me show it to you,' I say to her. But she picks up a book and walks away from me, her long, slim brown legs taking her away from me remorselessly. I stare at her slender back, at the thin neck, where little curls grow, endearingly feminine, giving her a childish, vulnerable look. I long to fondle her, to pass my hands over her neck. But I am afraid of being rebuffed. I know she won't respond. I don't have the key to open up this beautiful child, though she is mine. I don't have the key to her father, either. It is as if I am, in my own house, confronted with two closed rooms. I am condemned to sit outside and gaze helplessly at the closed doors.

I force myself to get up. I begin rummaging among my things for the peacock's feather. I have lost, misplaced so many things in my life, but I find the peacock's feather. As I look at it, I am overcome by an onrush of memories. My grandmother used to take me to a temple. I would go with her, quivering in delighted anticipation, for there were peacocks there. I had taken it for granted then, but now I wonder—peacocks in a temple? I can remember how breathless I would be when I reached the temple. Would the peacocks come out and dance for me?

'Can I get a feather? Can I?' I would ask over and over again.

'If you're a lucky girl,' she would say.

And one day I did. I want to share it with my daughter—the peacock, my excitement, the memory of my beautiful grandmother and the peacock's feather. But she won't listen to me, it's too late.

Sometimes I think we are all chameleons. We change colour, become different beings with different people. With my servants I am authoritative, with my parents, irresponsible, happy-go-lucky, but with my husband and child I am foolish, stupid, inarticulate. When I am with them, I become dull and brown—no, not even that. I lose colour completely. And with his family too. They can never forget that he married 'beneath him'. Neither can I. Before they visit us, I take endless trouble to tidy the house. But it remains dull, dead. Till he, or the child, does something. A small touch and the house looks different. I slog in the kitchen for his family; I must impress them, show them he's well looked after. They sit at the table, carelessly eating the food I have prepared, and talk of many things, ignoring me. The talk flows above and around me, leaving me untouched. An outsider in my own home. Have they locked me out or have I locked myself in?

I am full of guilt these days. I am a failure—as a wife, as a companion, as a mother. Between my husband and myself, there is a blankness—we never even quarrel. And with my daughter, I am helpless. Her fits of excitement, her questions, her rage, her tantrums, her ideas—I can cope with none of these. She fills me with the same delight the peacock did. And I have no more in common with her than I had with the beautiful peacock I saw that day in the temple.

Now she is asking her father about the robin. She listens eagerly as he talks and explains. They are looking at a book, their faces eager and alive. The reading lamp casts a halo of light around their glowing faces but the light does not reach the corner where I am sitting. I am conscious of an ache within me, an ache I cannot dignify with the name of grief. Even my emotions and feelings refuse to take on larger dimensions. But nothing can ease my ache. I get up and go closer to them. The vivid colour of the birds in the book dazzle my eyes after the dark. I am suddenly reminded of my childhood, filled with nostalgia for a home that exists no more.

When I was a child, we lived in a house surrounded by trees. I often woke up to see a sparrow hopping into the window near my bed. Plain, brown and dull, it was sure of itself. Self-assured and confident. And there were also vivid streaks of colour flying out of trees. I never knew the names of these birds, I could never identify the various cries that blended in some mysterious way into a harmonious melody. But they were part of my life. Now, listening to my husband telling the child about the robin, I am conscious again of my ignorance.

'Let me tell you about the peacock,' I had said. But what could I have told her? Only that I saw it dancing once, brazenly exhibiting the glory of its fan, the sunlight flecking the blue and green and bronze with a golden dust that dazzled my eyes which made it for me, forever, the most enchanting moment of my life. But I cannot say any of this to these two—my husband and my child. We belong to different species. I am an interloper. I do not belong. I move away from them resolutely.

I dawdle over my work deliberately, so that am late going to bed. Two single beds. Two islands that nothing can bridge. Not the child. Not even the bridge of passion. He has not come to bed when I go into our room. He sits and listens to music every night. I lie on my bed, eyes open, listening to the music streaming across the dark. I cannot understand this music, it is as incomprehensible to me as he is. At first, I wanted to sit with him, to try and share his enjoyment, to ask him to open my ears to the sounds so that they would become a melody. But I was afraid. Now I know I will never do it. It is his special place, his retreat, the place where he can be most alone. I will not intrude. And the worst, most frightening thought is that he may ask me—what do you want?

What do I want? What a large, what a cosmic question that is! What do I want? I will have to live the whole of my life to know what I want. And even then I will have no words to frame my wants. And now I realize I have no wants. I have whittled them down out of fear. I have hoped to give myself a stature I think I do not have by self-abnegation. Instead, I have dwindled. Without wants, there is no 'I'. That is why they so often look at me without seeing me.

The music comes to an end. He comes to bed. I lie still, not wanting to reveal that I am awake. After some time I hear his steady breathing. I can look at him now. He is lying in his usual hunched position, his back towards me. The back is mute, but his neck is like the child's, thin and somehow vulnerable. It makes him seem accessible. I can almost imagine myself going to him, talking to him without inhibitions, without fears. But I know I will not.

As I try to force myself to sleep, I hear a muffled sound from the other room. I hold my breath, waiting for the cry to be repeated. Perhaps he will hear, perhaps he will get up. When she was a baby, he woke up for her feeds, he never let me do it. I hear the sound again, but he does not stir. I know now that she is crying into her pillow. I hesitate to intrude, but the sounds tear at me. I stare, almost in anger, at his humped figure, willing him to wake up, to go to her. As I stare at the motionless figure, the conviction grows within me that bridges have to be built. They do not come out of nothing, they have to be created.

I get hurriedly out of bed, I pull my sari around me. The ground feels cool and smooth to my bare feet.

Her face is buried in the pillow. The young body is utterly still, but there is a tenseness about it that tells me she knows

I am there, though my feet have made no sound. I bend down and call her name. She does not respond.

'Shall I get Papa?' I whisper, remembering how, when she had the measles, she had wanted him all the time. She gets up abruptly, showing me her tear-stained face. She has given herself totally to grief. Whatever the cause, her grief is large, real.

'No,' she says. 'No, not him.'

'You want me?' Joy is surfacing through the scum of my distress.

Her eyes are distant. 'No,' she says again. 'No one.' Suddenly her eyes fill with tears, they spill over. Her face is contorted, her mouth is working. She looks almost ugly. I sit down and put my arms around her. 'What is it?' I ask her.

When she can control her sobs, she tells me. I look at her with conflicting feelings. My daughter—on the brink of womanhood? This child a woman? Suddenly I feel joyous, exalted, as if I have found one key, opened one door. But her frightened eyes bring me back to myself. I remember how I had once tried to tell her about the process of growing up. She had impatiently rebuffed me. 'Pooh! That! Who doesn't know about all that!'

Now all her self-possession has deserted her; she is only a woeful, frightened child. It is as if she is facing forces she cannot understand or control. I talk to her gently, trying to make her feel it is natural, a part of growing up, something to be welcomed, accepted. She listens to me silently, lying with her knees drawn up to her chest. Like an unborn foetus waiting to be born again.

'I have a pain,' she says. The tears spill over. I wipe them with the end of my sari. I make her get up and show her what is to be done. I get her a hot-water bottle for the pain. I bring her a cup of hot milk and sit by her side as she drinks it. She is unexpectedly docile and childlike, this child who has just become a woman. But the clouds of hurt and bewilderment are dissolving from her eyes. As she sips the milk, she sits up with a new dignity and grace that shows me she is accepting what has happened.

'Can you sleep now?' I ask her when she finishes the milk. She does not reply. I switch off the light and go to cover her up. Her fingers suddenly tighten round my hand. 'No, don't go,' she says with her old vigour. 'Talk to me, talk to me of something.' And suddenly I am my old self too. What can I talk to her about, what can I tell her?

'Were you frightened too?' she asks me shyly.

Yes, I tell her. I tell her how I too had cried and how my grandmother had held my hand as I am now holding hers.

'Your grandmother . . . ?' she says wonderingly, as if surprised I had one. 'Tell me about her.'

'She was beautiful,' I say. 'You look like her.'

'Do I?' I can't see her distinctly, but I can visualize her lips curving into an enchanting smile. 'Tell me about her,' she repeats.

I begin to talk. I tell her how I went to the temple with her every day. And how one day I saw the peacock dance. I tell her how the sunlight had glinted on its many-hued fan and dazzled our eyes so that the world had become a different place. 'I still have the peacock's feather,' I tell her.

Bridges have to be built. I feel I am doing just that.

'Show it to me tomorrow.' Her voice is slurred with sleep. Drowsily she says, 'I'll ask Teacher—why not a peacock?'

'Why not a robin?' I say slowly, trying to formulate my thoughts. I remember the sparrow that had hopped on to my window sill every morning. What if it had seen the peacock? And what if the peacock were more beautiful? It would have strutted just the same.

'Why not a robin? We all belong.'

But she is sleeping, her fingers loosely clasped round my hand. I sit still and quiet. Unmoving.

An Antidote to Boredom

'DO YOU WANT more sugar in your coffee?'

'Sugar? No . . . no. Maybe a little bit.'

'Half a spoon?'

I got the sugar, stirred the coffee. And suddenly, standing there, my sari tucked in at my waist, the picture of a solicitous wife serving her husband, I retreated into a wild flight of fancy. What if I came up to the table, I asked him silently, walking on my hands, your coffee balanced on my feet? I concealed a small smile at the vision I had conjured up, knowing fully well that he would do nothing, because he would notice nothing but that he had been served his coffee. No need to conceal my smile, either. For that again was something he would not notice. Whereas *he*—no nuance of my expression ever escaped him.

'Why are you smiling?' he would ask, his tone tender and cajoling. I would hesitate, afraid of sounding ridiculous with my fancies, but he would make me tell him. And when I finished, he would, I knew, laugh aloud, genuinely amused and, relieved and happy, I would laugh too. And this—this shared laughter would become one more link between us; one link less between this man, who sat silently eating, his jaws moving rhythmically, and me, his wife.

I knew what he would do now after eating. He would wash his hands, rinse his mouth and sit down with the newspaper for exactly five minutes, while I moved about restlessly, wishing he would go away so that I could get on with my day's work. When his five minutes were over, he would pick up his bag and saying 'See you in the evening', would walk out. And in the evening? I knew how it would be.

'Any letters?'

'Yes.' Or perhaps, 'No.'

'Rahul home?'

'Yes.'

'What's for tea?'

One day, I often told myself, I would reply, 'Toads and mice for tea today.' And what would he do then? Give me a startled look? Or his painstaking smile to show that he understood it was a joke? Once I had thought I would fling myself at him and say, 'I've missed you.' But I knew what his reaction to that would be. He would be painfully, horribly embarrassed. Now I no longer thought of saying that. It would no longer be true.

No, I was never lonely now. As I moved about the house doing my chores, I stored up jokes, little bits of my day to tell him, the other. We could talk of anything, nothing was too trivial or too intense for us. There were only two things we never spoke of. We never once mentioned those two little boys, at once the bridge and the chasm between us. Only that one day . . .

'You're thinking of something. You've gone away.'

'No, not really.'

'You're thinking of Rahul.'

'No!' My negative had been fierce, abruptly torn out of me. No, I never think of Rahul when I'm with you. I push him away to the remotest shelf in my mind. But I could not say this aloud. And yet, it was because of our boys that we had met at all.

'Do you have to go to see Rahul in school?' my husband had asked me in irritation.

How explain that the thought of your gentle, sensitive five-year-old all by himself in a crowd of big, rough, hustling, pushing boys tore at you? I couldn't, I prevaricated instead.

'You're making an unnecessary fuss. Leave him alone. He'll settle down fast enough.'

'I know that. But . . .'

'The teachers must be fed up with you mothers.'

But we weren't all mothers there. He was often there too. A father. Waiting patiently to meet the teacher. Why, I had wondered, did his wife never come? Then one day, we had found our children walking around, their arms round each other's shoulders. We had smiled, pleased, not really seeing each other. Only our children.

'I never see his mother,' I had idly remarked. There was a little pause before he replied, 'She's dead.'

'Oh God, I'm sorry.'

Filled with shame, I had taken Rahul and his new friend to the canteen for ice cream. He had said nothing, had followed us silently, then got me an ice cream with a smile. That had been the beginning.

The beginning? Of what? Nothing, really. Just that we met and talked and laughed. Just that I felt I had to see him. I knew he felt the same. So that, without any words, we found ourselves going to the school twice a week, the same time, the same day, knowing fully well that our children didn't really need us any more. Yet I would pretend to myself it was Rahul I went to see.

With a kind of guilt and shame at making use of him, I would rush up to him, rumple his hair, stay with him for a while, and then, with a throbbing heart and pulsing excitement, go to the courtyard where I would find him waiting for me under the large clock.

Once Rahul had followed me. I had already dismissed him from my mind, and was walking fast, full of the fear that was always in me that he would not be there. But, of course, he had been there and at the sight of him, smiling at me, I had almost broken into a run. Then, hearing a scuffling sound behind me, I had turned round sharply.

'Rahul!' I had gasped. 'What do you want?'

He had stopped abruptly and giving both of us a curiously adult look, remote and wary, had fled. That day it had all been spoilt for us. We had gone in his car to our usual place, a quiet road where there wasn't much traffic. I had sat and said 'yes' and 'no' and he had watched me anxious and worried, but said nothing. That was the day, the only day, he had mentioned Rahul's name to me. And when it was time for us to part, he had suddenly said, 'It's bad for you, I know. But don't think it's easier for me. The dead clamour for loyalty as much as the living.'

But it was rarely like that between us. Depressing or tragic. No, it was more often joyous, exciting. And the thought of meeting him kept me keyed up to a more intense pitch of living. His frank admiration was as refreshing to me as cold water on a hot day. Until then, nobody had cared what I wore, how I dressed. My husband denied me nothing; but there was not one sari with associations. Not one sari that was special to me because of something we had done together, something he had said to me.

Now . . . 'I love you in blue,' he would say. And the next time I went shopping, I would go looking for a blue. I would drive the salesman mad, for he would have all the shades but the one I wanted. He would press all of them on me, talking glibly the way all salesmen do. The saris would mount up on the counter and my husband's eyebrows would draw together in an irritated frown. 'What does it matter what colour it is,' he would exclaim in irritation. But I would be stubborn until I got the colour I wanted, thinking of him saying to me, 'I love you in blue.'

If only my husband had been more demonstrative of his affection, I often thought . . . But what if there is no affection at all, the only things holding us together being habit and a child?

If only my child had been more demanding . . . But he had never been that. Always quiet and self-sufficient.

If only that other child of ours had lived . . .

If only his wife hadn't died . . .

If only . . . If only . . .

But I was fooling myself. There was a sweetness in our relationship that made it impossible for me to wish it away. I knew it was the same with him. He even spoke to me of his wife and I loved him for doing it.

'When she died, I felt it was the end of the world. Other women didn't exist for me, I never saw them. Until I saw you that day eating ice cream with the children. Sometimes I have a strange feeling she doesn't mind. But you! I feel bad for you. To carry a load of guilt . . .'

'Guilt,' I had said bitterly. 'No, there's no guilt. Why should there be? As long as his world isn't disturbed, at least obviously, he doesn't care. Sometimes I feel like shocking him, shaking him out of his lethargy by screaming in his ears . . . I have a lover, yes, a lover.'

He had laughed and said, 'And what would you gain by that?' And then, seriously, 'Lover? But that wouldn't be true, would it?' No, because we weren't. What prevented us? At first he had been quiescent, his importunities slight. Now I could feel his need for me strong and pulling. He wanted me. It was a wonderful feeling. I wouldn't be just a habit with him, a body to be loved once or twice a week, so that love-making became just another chore. Dull, like treading a path one had walked many times before. So that at the end I would lie awake, wondering, thinking about those women who did it for money and did they have the same feeling of being cheated, of being defrauded of something that was the right of our womanhood?

No, it would never be like that between us I knew. And yet I hesitated. Tried to ignore the feeling that often came between us. I was no inexperienced girl, but a woman married for twelve years, knowing all there was to be known, aware of passions and desires, though they had passed me by. Knowing fully well that two persons, a man and a woman, could not look at each other the way we did, could not refrain from touching each other the way we did, without something having to happen some time.

But I was content to drift. Events must take their course— I repeated the sentence to myself a thousand, a million times, till it became a meaningless jumble of words. And still I hesitated, because I knew how it would be afterwards. I would never be the same again. I knew I would sit in my own home feeling an interloper, the very fringe of the bedspread on our bed staring me out of countenance, making me feel a criminal. And there was the thought of Rahul too, some awareness in his eyes, a recent withdrawal from me, which made me wonder how much a child could see and understand. The very thought of it made me feel guilty towards Rahul. But I felt no guilt towards my husband, because I would be depriving him of nothing, nothing he wanted. How often had I felt in myself a boundless capacity for loving, for giving. But I had felt in him an incapacity to receive and for that I hated him at times, though I knew I wronged him by that. For he was not a wicked man, not harsh nor cruel. Only unperceptive. And dull. And dullness is to me an unforgivable crime.

Sometimes terrible thoughts plagued me. I wondered whether it was only the demon of discontent which had brought me to such a strange situation, sitting with a strange man in his car, exchanging pleasurable glances with him, hiding my face guiltily at the sight of what seemed a familiar face. And at times there was the even more shaming thought that it could have been any man; if not this, then another. Because this was for me, perhaps, only an antidote to boredom, something I enjoyed because of the excitement it brought into the dull routine of my days, the unchanging pattern of my life.

But when I was with him I never spoke of these things. We never mentioned our own separate worlds. Instead, we built a new one of our own, a third that was ours only, one in which our usual personalities changed, so that we became different beings altogether, at once more interesting, more vital, more sparkling. So that I would come home, humming a little tune, smile at myself in the mirror, wondering that I even looked different. The glow would stay with me till the evening. Then the bell would ring. 'Any letters? Rahul home? What's for tea?'

And I would feel the sulky furrows coming back to my forehead, the little droop returning to my mouth. A long, dull evening would loom ahead of me, teeming with dull barren silences. And I would think of our life together, and of how we could go on like this for years and years, until we were both old and withered, with even Rahul, the only meaning to our relationship, an occasional visitor. I would feel like yawning and yawning. Face-splitting yawns.

I often thought of these silences when we sat in his car and a little silence grew between us. These silences were never barren; they were replete with meaning, making us more at ease with each other.

Strangely enough, we never once spoke of love. This was the other thing we never mentioned. Love—how often they use the word in books and movies, how carelessly people fling the word at one another there. But how wary we are of the word in real life! I had thought I had grasped the thing that was the word in the youthful, fevered excitement of my honeymoon days. But it had proved to be an illusion. And now the word was stored away at home, a skeleton in the cupboard.

But now, the phantom that had eluded me was beginning to take on features and a face once more. Though I knew it would be a blurred picture, a misty image, until we spent long unhurried hours together, exchanging not only long, passionate kisses, but nibbling, little kisses as well, my hair spread out on the pillow, the warm length of our bodies against each other. Instead we sat in the car, carefully distant, the tension between us growing daily, until some days back, when something snapped in him and he pulled me close. It had amazed me. Kisses—I had thought them the preserve of the young, of people in books and movies. For the rest of us, they were something to be indulged in behind closed doors, a prelude to something else. Now, for the first time, I found that a kiss could contain in itself as much pleasure and excitement as anything between a man and a woman. That whole night I had lain awake, ashamed of my earlier ignorance, of my innocence.

The next day I had told him, 'He's going to Delhi next week.'

'Oh!' He had refrained from saying anything more, careful not to prod or question me, letting me take my own time, my own way of coming to things.

'And Rahul always spends a day with his grandmother.'

Again an 'Oh!'

'What floor is your flat?' I had asked in a burst at last, careful not to look at him, ashamed of seeing in his face that I had cheapened myself. And then, I had nerved myself and looked up and seen such joy on his face that I had found it hard to bear. Once the fact had been settled between us, we never spoke of it. Just waited quietly for the days to pass. As I moved and worked in my home, kneading the dough, or cutting the vegetables, my mind moved forward, leaped through the intervening time and I thought of the day and how it would be. And whether his boy too had a convenient grandmother and what we would do and what we would say, until I was filled with an impatience for the time, and yet, a fear of it too. And he, my husband, noticed nothing, not my excitement, nor my restlessness, just as my earlier boredom and discontent too had passed him by. For the first time I was glad of his passivity, his blindness, his stolidity. And I was good-humoured and patient with him. Yet, perversely, sometimes I wished he could see, wondering what he would do, whether he would mind at all. And surprisingly, the most humiliating thought was that he would not mind at all.

And at last there were just four days for him to go and my mind was in a fearful state, half guilty shame, half joyful anticipation. I was sitting with Rahul, helping him with his homework when he suddenly said, 'Why don't you come to Delhi with me?'

It was too sharp, too sudden, too swift an upsetting of all my plans and I blurted out foolishly, 'I . . . I can't!' Then I looked up fearfully. Did he understand? But his face was as calm, as bland as ever. 'Why not?' he said. 'Weren't you saying you were bored? Mother is prepared to look after Rahul for a few days. You don't mind giving your mother a holiday, do you, Rahul?'

And Rahul, ever reasonable, shook his head, while I desperately cast my thoughts about, wondering what excuse to give, clutching even more fiercely at the dream that was now receding. At last I said, after a pause, trying to sound casual, as if I didn't care either way. 'Next time, perhaps. I don't feel like it this time.'

'If I were you, I would make it this time.'

The words sounded suddenly menacing, and I looked up startled. The same face, the same voice, but for a brief second I saw a dull, red light flicker in his eyes, like a warning, a challenge, then disappear. And I felt as if I was standing with my back to the wall, no room to move, no air to breathe, the two faces watching me steadily, warily. And then I knew that he knew, that he cared, and as if a dam had burst, a flood of shame and guilt swept over me, drowned me. I let go of the mirage I had tried to grasp so long, and now I realized, when it was too late, the most piercing thought of all—that it had been no mere antidote to boredom, but the best part of my life. And I let it go.

It Was the Nightingale

THE LAST TIME, I say to myself, as I fit my key into the latch. Then I smile at myself—what a portentous phrase! I have always had a hatred of exaggerated emotions, I have learnt to play down my own—most of the time anyway. Today is one of those other times when I can't. I'm brimming, spilling over with feeling. Before opening the door, I make a fierce attempt to cork them in. I succeed, but it makes no difference. The atmosphere in the house is redolent with emotions His resentment and anger come across to me, nebulous like a rising mist, but tangible enough to choke me. All the way home I have been indulging in a savage self-flagellation. Thinking—how shall I excuse myself? How shall I show him how desperately sorry I am about coming home late? Now, seeing his face, everything dries up in me. There is nothing I can say which will undo what I have done. And yet, there is no anger on his face. Only I, who know him so well, can sense the storm behind the imperturbable calm. I know his very stillness is intended to be a loud reproach.

I go quietly into the bedroom without speaking. My packed suitcases stand with an air of finality against the wall. The room has the desolate look of one denuded of all personal articles. His things are still there, but it suddenly strikes me how abandoned they look all by themselves. Hurriedly I throw my bag on the bed and wash my hands, my feet, my face. I am wiping myself with the towel when he enters. And all at once the silence between us is unbearable.

'I'm sorry, I'm very sorry,' I stammer out. 'Don't, please don't make a thing of it today. Not today, please, not tonight.'

His calm breaks and the words cascade out of him. 'I could say the same to you, couldn't I? Why couldn't you have come early today? Why did you come late, today of all days? Do you know what time I returned? Do you know how often I've looked at my watch? Do you . . . ?'

'I couldn't help it. I'm sorry. You know I didn't do it deliberately. There was so much to do, so much to clear up . . .' My voice trails away.

Ever since I decided to go, there has been this vague something between us. We had just managed to come to terms with it. Why did I, I ask myself angrily, have to bring the shadows in again?

'So much to do! And I, I suppose, had nothing!' The rage in his tone withers me. 'I had planned,' he goes on after a silence, in which I can see him trying to compose himself, 'to go out to dinner. It's too late now.'

'I'll have something ready. It won't take any time.'

'Don't trouble yourself. I've put the cooker on.'

I feel guilty and resentful. Every way I turn, there's a 'No Entry' lane. He is obsessed with his hurt. I have accepted that. And yet his pain pierces my armour of understanding but not caring. As I set the table, I teeter on the edge of self-abasement. Anything to get over this sullen, hurt-filled silence. Instead I say, 'Dinner is ready.'

We sit down to eat. Now is the time to talk of practical details, business matters. But we have been so long preparing for this time that everything has been said and there is nothing left for this last night. Only those futile protestations, those unending demands, those eternal promises all lovers make when parting. These are not for us. What promises can I make him? Or, he make to me? This is the price we have to pay for too deep an understanding. We can never use the small change of love. And yet I know I have to speak now.

'I . . .' I begin and choke over a mouthful. He looks at me inquiringly, waiting patiently for me to go on, his raised eyebrows mutely asking a question. I will see him like this so many times, looking at me with that quirk of his eyebrows. And the memory will pierce me like a knife, leaving me limp with longing. Will the memory blunt one day and cease to stab and hurt? Suddenly I'm aware of what I'm doing. I'm putting two years between us. A fearsome period. Two years of experiences we will not share. And each one a brick that can ultimately become a wall between us. It isn't quarrels that shatter a marriage, it's doing things apart. Can we stand two years of separateness? Confronted with this thought, the link between us seems tenuous.

'What were you saying?' he asks me, polite as a stranger. No, no stranger. I will break down the wall.

'You have beautiful eyebrows,' I say. He stares at me in comical astonishment. I begin to laugh. But as his look changes I begin to feel the fluttering in my stomach that is for me the harbinger of desire. Thank God, we are eating at home. Thank God, we have not gone out. He is so impatient he scarcely lets me wash my hands or rinse my mouth. 'Oh, don't, don't . . .' he cries out and suddenly I leave everything and go to him. 'Why do you . . . ?' he mumbles and stops as his mouth finds mine.

And then we are lost. No, not lost. Found, because this is where we really find each other. We do not have to search. Each goes out to the other and we are merged in a oneness that is absolute. I give all of me until I am only a hollow ecstasy. And pain. And then I realize he is holding back. I will not let him do that. I am stronger and fierce and fiery until he melts and responds with equal intensity.

Later we lie in the usual serenity and peace that descends on us after loving. But I know it is ephemeral and spurious.

His hand lies heavy, limp and unresponsive in mine. And now I know I must speak. My body has receded into the background, my mind is active and alive.

'I wish,' I say angrily, 'you had refused to let me go.'

'How could I?' His voice is drowsy. But it is lassitude, not contentment, that makes it so. 'If you had once, just once, showed the smallest doubt . . . But, there never was a doubt, was there?'

Never was a doubt . . . He does not know, he will never know, how I have fought myself. How I have longed to give ambition and success the go-by and stay with him, throttled by his love. No, not throttled, that's not fair. It's a soporific, his love and mine, which makes me long to lie down in lethargic bliss. And I would, but for that savage in me, the savage I myself have nurtured, which kills all such self-destroying doubts.

'No,' I say, hating myself for saying it, 'I had no doubts.'

'But what intrigues me, Jayu,' he goes on, his tone no longer angry or argumentative, but reflective, 'is this . . . why are you really going? Is it really going to make all that much difference to your work? You know you've just begun feeling your own way. And you don't crave for a foreign-returned tag . . .'

'You know why I'm going,' I say lightly. 'To get a bigger salary when I return.'

'And when have you done anything for so simple a reason as that?' he asks equably.

He knows I am frightened of myself. If I give in once, if I give way once, I will walk that road of self-abnegation forever. And shall I then end up like my mother who stripped herself of everything and cried out against us as denuders?

'To go when you need not have gone, when we had made other plans . . .'

Other plans. To have a child. Now the child will have to wait. We will not let it be born yet. Can you feel a traitor to someone who does not exist?

'I couldn't miss this chance,' I say, sensing that my tone is petulant. 'If you had been me . . .'

'. . . I would have put ourselves first.'

Of course. A wife and mother first. Like his mother.

'Don't let her put you against me by her constant criticism, will you?'

'Who?'

I stifle my laughter at his facade of ignorance. 'Your mother, of course.'

I am thankful she will be here tomorrow, not today. I am thankful I have these last moments with him alone.

'She doesn't criticize you, Jayu. You're prejudiced. How a woman as rational and intelligent as you can be so prejudiced . . . !'

I laugh again under my breath at his doggedness. To his last breath he will assert his mother likes me. Just as, I suppose, he tells her I am fond of her. But we understand each other better, she and I.

'No, she won't criticize me directly. But she will tell you that story she has narrated to me umpteen times. Of how— "I never went to my mother's house even once after my mother-in-law died, because if I did, who would look after HIM?"'

I say it all in one breath and become breathless. He is silent. I can imagine the blank look on his face. He is intensely loyal. Does he have the same look when she says or hints at things against me?

'You should try and understand her, Jayu,' he speaks placatingly. 'For women of her generation, life held nothing, literally nothing, apart from husband and children. She can't understand how a woman can see beyond that.'

How can she when even he cannot? To me, our lives are intertwined, yet they are two distinct strands. They are like two lights that shine more brightly together, but to keep my light burning is my responsibility and mine alone.

'I wish,' I say slowly, 'that you had met my mother. She died a year too soon.'

Now, from this distance, I can understand her. Even feel sorry for her. Then, there was only dislike and contempt. And anger at what she was and what she was doing to me. A woman who had nothing of her own. Who tried to live her life through her husband and daughters. Who was shattered by any tug at the bonds. Who tortured herself and tormented us. Who made her own hell and gloried in it. And so, for me, each step out of home had been a battle, each success a treachery towards her. Now I am free, but the fear remains . . . will I shackle myself? Or others? And often there's an abashed feeling that I'm making gestures of defiance at a person who doesn't exist.

'Forget it, Jayu. You've made your plans and they can't be changed. Let's not talk about that now.'

And so we lie together and talk the whole night through of other things. And I know that however often I will long for him when we are not together, the physical longing will be nothing compared to the craving for this intimacy, this effortless communing. As we talk, we doze and wake up again to each other. And once I wake out of a little dream, short and forgotten in the very second of waking, yet leaving behind an impression of sweetness and intense happiness. And once he talks to me of his grand-aunt who looked after him when he was a child. He does not know why he thinks of her now, but I do. He had often told me how totally selfless, totally loving she was. To him, she is always the ideal woman. And though he loves me, he finds it hard to accept me as I am, so unlike that woman who mothered him when he was a child.

And I cannot change. He knows this too. And more. For once he says, his mouth so close to my ear that his breath tickles me, 'You know, Jayu, I believe it is not pride or ambition but obstinacy that is your real vice, after all.'

We long to be understood, but only if that understanding encompasses our virtues. When our vices are uncovered, we are indignant and abashed, as if surprised in the bathroom. Why, I ask myself, did God make me a creature of many parts, not of one alone—and that ambition?

At last I can see through the window that the night is coming to an end. He sees it too. 'Time to get up,' he says.

'Believe me love, it was the nightingale,' I murmur against his shoulder.

'What?'

'Not me. Juliet. She said it, trying to hold Romeo back. Believe me, love, it isn't the lark, it's the nightingale.'

'You wouldn't ever say that, would you? If it's the lark, you'd say it is the lark. You wouldn't ever fool yourself, or others, and say it's the nightingale, would you?'

He sees the hurt in my eyes and bending down swiftly to me says, 'But who will now quote Shakespeare to me in bed?'

And so we get up with laughter. We leave the house and reach the airport in the same mood. Two years, I tell myself, are nothing. Lovers have parted since time began and people have stayed apart for ten times two years and come together again. Why am I making such a big thing of it? But I know that each parting is a little dying. And so it is for him and for me. And this is my doing and all my life I will carry the burden of this guilt.

Inside the airport there is a crowd even at this early hour. A babble of noise. Garlands lie in trash bins like coiled snakes. The smell of flowers is heavy and sickening. He gives me a wry smile. 'All these people. And for you, only me.'

'That's how I wanted it.'

And that is why I discouraged all the others from coming. Even my sister Sumi. But now I wish there was someone to go back with him. It saddens me to think of him going back to the empty flat alone. With the pillow having the impress of my head still upon it. The bathroom smelling of talcum. And my teacup, unwashed, on the dining table. But, perhaps, these little things don't mean so much to a man. But I am glad I am going to a place where there is nothing of him. I will be starting on a blank sheet, a clean page. No. I'm fooling myself. The memories of hurt are bottled inside me, I will carry them wherever I go.

At last it is time for us to part. Now I will tell him how little I really want to go. How much I want to be with him. Now I will explain that my going does not mean I care for him less. But the finality of the moment carries away my words. I can say none of these things. I can only cling to him. Even as he holds me close, I feel the reproach in him. And perhaps he can feel the guilt in me. Will they always come between us? We let go of each other and I walk away, my bag cutting into my shoulder, my eyes tearless and dry and burning.

The Stone Women

LOOKING OUT FROM the cool darkness of the arched entrance, I am blinded by the glare. For a moment I can see nothing. Slowly things come into focus and I see a shining, chiselled jewel, gleaming in the sun, rising out of the earth, offering itself to me. I blink. The illusion disappears and it becomes what it is—a temple. I hear his voice calling out my name and I see he is already in the centre of the courtyard, vainly trying to shelter himself in the narrow shadow cast by the pillar of lights. Guiltily, I move forward. The sun strikes my head with savagery, the stone under my feet scorches my soles. I take quick steps, end up running and reach him in a rush. He holds me to steady me. His hands linger. Once again, for a few seconds, we ride the waves of physical pleasure together.

'Guide, saar?'

We turn away from each other. A young man, dressed in a kind of slick smartness, is smiling ingratiatingly at us.

'I can explain everything, inside the temple, outside, in any language—English, Hindi, Kannada . . .'

'Shall we . . . ?' He looks at me questioningly.

But even before I can reply, he begins to discuss terms with the guide and I retreat into the world that's always waiting for me these days—the world of the wonder of the two of us, the marvel of the two of us together. The time before this seems so distant, I can scarcely connect myself with it, to the girl I was then.

'All right, let's go,' he says. Abruptly he stops and looks at me. And smiles. 'You've lost,' he says.

'Lost? What?' Realization comes suddenly. 'Oh God, was I humming again?'

'You'll never win,' he says triumphantly.

The guide, waiting for us by the stone lions at the entrance, clears his throat impatiently and we hurry to position ourselves before him. He gives us a satisfied look, passes his hand over his sleek, oiled hair and begins in a tone quite different from his normal one.

'This temple was built by King Vishnuvardhana of the Hoysala dynasty in the year . . .'

'You'll never win . . .' Was there contempt in that? No, the feel of his palm against mine, warm and reassuring, tells me he isn't really displeased. I relax. But I must conquer this silly habit, I warn myself. Why a tune gets hold of me this way, I don't know. But there it is, a different one each day, dancing about in my head all day. Always Hindi film tunes. 'Silly jingles,' he says. 'One day,' he's challenged me, 'let's see if you can control yourself just one day.' I've stopped listening to film songs, I try to crush the tunes whenever I know they're there, but they're always biding their time, waiting to spring out, taking me unawares Why, even now, as I'm listening to the guide narrating facts in a drab monotone, I can still hear the song going on inside my head. God, I must stop it. I give him a quick guilty look to see if he's hearing it too. No, he's listening intently to the guide and I force myself to listen as well.

'Now these ladies you see above you . . .'

Obediently I look up and—what did he call them? Ladies? God, no! They're women, lush-bodied, high-breasted women carved on rectangular stone panels, leaning provocatively out of them, towards us, it seems. Women in all kinds of poses—

looking into the mirror, doing their hair, playing on musical instruments, dancing, hunting. I walk along, looking at them, as if mesmerized, while the man goes on describing each carving in meticulous detail.

'Madam will know this hairstyle,' he stops before one to say and names a film star who made the style famous. 'Ladies are always the same,' he adds and the two men exchange smiles. Must I smile, I wonder? But the men are not looking at me and we move on. The guide points out tiny details, like the fly on a woman's arm, the seeds of the fruit a parrot is eating, the tiny bells on a woman's anklets—'You can see how they seem to be moving,' he says. But it's not these details in the carvings that amaze me, its what we're seeing here—the joyous, playful, narcissistic existence of these women. Were they really like this? Could any woman ever have been like this?

'Beautiful.' I hear the word over and over again and I look at the women with their high, firm breasts, tiny waists, straight noses and elongated eyes and wonder—are they? I suppose they are. But they don't look real, a voice inside me protests. And yet . . . no, I don't know. Sometimes I think that's the truth. I don't know.

'What an ugly thing,' he'd said soon after we were married, touching the silver bracelet I was wearing.

Was it ugly? I had never known. In fact, I'd been wearing it for so long, it was like part of myself; I scarcely saw it. But I put it away that day. Yet even now, in idle moments, the fingers of my right hand grope for it and there is a sense of loss when they miss its familiar contours.

As we go on, from one panel to another, I find myself overcome by a sense of uneasiness. A strange feeling that the stone women are converging on me, pressing on me so that I can't breathe. Is it the heat? Yes, it must be the heat, for I am conscious now of the faint beginnings of a headache.

I have a feeling of relief when we go inside, into the temple. There is a sense of space here. The guide takes us to a smooth, shining dark circle. 'This was the dance floor,' he says. And then, 'Look at the roof. The most beautiful carvings are here.' I look up at the canopy of complicated intricate carvings and have a sense of vertigo. I clutch at his arm and am conscious that my palm is clammy. I can no longer pretend. I am feeling sick. I retreat into a kind of daze and words come to me disjointed and fragmentary.

'There was a queen who used to dance here,' I hear the guide say.

'The king didn't mind?'

'She danced for the gods, saar.' The voice is reproachful.

'Danced for the gods.' At the words, I have a bizarre picture of a woman dancing on that smooth polished floor, a galaxy of gods lolling before her, dressed like the gods in TV serials, in plastic heads and tinsel crowns.

At last it's over. Thankfully I begin to move out.

'Madam, you don't want to do puja?' the guide asks me in surprise. For the first time I realize that this is a temple with gods to be worshipped. No, just one god. 'Chenna Keshava—the most beautiful god,' bejewelled and beflowered, flanked by his two wives. As we wait for our offerings to be accepted, my uneasiness congeals into a heavy oppressive weight that threatens to suffocate me. I make an involuntary sound.

'What is it?' He turns to me.

'I'm not feeling well.'

Solicitously he helps me out, the guide following us. I can hear him murmuring, 'It's the heat.'

'Shall I get some water?' the guide asks when we get out.

'Water? No, wait, is there any tender coconut here? There is? OK, you wait here, we'll get you something to drink. All right? I won't be long.'

They leave me on a platform below a tree and go away. The cool breeze chills my wet, sweating body. I wipe my face.

'Not feeling well?'

It's a woman, sitting cross-legged, a child sleeping on her lap, looking at me curiously.

'A little.'

'Must be the heat. Shall I give you some water?'

'My husband has gone to get me a tender coconut.'

I can see the two of them standing before the coconut seller. They seem remote, there's a dream-like quality about them, about the whole scene. A pleasant dream. I feel suddenly more peaceful.

'Just married?'

'Five months back.'

Where do I live? What does my husband do? Where are my parents? And my in-laws? And am I working too? Really? And what do I do? The questions gush out of her. My monosyllabic answers don't seem to discourage her. I can see the guide coming towards me, a coconut in his hand.

'This is your husband?'

'No, he's the guide.'

I sit back and sip the cool liquid, letting her words flow over me. The sound of the rustling branches is infinitely soothing. A twig gently drifts down into my lap and I realize that this is a neem tree. The woman is telling me about herself now. 'My grandchild,' she says, tenderly passing her hand over the sleeping child's hair. The child stirs and her voice drops a decibel. There's such an air of ease and comfort about her, it's as if she's in her own home, conversing with one of the family.

He comes to me, putting his wallet back in his pocket. 'Feeling better?'

'Yes, much better.'

'Shall we go?'

'Your husband, huh?' she says rather than asks. I nod. 'Look after her,' she tells him.

'What does she mean?' he asks me as we move away.

I smile. 'She thinks I'm pregnant.'

'God!' He makes a face. 'I could see her going yak yak yak. She must have bored you to death.'

'No, not really,' I say. I can see he doesn't believe me, but it's the truth. There was something about her, a kind of rough warmth, that reminded me of my mother.

I go for a bath as soon as we get back to our room. I have a sense of washing away something more than just the sweat and the dirt. When I come out, I see he's ordered some tea for us. I sit by him and pour it out. A new song enters my mind: *Isi liye mummy ne meri tumhe chai pe bulaya hai* . . . I stop it, crush it, refuse to let it go on. He puts his arm round me. 'You smell wonderful,' he says, nuzzling into my body. His hands move over me. Suddenly he stops and moves back.

'You're wearing something new. I don't like it. It hides you,' he says, his hands moving as if tracing the shape of my body. For some reason, when I look at him, eyes narrowed, mouth pursed as he gazes at me thoughtfully, my mind leaps back to those stone women in the temple. This is how they must have looked, I realize, the men who sculpted the women in stone, as they shaped them from their imaginations. As if I have evoked the sound, I even hear the tap-tap of the hammer as the men chipped away at the stone, working out their fantasies on it, creating women with unreal bodies, women who played and sang and danced all day. For a moment, while he looks at me, I am overcome by a sudden fear, as if I am becoming one of them too, women frozen for all time into a pose they have been willed into. Then I lean back and say, 'It's comfortable, I like it.'

We go on talking but I can see a faint shadow on his face— he is puzzled and doesn't know what it is that is puzzling him. I move closer to him, into his arms and the shadow is gone. And the tune comes back, flows into my mind, on to the tip of my tongue.

Mirrors

I HEAR THEY are now calling it a revolution. Actually, it was the court poet who used the word in his poem. I didn't hear the poem, I didn't need to, for I knew what it would be—a poem celebrating the victory of Indra against Nahusha. A song chanting the triumph of the hero against the tyrant. Can Indra's court poet do anything else? And now that he has used the word 'revolution', that's what it is going to be. I think I'm beginning to understand why men of learning, men who write, are given so much importance. It's not only because of their knowledge or their ideas; it's because, by putting these into words, they bring them into existence. Without words, things can be swallowed up in silence. Like you. You have no place in any of the stories that are being told about what happened, none at all in the court poet's poem And it is as if you never existed.

When I think of this, I feel the burden of guilt. Have I the right to remain silent and let the truth be concealed? I know that Indra was no hero but a desperately frightened fugitive, I know that the minister was not Indra's loyal ally but a partner in many of Nahusha's misdeeds, I know that the person who really ended Nahusha's misrule was you. I also know that if I don't speak of these things, they will never be known.

But to whom do I speak? Things said here, in these rooms, die within these walls. And even if, by some miracle, my words do find their way out of this place, if they are heard and not dismissed as 'mere women's talk', even then will people understand what really happened, will they realize what you really did? No, they will think you did it out of anger. Spite. That you were jealous because your husband desired me, because he wanted to replace you with me as queen. Will even one person understand that you did it because you wanted to set things right? No, a woman has no place in any story except as a devoted wife. Look at me—I'm there in the court poet's poem as the *pativrata* who waited patiently for her husband to return. The good woman who spurned an alien man's proposal. I can see the pativrata when I look into people's eyes, that good woman seems to accompany me wherever I go, like my own shadow.

Only two people know the truth of what happened: you and I. You have already gone back to your own home and I know you will never speak. I seem to know you so well—though we met only once—that I am sure you don't even want to think of what happened. Your face when you said, 'He was not always like this, he was a good man once,' comes back to me often and I know the depths of your sorrow for what happened to your husband. It is because of you, because of your sorrow that I remain silent. Yet, sometimes, when I think of how your name is forgotten, I become restless and uneasy. Buried in silence, you have become just one more of those nameless queens whose identities came out of the kings they married. In fact, I wonder whether anyone knows your name at all. You were always, to everyone, to me as well, Nahusha's queen.

Nahusha's queen. The queen. I can confess now that it made me angry to hear those words. How could you be the queen? I, Sachidevi, Indra's wife, was the queen. I am ashamed to think of how long and painful a time it was before I realized

I was no longer the queen. It was my stupidity and obstinacy that kept me from seeing the truth; I should have seen it coming. But when you seal yourself into the rooms of power, you become both deaf and blind. And for some time, even after Indra's disappearance, there did not seem to be any change. But soon it began. I had a sense of being ignored. As if Indra had been the filter through which they had seen me, I felt myself becoming invisible without him. It's not for long, I told myself, trying to give myself courage. Indra will return and things will again be normal.

But Indra didn't return. Soon, there were no more visitors, even the number of servants dwindled. And I began hearing the name 'Nahusha'. I can remember the day I heard they had chosen Nahusha to be king, I can hear the shouts on the streets, the people cheering their new king. And queen. It was a day of mourning for me; I felt as if both Indra and I had died, that I had lost everything, even my self. The words which I had heard continually—beautiful, gracious, generous—these words no longer fell on my ears. And I wondered whether, like my title, they had gone to you as well. I became fearful of seeing my reflection, I feared there would be nothing, only blankness, I kept touching myself to reassure myself I was real, that I existed. The question came up in my mind over and over again: if I was not what they had told me I was, who was I then? A huge anger began building up inside, anger against you, for it was you who had taken away this self from me.

Did you guess my thoughts, did you have some idea of the way I felt about you? Was that why you came to see me, to make me understand you were not my enemy? I can still remember how, the moment our maids went out at your order leaving us alone, you burst out, 'But you are very beautiful!' There was nothing but a kind of surprised pleasure in your tone; there was no envy—no, neither in the words nor in the tone. And I was surprised too. Didn't you hate me? Didn't you know about your husband's desire for me?

You knew, yes, you made that clear to me in the very first few moments of our conversation. Of course you knew. 'Are there any secrets in palaces?' you asked me wryly.

'You don't hate me?'

'Do you hate all those women your husband pursued?'

You were the first to speak to me of it so openly, so directly. But, of course, everyone knew of Indra's womanizing; was there anyone who didn't know? I had learnt it soon enough myself. But, blinded at first by his looks, his charm, his power, I thought it natural that women should be attracted to him. As for those women of pleasure he had in his court, they didn't really matter. It shames me now to remember how little I thought of them, how scornful I was of them, how superior I considered myself to them. They were no more than the king's possessions; they didn't threaten me. It was those other women . . .

It took me some time to know about them. His brief disappearances, sometimes for a day or two, didn't mean anything at first. And then I began to notice a kind of furtive triumph in his bearing when he returned. Bringing with him, I slowly realized, the smell of women's bodies, of sweat and that other exudation that spoke of his fulfilled desire. I began to see too the marks on him, marks of love, I thought, though I should have seen that they looked more like the marks of a woman's resistance. But I thought of them as love scars. And a savage anger filled me; I wanted to shout out my rage, to scream, to tear him apart.

I did none of these things. I withdrew instead behind the mask of the loving wife, into the shell of the dignified, gracious queen. But behind the mask, within the shell, was a bewildered woman asking herself, 'Why? Why does he need those women?' I could understand his enjoying the skilful beautiful women he had in his court, but these . . . ?

I saw the wife of a rishi once. A tired, middle-aged woman, her face coarsened and darkened by the sun and wind, her body hardened by work. Were they all like this? How could he desire women like these? As I kept staring at her, I had a strange feeling that this woman was real, while I, I was only a painted clay doll. I was not living, I would not die; I would just disintegrate into a bit of coloured earth.

To my own surprise I found myself speaking of all these things to you that day. To you, Nahusha's queen, the woman who had taken my place, the woman I had thought was my enemy. How was it I could tell you things I had never revealed to anyone before? Yet, there was something I did not tell you, one thing I could not talk to you about. It was about how I'd learnt, since your husband had begun importuning me, that a man's passion, that his desire, even when it is unwanted by the woman, creates a link between the two of them. I had begun feeling this, begun understanding that Nahusha's passion, which I hated so much, gave him some kind of a power over me. And so, much as I hated him, repulsive though I found him, he could, even against my will, reach to some inner secret part of me. I could not say this to you. But perhaps you guessed, for you began to speak, telling me about the man Nahusha had been.

'He was a simple man. And he knew what he was and what he could do. He has changed. I wish they had left us where we were, they should have left us alone. My husband was a good king, yes, he was. Wasn't that why they chose him? When they came and asked him to take Indra's place, he confessed his doubts to me, he told me he was not sure he could rule this kingdom. Now, he refuses to admit those doubts, he cannot bear to be reminded of them. The fact is, he is trying to become what he is not. He wants to become Indra. And he is afraid to face the fact that he cannot become Indra.'

And then you said it, what I had been afraid of. 'And now he has begun to think that if he kills Indra he can take his place.'

So Indra was not dead? I looked at you hopefully, trusting you to tell me the truth.

'No, he's alive. But Nahusha's men are searching for him everywhere. I am afraid they will find him. And then . . . No, I can't let that happen. That is why I came to see you. I decided I would find out his hiding place before the king does. And then it is for you . . .'

I think it began then, my realization of how hollow my idea of being the queen had been. Only the facade, only the costumes, nothing more. To be beautiful, dignified and gracious, to add to the king's glory, to be available to him when he wanted me—that was all! I have had much time since then to think of what you did, of what you thought that you, as the queen, had to do. And to remember my own role when I had been queen, to be ashamed of it.

Vritra—that is the name I think of, the name I can never forget. Nobody spoke the name aloud, specially not in my presence. But even I could not ignore the fact that the name fluttered about us, the whispers like a bird's wings in the quiet of the night. I could not but notice the silences that suddenly closed about me as I moved in the palace. My husband told me that Vritra was an evil man, a man who had come to avenge his brother Visvarupa's death, that they were both the sons of his enemy.

I swallowed the story that Visvarupa's death had been an accident. When Vritra died, I accepted the fact that he had to be killed before he killed the king. But I am no fool, and I could see how the faces turned sullen, yes, even in the palace, as if the light that Vritra's name had lit had been extinguished. But it was easier to believe my husband, simpler to be on his side, most comfortable not to argue. And, after all, was any of this my business? And so, even after I heard the murmurs, I held on to my belief that Vritra had been our enemy, an enemy of the king, of the country, of the people. When the murmurs swelled to a roar that came nearer and nearer, and finally Indra disappeared, even then I did not ask myself the question: Why does an innocent man need to run away?

I think of these things now and ask myself: Suppose I had admitted the truth to myself, suppose I had said, 'Yes, my husband is a tyrant and Vritra was fighting this tyranny'— even then, what could I have done? When I could not stop my husband from ravishing unwilling women, when I could not change things in my own life, how could I change the lives of others? I could have spoken—there is that. I could have spoken instead of being silent. You showed me that courage. But I lacked it. And I did something worse than remaining silent; I became the mirror that showed Indra what he wanted to see, I showed him the image of a hero, the irresistible conqueror of men and of women. The king who could do no wrong.

Yes, now I know if I could have done nothing else, I could have spoken. Perhaps, if I had done that, I would not have despised myself as I do now, I would not have felt the guilt at having sacrificed my humanity to preserve a man's idea of me as a woman. I think of you—and I have a great deal of time to do so now—and I wonder when you learnt that your humanity was more important than your womanhood, when you looked for your own strength as a human being and found it. I suppose we all come to this knowledge in time, but only if we are ready for it. If we do not want to know, we will never recognize the moment when it comes.

For me the moment came when I saw Indra in his hiding place. I remember the look you gave me when I asked you to tell me where he was. You had just confessed to me that you had found him out, that this was why you had come to me. 'Where is he?' I asked you and you were silent, your look pondering, doubtful. Wondering, I now imagine, no, I now *know*, whether I would be able to do what you wanted me to. But you gave me the information I wanted finally; you even sent a man to guide me to the place.

It was a small hut, so dark inside that I could scarcely see the man who was there at first. They say now that Indra was ashamed of having killed Vritra, that he went into hiding to cleanse himself of his sins, that he was repentant. But that day when I went into the hut, I knew that it was neither guilt nor shame that filled him, but fear. The hut reeked of the smell of fear, the very sound of his breathing in the dark spoke of it. He seemed, too, a much smaller man than the one I knew, as if, without his king's accoutrements, he had shrunk. I remembered then your words about your husband, about Nahusha. 'He was not like this,' you had said. 'He has changed.' Then you had paused and said, 'Or, has he? Do you think this cruel man, this lecher was there in him all these years? Do you think they were just waiting for such a time to emerge?' And I thought—had this small frightened man always been there in Indra?

That night Indra spoke to me of his innocence, over and over again he told me he was innocent of the killings of Visvarupa and Vritra. When I was leaving he clutched at my hand with the desperation of a drowning man. 'A second chance,' he said. 'That is all I want. Things will be different after this, I promise you they will.'

I knew then he was speaking of us as well, of the women we had never mentioned in all these years.

I didn't believe him. I knew things would not change, that, even if, for a while, he became a different man, he would go back to his old ways soon enough. No, I did not believe him. But we had agreed, you and I, we had decided that this was the only way we could change things. I had no choice but to make Indra think that I believed him.

It is a relief to say it now, even to myself, to put the record straight: it was your plan, all of it. All I did was carry it out. And so I told Nahusha that, yes, I would become his queen. But I would not go to him, he had to come to me, the way a great king should. The way no king, however great, had ever travelled. I told him that he had to come to me carried by seven venerable rishis. My heart quakes even today to think that I dared to ask for such a thing; how did I even speak of it?

Now, after it has moved into becoming the past, I find myself wondering: Did you know what you were doing? Did you plan this with the knowledge that it would destroy your husband? Was this to be your punishment for him? I don't think so, I don't think it was punishment that you were after. What was it you wanted then? To give your husband another chance, like I gave mine? Perhaps you gambled on the chance that the better man in Nahusha would win, that he would draw back from what I suggested, that he would refuse to do what I asked him to do.

It didn't happen. Nahusha agreed to my conditions. I admit I was frightened, I longed to have you with me, to take courage from you, but that was not possible. Waiting in my room, all decked up—for I had to play my role till the last minute—I thought fearfully: What will I do if he gets here and claims me? Had you thought about this? Maybe you had; I will never know now.

It worked; Nahusha never got to me. They speak of it even now, the story has been told and retold so often it has swollen beyond recognition, gone way beyond what really happened. Do you think about it, do you dream, do you have nightmares about it like I do? Is that why you went away so quickly so as not to hear people talk about it? I am spared nothing, neither the talk, nor the nightmares. For the first few days, even in my waking hours, I could see the picture of Nahusha in his royal palanquin carried by those seven venerable men. I saw those proud men, so unused to carrying burdens, bearing the palanquin on the narrow hill paths. Stumbling at times. Angry, resentful. And Nahusha, arrogant, drunk with power, blinded by lust, goading them on, abusing them when they faltered, even, the story goes, kicking them . . .

It was Agastya who took the decisive step—I have heard that. I wonder whether they had planned it earlier. Or did it happen on the spur of the moment, suddenly, when they saw the deep abyss? I can imagine Agastya nodding at the others and they, understanding him immediately, shifting the palanquin from shoulder to shoulder until they are all on the same side. The palanquin tilting, Nahusha, angry at first and then, as the palanquin keeps tilting, afraid. Crying out in fear. The terrified screams when Nahusha knows he is going to fall, the screams becoming shriller as he feels himself being thrown out of the palanquin, the cries fainter and more distant as he plunges into the gorge. And then, finally, a fearful silence.

A revolution. Does a revolution mean a complete change? Or does it mean completing a circle so that you come back to the same point? This is what has happened to us. We are back to where we were before Nahusha came. There are the same people in the halls, the same crowds thronging outside the gates. The minister moves freely through our palace once more, the palace he had shunned like a bad smell all these days. He bows respectfully to me, he calls me 'Queen', daring me, I sometimes think, to recall what he had said to me when Nahusha was king. Indra believes he was on my side, he thinks that he was with us all the while; I have no desire to disillusion him. What if I were to tell him that the minister had advised me to accept Nahusha as my husband? Will Indra believe me? But it makes no difference to me any more. It is enough for me that I know the truth.

Did I say nothing has changed? No, that's not true, for *I* have changed. It seems odd to remember now that I thought of you as the woman who had stolen my self. The truth is that it was you who really gave my self back to me. We destroyed that splendid shell of the queen between us that day, you and I. Now, without that cover, I see things I've never seen before. It's not a comfortable state, I admit that; no, it is disturbing to see the lies, the cruelties, the deceptions, to know that only the dishonest and sycophants can survive and flourish here. And there is Indra—I see him clearly as I have never done before. Right now, he is a subdued, chastened man. But this will not last; I know that he will disappear one of these days and come back with the odour of a strange woman about him, a woman he has raped. Yes, raped, I have to use that word now, I can no longer blind myself to what he does. What will I do then? What will I do if another man is killed like Vritra was because he dares to raise his voice against tyranny?

It seems worse to be able to see things and to be unable to do anything, terrible to know your own powerlessness. Yet I cannot forget that for a brief moment power was in our hands, yours and mine. That was no illusion. I also know that the power came out of your courage, your strength. I don't have them, no, not as yet. But, perhaps some day . . .

The Inner Rooms

PERHAPS SHE LOOKED a little mad. The little boy she had met grazing his cattle had stared at her curiously—only for an instant though. The curiosity had soon turned to something else. Pity? Then he had smiled, a friendly smile. There had been a momentary impulse to sit with him, to talk to him. But he had turned away and she had gone on with her emptiness.

Strange, it was only the small things that mattered now—the thorns that pricked her feet, her dry throat and tongue, her burning eyes and aching muscles. Pride, anger, hatred, revenge—what were they compared to these? They dwindled into foolish toys she had played with for too long. Even the thought that had thrust itself on her when the child had smiled—if not for Bhishma, I would have had children—had not hurt. She no longer had any desire to bring children into this world. A boy who would become a man, playing the game according to some foolish rules made by men long dead, losing his self in the process. And if she had a daughter? She would only become a pawn in the game, to be moved and discarded as their rules demanded.

No, she was glad she had no children. For a brief moment, the thought of her mother came to her—a woman who had had to watch her daughters being carried away by an old man. Had she cried? Protested? In any case, neither her tears nor her protests would have had any meaning, for they would not have reached the world beyond the rooms in which she lived.

Those inner rooms—how she hated them! As a child, she had imagined that the whole world was hers. But gradually, relentlessly (don't, don't, you cannot), the world had closed in on her, pushing her into the women's rooms. From the first she had felt trapped in them. Today, when she walked out, she had been amazed to find how easy it was. A sense of peace had descended on her. Why hadn't she done this earlier?

Once out, the freedom she had never known had gone to her head. For a while, she kept the thought of what she had to do at bay, revelling in the almost forgotten emotion of happiness. How foolish I was, she thought, to let my happiness depend on other people! My nurse at first, then my mother, my father, my sisters and finally Salva. What a burden to put on others, the burden of your own happiness. She felt a fleeting pity for the sisters she had left behind in the inner rooms, stoically waiting for their husband to visit them at night, living in the constant hope of bearing him sons. At least she had escaped *that* degradation, by rejecting that same husband in an open assembly.

His face, when he had heard her words, came back to her now—hurt, shamed and finally angry. It was the anger of a weak man, a man who had lived in the shadow of a much stronger personality all his life. Poor Vichitravirya, calling himself king, when everyone knew he was but a puppet in the hands of his much older half-brother, Bhishma. But then, Chitrangada, braver and much more of a man, who had been king so briefly before Vichitravirya, had been Bhishma's puppet too. Suddenly Bhishma's 'great' act of renunciation appeared to her in its true colours. Of course, she thought, I now know what it is. By renouncing his right to the throne, to have children of his own, so that his father could marry the fisherman's daughter, Bhishma had let go of the shadow and grasped at the substance. He gained power over all of them, his father, his stepmother and their two sons. Power-drunk, he had become arrogant, uncaring of how he sacrificed others to his own ideas. To bring my sisters and myself here as mates for this idiot, she had thought angrily when she saw Vichitravirya. How dared he, how dared he!

Her sisters had submitted in silence, but she had declared angrily, 'I cannot marry this man.' And then she had done what seemed to her unimaginable now—she had invoked their rules to aid her. 'I had already chosen Salva, king of Saubha, before I was brought here. I had already promised myself to him. You had no right to bring me here.' Heads had nodded in reluctant approval and, looking at them, Bhishma had let her go. She had been exultant. She was the winner. And how easily victory had come!

But she had been foolish. The victory had been as illusory as her belief during her swayamvara that she held her life in her own hands. Why and when had she begun to dream of Salva? It was too distant now and she could no longer remember how it had begun. But her eagerness as the swayamvara approached was still distinct. Now it is in my hands, she had thought. I will garland him and become his wife. Now they cannot say, 'Don't, you cannot.' As she had entered the glittering, crowded hall, her two sisters a little behind her, she had been conscious only of the soft feel of the garland in her hands. How difficult, impossible almost, to move slowly, to keep her eyes decorously on the ground. She had felt, rather than heard, her two sisters whisper softly to each other. She had known they would be stealthily trying to look at the faces of the princes in the room. No need for the men, however, to give the three sisters furtive glances. Their bold, staring eyes had seemed to pierce through her.

Not that she had cared much about these things. For her, there had been only an impatience to hear the mention of Salva's name. But when Bhishma's name had been pronounced, she had come out of her abstraction with a jerk. Bhishma, the so-called celibate, the lifelong bachelor—could it be he? Yes, there was no mistake. 'Bhishma, son of King Shantanu.' There had been roars of laughter at the name, drowning out a few angry murmurs. Under cover of the noise, she had heard Ambika's giggly, throaty whisper to Ambalika, 'Go and garland him, child.'

'Not for me. He's for Amba. She's the eldest, isn't she?'

She had ignored the jibe. She had been looking at Bhishma's face on which outraged pride and fury had battled. And she had sympathized. Yes, ridicule and humiliation were hard to bear. The moment of sympathy had never recurred. The hatred which replaced everything else in her life had been born soon after.

At first, though, there had been only anger. Even when he had driven off with them in his chariot, the three of them tumbling about in an ignominious heap, there had been nothing but anger. Ambika had been in tears, Ambalika excited, but she had cried out furiously, 'Stop, old man, stop.' He had disregarded her; even the calculated insult of 'old man' had not roused him. He had sped on, hair blowing behind him in the breeze.

It was then that the anger had begun. She had understood. He would not dignify her anger by noticing it. She was only a woman, she was to be disregarded, ignored; her will, her determination had to be set aside as nothing because she was a woman. Whereas, one shout from Salva who had chased them had sufficed. Bhishma had brought the chariot to a sudden halt, with a rumble and a jerk that had sent vibrations through her head. She had hit it against something then, and there had been a whirling darkness, from which she had emerged to the sight of Salva walking away defeated, head hanging down. Ambika crying softly. And then Bhishma, still with no word for them, had picked up the reins and driven on again.

Even a man's defeat had its consequences. The three of them were, she realized, Bhishma's by right after that. Or rather, Vichitravirya's, the man on whose behalf Bhishma had fought.

'This weak, this feeble . . . creature, this puny boy—how can I, princess of Kashi, marry him?'

She had laughed in scorn and the boy had winced. But Bhishma had listened stolidly, sure of himself and his power. Perhaps he had thought—she will soon come to her senses. Where can she go? 'Send me to Salva,' she had declared. 'He is the man I chose to be my husband.'

And then, irony truly, the very rules she had invoked in her favour, worked against her.

'I can't marry you,' Salva had said. And surely, the face had been that of a petulant, sulky boy. Was this the face she had dreamt of for so long?

'Bhishma defeated me. You now belong to him. I will be dishonoured if I take you for my wife.'

As she went back to Bhishma, the very dust that surrounded her palanquin seeming to be a cloud of shame, she had thought—honour, dishonour, right, wrong—what are these but words used by men to cover their real emotions? Bhishma was angry, Vichitravirya humiliated and now Salva is ashamed. Where is the honour here? Or, the dishonour?

'The king of Saubha refused you?' the boy had asked, triumph glinting in his eyes. 'And so you come back to me. But I can't marry you. How can I when you have loved, when you still love maybe, another man?'

And once again heads had nodded. 'He is right, what he says is honourable.'

Right! Honourable! The words had angered her. It had been nothing but the petty revenge of a humiliated boy. Can they not see that, she had wondered contemptuously. With a fierce desire to break through this meaningless rigmarole of words, she had said to Bhishma, 'You marry me, then. It's you who have done this to me. You must make amends now.'

For a moment she had seen something in his eyes. What was it? Fear? What was he afraid of? Then the shutters had come down and he had looked at her with a bland, inscrutable face. 'You forget my vow of celibacy. I can't break it. That will be dishonourable.'

The mask had slipped only for an infinitesimal moment. It would not do so again. He had become once more a stuffed figure, filled with ideas and words, trying to deceive himself that they were a substitute for passions and emotions. And then she had known he was trapped too. Not behind walls, as she was, but inside words and ideas. Other people's ideas. He would never get out; she would never get to him.

After that there had been nothing left for her but her hatred. A hatred of Bhishma that filled her life as nothing else had done till then. Even her love for Salva became a childish, foolish dream.

'You have destroyed me, I will fight you,' she had cried out to Bhishma.

'I do not fight women.'

Oh God, to be and not to be seen; to speak and not to be heard. It was like being a child again, trapped in those inner rooms, raging against them.

Now, as she came to a stop, thinking that surely this was far enough, this could as well be the end of her journey, she knew that, at this moment, nothing was left to her. Her mind was empty and blank, like the sky before the first star came out. Her hatred that had been all of her—why, that was gone too. She tried to bring it back, but it was no use. It had receded too far.

No, there was nothing left now but her self. But what was that and who was she? Daughter of the king of Kashi. Amba, the princess of Kashi. There had been an immense pride in those words once. It puzzled and angered her that they seemed to have nothing to do with her any more. She was neither a daughter, nor a wife, nor a mother. What was she then? Amba, Amba, Amba . . . the name came to her from a distance, like a faint echo. It was like hearing her sisters call after her as she ran ahead. But surely, that had been long back? And why did she feel she was one of them too, one of those calling out 'Amba, Amba, Amba'?

She relinquished the thought. It was too late now to think of such things. Too late, and besides, she was too weary. Her very weariness gave her a serenity she had imagined she had lost forever. When the thought of what she had to do now came into her mind, it was like a twig being dropped into tranquil waters. The ripples spread and filled her. Yet, there was no confusion. There was only a stillness and calmness that absorbed those ripples too.

Yes, the time had come. The place as well. It was a long time since she had met any humans. Hours since she had seen even those dark people of the forests. They had looked through her incuriously and it had increased her sense of isolation. She did not belong to their world; she did not belong to the world she had left behind, either. The world where life was lived according to rules that made no sense to her. She had denied those rules. All the same, it had not prevented her from being a pawn in their game. Oh well, she thought as she got up and began to gather faggots, she would sacrifice the pawn herself. The act would be her own. At least this one thing would be of her choosing, the way she wanted, at the time she chose.

The thought carried her on for some time until she had neatly arranged herself in the midst of dry wood, dry leaves carefully spread in between. Once again, the minor discomforts mattered most. The sharp twigs hurt her body, her hair was entangled somewhere. In her impatience to be free of these small pains, she rushed to the task of lighting the fire.

A spark, a small glow. And suddenly she was confronted by flames. There was a moment's panic as she realized she was trapped again. But where would she go?

She closed her eyes against sights, her ears against sounds, her mind against doubts and fears and lay still, submerged in nothingness. The wood had been dried by the heat of summer and the fire blazed fierce and fast. She was calm until the flames touched her. Then she began to scream. Shrill, anguished cries that were her last tenuous link to the world she had so angrily rejected.

In a little while the cries were stilled, the crackling sounds died down and there was nothing left but silence.

A Wall Is Safer

IT IS A narrow ribbon of a road. A little earlier, it had been only an incision in the full-grown sugar cane. Sitting in the minibus, you could hear sibilant whispers as the cane brushed against its sides. With the cane gone, there is nothing to demarcate the road from the flat expanse of land on either side. The lone cyclist is like a marker now, showing me where the road is. I know he is coming here, not only because I can identify him as Ramachandra, but because there is nowhere else he can go. The road ends here with us. The sun glances off his white clothes in a blinding glare as he comes nearer and I am forced into the house. As I wait for him I wonder whether he can tell me why Sitabai hasn't come today. I have been struggling against both exasperation and anxiety since the morning, waiting for her, watching the work pile up.

The tinkle of the cycle bell sends me out. He hands me a note with an ingratiating smile without getting off his bike. 'From the sahib,' he says and rides off, without giving me a chance to say anything. He is afraid I will question him about his domestic tangle—or, is it triangle? It amuses me sometimes, the thought that even here, in this God-forsaken place, there is this problem of 'the other woman'. 'Sex rearing its ugly head' Vasant calls it and laughs. Poor Sitabai! And yet her belligerence keeps sympathy away.

I open the note . . . it is from Vasant . . . neither curious nor expectant about its contents. I know it will be only to tell me that there will be a guest for lunch, tea or dinner. We have more guests here than we ever had in Bombay. Anyone who comes here to meet Vasant has to be brought home for some sort of a meal; there is nowhere else they can go. I am used to it now and it means nothing more to me than having to cook a little extra. The men don't expect anything from me at all. They are here to talk to Vasant and they do just that. When they have to speak to me, they are uneasy. Unnatural, forced smiles flicker across their faces as they talk to me, staying on even when there is no need. They turn away from me with almost audible sighs of relief and I sometimes wonder whether they will recognize me if they see me at another time, another place.

Now I read the note mechanically, thinking—hope it isn't someone for lunch, the vessels are not washed, the house not swept . . . Oh good, it's for tea. And what shall I make for tea? Then suddenly the news penetrates, getting through my housewife's armour. It's Sushama who's coming, Sushama . . . All at once, the texture of the day seems to change, it's pace quickens and livens. Sushama coming to stay an evening and a night. I hurry energetically through my tasks, so fast that when Sitabai eventually turns up, I have done most of them.

'Why didn't you wait for me?' Sitabai asks. 'You know I will always come. Unless I'm dead or dying.'

She isn't being melodramatic, I know she is speaking the literal truth. When she first told me about her pregnancy, my heart had failed me. To look for another woman when I had just got used to this one . . . But now I know she will keep coming. She needs the money and the food. Ramachandra gives most of his pay to 'that woman'.

Sitabai and Ramachandra—apt names for a couple. But, of course it isn't a happy coincidence. Since he was Ramachandra, the woman he married was named, renamed rather by his parents, as Sitabai.

'And that is why I have all these troubles,' she had said phlegmatically once. 'What can you expect when you're named Sitabai but troubles?'

She had used the word vanvaas for troubles. I thought of its literal meaning—'stay in the forest'. Exile. I had toyed with the thought for a while—to be a Sita who follows her husband into exile—would it help? It didn't. I had to laugh as I abandoned it. Me a Sita? I'm here, not out of choice, but because there was none.

'Your husband was just here,' I tell Sitabai. 'I wanted to ask him about you, but he was off like a shot.'

'He?' she spat out the pronoun. 'He hasn't come home for three days. Good riddance, I say. Who wants to see his face? She can have him.'

We get on with our work, the two of us, her monotonous voice providing a soothing background to our tasks. I clear up the children's room, make up Raju's bed for Sushama. He can come in with us. By the time they come—the minibus brings them all at the same time—I am ready for them. Sushama is the first to get off.

'You've lost weight,' she says at once. It is said as if it is an accusation.

'And you're still eating those greasy office lunches.'

'You're darker too,' she goes on, ignoring my words and welcoming smile, still scrutinizing me.

Well, of course. It's the sun. In Bombay you don't really get to know the sun. It keeps it's distance. When it approaches you, it does so deviously—from between buildings, through chinks in curtains, filtering through sparse foliage. Here, there is nothing, absolutely nothing, between you and the sun. It attacks you directly with its two weapons: heat and glare. And you have nothing to fight back with, except the pigment in your skin.

The next hour is chaotic. I have to cope with tea, the children's excited conversation and Sushama following me about chattering. I can relax only when the table has been cleared. The children instantly go out and resume some game of theirs. The three of us sit out in cane chairs, the only sound at first being the hissing noise Sitabai makes between her teeth as she washes up, squatting at the low tap a little distance away. We watch the sunset. The vast panorama of the sky is always overwhelming here. Now, it is dramatic too, a corner of the stage illuminated as if a spotlight has been turned on to it. It is like a flamboyant finale when the sun finally goes down in flaming colours. Each time I see this, I feel some kinship with those ancient Aryans who sang paeans to the Being who made all this possible. A tinge of freshness touches my jaded mind. All at once it is evening. There is that curious hush which is only an interlude before the night sounds begin. We speak in low voices now as if it would be wrong to break this stillness. The children are unaffected and their high, excited voices punctuate our conversation.

'God, it's wonderful here,' Sushama says. 'Peaceful. All the same I wouldn't like to live here. Terrible.'

I know what she means. Everything here is limitless, immense. Your eyes go easily all the way to the horizon. The immensity makes nothing of you and your concerns. Sometimes it soothes me, this idea of my own insignificance. Often, however, I am angered that it makes so many years of my life take on the grey colour of futility.

Vasant is now arguing with Sushama and she retorts with spirit. She says, 'Your agricultural research station' and 'You research scientists' with a sharp note of sarcasm in the words. 'You Bombay people,' he says disparagingly, and I know he will soon go on to 'You lawyers' and the final withering 'You women lawyers'. He gets to it at last and then says, 'And as if that isn't enough, you have to turn into a feminist as well.'

I wonder why the word 'feminist' invariably sounds derogatory. Is it the way it is pronounced? But Sushama is irritated by the very word. 'I'm not a feminist,' she says firmly. 'That's too vague. What we're trying to do is very concrete. We want women everywhere to become aware of their legal rights. Nothing more.' She has already told me she is here to attend a meeting in a town very near us. 'We've roped in the local women's clubs and associations,' she says and tells us what they're planning. Even Vasant gives up his supercilious pose and listens. Seriously. And I remember their last encounter.

She had fought against his decision to take up this job which brought us here. 'Look,' she had said, 'you have an alternative. A perfectly good job in Bombay. But if you go there, what about Hema? What can she do there in the middle of nowhere?'

'She can teach. Or something. There are schools in the next town.'

'For God's sake, man, she's a lawyer, not a teacher. Would you change your profession that way overnight?'

'It's not the same.'

'Why?'

Unable to move him, she had turned on me. 'You're a defeatist,' she had said. 'You're just giving up.'

'Well, what can I do? This is the work he always wanted to do. So he's going anyway, in any case. Period. Maybe I can continue here with the children—I've thought of it. But it means two establishments. Money problems. A weekend, not a vacation marriage. The children without their father for months, me without a husband for months, he without a wife and children for months. So . . . ?'

Now, after listening to Sushama, Vasant suddenly turns to me and says, 'Look, Hema, why don't you get involved with this thing of Sushama's? You can go once a week, maybe . . .'

You don't have to feel guilty, I want to say to Vasant. It's my doing, this coming here. Nobody pushed me into it.

'Sorry, Vasant, it won't work,' Sushama says.

'Why not?'

'Ask Hema.'

I move indolently in my chair while I think of what to say. I'm a pure professional, I want to say. Like you. I'm a lawyer, not a social worker. But I don't say any of this. Instead I mumble, 'Oh, I'm all right as I am. After all, I'm a good housewife now.'

I'm not being bitter or ironic. I mean it, but somehow it silences the two of them. After an awkward pause, Vasant changes the subject. 'Oh yes, I forgot to tell you. They're starting on the fence tomorrow.'

I have been asking for it for quite a while now. When we first came here, I had had a queer feeling that there was something wrong with this house. Something more than the fact that it was squat, ugly and purely functional. It took me a few days to realize that it was the lack of a fence. You stepped out of the front door and were immediately swallowed up into immensity. It had daunted me and I had begun agitating for some sort of a fencing.

'Oh good!' I say.

We are on a safe track now. Vasant tells Sushama about his work and Sushama, impressed, but determined not to show it, says lightly, 'Well, well, I can see you're heading for a Padma Shri at least.' He protests laughingly, but I can see he is pleased. And Sushama goes on, 'And here she is, the woman behind the successful man, the one to whose support you owe everything, the devoted, self-effacing wife . . .'

'Oh shut up!' I say, smiling to show I know it is a joke. But the words stay with me. Self-effacing. Suppose you go on effacing yourself until you're wholly blotted out? For some reason I think of the cry of the newborn. A triumphant assertion of being. Of existing. And I also think of how there is no difference between the cry of a female baby and a male one. When does it become a virtue to stifle that cry?

I don't know the answer to this question. I only know that I bitterly envy Vasant when he comes home tired, satisfied and full of what he has been doing. Formerly he used to share his day with me. Not any more. I wonder why. Maybe, it's because I have nothing to offer in exchange. The small cash of my day seems paltry in comparison.

At night, after the children and Vasant have gone to bed, Sushama puts me through a cross-examination. Am I happy here? What do I do with myself? Can I go on this way?

'I'm busy,' I tell her. 'I have enough to do. I cook, I clean, I wash, I iron, I read, I listen to music, help the kids with their lessons, I visit . . .'

I am forced to stop for lack of breath and Sushama pounces on me. 'Visit? Who? Or, is it whom?'

'Whom, I think. Families like us. There are a few houses on the other side of the farm.'

We visit one another with scrupulous regularity. I have now got used to the monotonous grind of the conversation, the sameness of the topics we touch. What I cannot get used to is the way I feel when I'm with them. It's like I do when the minibus moves away from me in the mornings, my own reflection sliding past me in a continuous series. So many identical reflections of my own self—they make me uncomfortable.

'For God's sake, Sushama,' I finally say, 'don't make me out to be one of your exploited women. I know all my legal rights.' She knows when to stop. She gives up and we begin to reminisce. I go to bed in a good mood, but I am surprised by a fierce surge of longing to be one of those women who carry their work about with them—a writer, a painter, a musician . . .

The next morning they are all to leave at the same time. I rush about getting breakfast ready, suddenly eager to have the house and the day to myself once more. The children shout warnings when they see the bus approach. Sushama smiles and says, 'Well, when are you coming to Bombay?'

'I don't know. Some time.'

'I may come here myself for another meeting.'

'Lovely,' I say, but somehow I don't look forward to it. In some way, Sushama threatens the tenuous peace I've built around myself. The bus comes and they all get in. It begins to move and mechanically I count my reflections . . . one, two, three, four. Then they are gone. I am sure Sushama is already looking through some papers. Vasant will be reading too, the children squabbling over seats. I go inside and Sitabai asks me, 'Have they gone? Your friend too?'

There is a gleam in her eye which tells me she is going to grill me about Sushama—is she married and how many children and where does her husband work? I hurry to offer her a bait that will turn her thoughts elsewhere. 'Sitabai,' I say, 'they are coming to put up the fence today. Barbed wire.'

'Barbed wire?' Sitabai sniffs in contempt. 'What's the use of barbed wire? They should build a wall. It's safer.'

A wall? As the work goes on and the fence goes up around us, I think of her words. Finally it is done. Five rows of barbed wire. And only then I understand Sitabai's words. A wall is safer. With a wall, you can't even see what's on the other side. But suppose the dangers are inside? What do you do then?

The Duel

HOW DOES A writer write about himself? Specially when he knows he cuts a poor figure? He fantasizes, I suppose, and makes himself out to be tragic, weak, wicked, evil . . . anything but foolish. But I can't do this. Something tells me that the fabric of my story can stand nothing but the truth. And didn't she say, 'You will write about me, won't you?' So here you are . . .

'Oh, come on,' I said brusquely.

We were sitting on the porch of her house. The setting was so picturesque as to be almost banal. Tendrils of the bougainvillea were trailing down the roof of the porch. Its flowers looked, in the moonlight, unabashedly artificial. A full moon had just risen and hung low in the sky, a large orange dollop, stagy and uneasy. Fragrances of various flowers wafted to us from the garden. The right setting for a declaration of love. And yet, as a writer, I wouldn't have used it. I'd have chosen instead a dingy restaurant, a crowded bus or a train. Anything to contrast. But, here we were, surrounded by this romantic melody, to which, I felt, neither of us was really attuned.

'Well?' I waited patiently for her response.

I've met with a variety of them in my time. This one was an almost total lack of response.

'No, thank you,' she said matter-of-factly. As if I had offered her something to eat. But it was she who had fed me to my repletion some time back. So that I should have been lazily content. Instead I was all on an edge. I picked an apple off the table between us.

'Why not?' I asked savagely. 'Surely you don't believe in all this morality business? A bourgeois concept like that?'

A good thrust, I thought. Nothing needles a person as much as being called a bourgeois. But she didn't stir.

'Or maybe you believe in a husband's monopoly?' I drawled.

'Monopoly?' The retort was sharp. 'What am I?'

After a pause she spoke again. And it was as if she had sheathed her sword. 'No, it has nothing to do with morality. It's more simple. I don't feel like it.'

Her voice had a kind of soft huskiness that added an odd significance to her simplest words. Now they lingered between us while I took another bite of the apple.

'Tchah!' I flung it angrily away from me. 'Flat!'

She suddenly laughed. Her face was in the shadows and I couldn't see it. But there was genuine amusement in that laugh.

'And now, I suppose I should say "like my life" or something like that, shouldn't I? If I were a woman in one of your stories, I bet you'd have made me say that, wouldn't you?'

I mumbled something non-commital.

'Actually, the only thing that occurs to me is that I've been cheated. Five rupees wasted,' she added reflectively.

'Philistine,' I spoke scornfully.

'Perhaps,' she replied equably.

'But to go back to my point. Why not?'

I don't know why I should have persisted. What was there in her? Nothing exceptional about her looks. A rather fleshy nose. A rounded chin. Eyebrows that had retained their natural shape. No, nothing unusual. A woman like many others.

One who fed her household, looked after her children and carried an aura of domesticity around her.

No, it was not her. It was me. I had this penchant for middle-class women. I enjoyed seeing them shed their inhibitions. I loved ripping off the thin facades of their morality. It gave me a thrill, an ecstasy almost, like writing on a blank sheet of paper. Or was it more like fighting a duel? I don't really know.

'Why not,' I repeated now to this woman with a maddening insistence.

'I just told you. And besides,' she suddenly roused herself out of her somnolence and retorted with spirit, 'if I did, what would you do but make use of me in your writing? Wouldn't you?'

I laughed lazily. 'Perhaps. And what's wrong with that? I get you out of my system that way and you get out of your frustrations.'

'Frustrations? I'm not frustrated.'

'If you aren't, you should be,' I said impatiently. What was the use of all this verbal sparring? 'I mean, everyone is.'

'I'm not. I'm just bored. Unutterably bored. There was a time when I tried to find a meaning in everything. Now I feel everything ends in absurdity. No, I can't believe in anything.'

'You don't have to believe in anything, do you, to go to bed with me?'

I brought her firmly back to the point.

She moved suddenly. I could see the stone on her ring flash in the dark. But I had an illusion that it was not her ring but her eyes that flashed fire at me. Now, I thought, we will see the outraged female.

'What!' she exclaimed. 'Not even in you?'

Her voice was unexpectedly rough. Was there a hint of laughter in it? Certainly, there was no shock or outrage in her tone. I tried to see her face, while she went on with her own thoughts. 'And anyway, that's so commonplace as to be almost a cliché isn't it? If you can call an idea a cliché?'

'What idea?'

'That a woman who is bored needs to have a child. Or lover. Or a mission in life.'

Strange . . . I couldn't see her face, but I could almost see those capital letters.

'Sometimes, clichés are true. Most often they are. That's how they become clichés.'

'You fool,' she suddenly flashed out at me. 'And I thought you were perceptive.'

'I am. I guessed you were bored. I'm offering you a panacea for it.'

'Like a doctor with a prescription. So many doses of sex for this woman.' Her voice rose. 'Is life lived only on the physical plane?'

'What else?'

'Yes, what else?' She moved restlessly in her chair. 'Which means my existence ends with my body's dissolution. When I'm gone . . . ' she said the words thoughtfully, lingering over them, 'when I'm gone, I will leave no trace behind.'

I could see her ring gleam and sparkle in the dark as she rippled her fingers lightly in the air. 'So what's it all about?'

I checked my impulse to laugh. This was a new line to me. You ask a woman for her body and she tries to lead you into metaphysics.

'Why do you want me?' she asked me abruptly, as if she had read my thoughts.

'Why? For one thing, I find you sexually exciting.'

That wasn't strictly true. I found the thought of arousing her out of her placidity exciting.

She met this calmly. 'What do I get from you that I don't get from my husband?'

Now I was outraged. It was all right for me to be cynical. Not for her. 'I bet you he's dull,' I said, purposely coarse.

'And you promise me you won't be?'

She moved forward into the moonlight. I could see that her eyebrows were raised. Her face, absolutely pale in the moonlight, looked not beautiful, but intimate. And I saw her for the first time as a human being, not as a woman. It was like a door opening and the room inside was very familiar. And suddenly, most unwillingly, I knew why. She had the same look of innocence my mother had had. To me, my mother had been pure and undefiled. Until that night.

Why had I been in their room? I don't remember. But I can distinctly remember that I woke up to hear odd sounds coming from the dark. I had been terrified, more so when I recognized my mother's voice. Hoarse, unrecognizable, saying something incoherent. And there had been another sound too. My father breathing loudly. Panting almost.

When do children lose their innocence? I was, I suppose, eight or nine then. But I knew what it was. I have never believed in the innocence of women since.

I thrust the memory away resolutely. 'Yes,' I said, feeling I was closing a door. 'I promise you I won't be dull.'

'You don't talk of love.'

She settled back in her chair. Had she realized I had closed the door?

'Love!'

'What would you writers do without love? And you say "love" like that.'

'I'm being honest with you. I don't wrap up my desire in fancy wrappings and coloured ribbons.'

'What you really mean is that to escape the pointlessness of my life, I should drift into an equally pointless affair with you.'

'Drift? No, I ask you to choose deliberately.'

'Choose?' Now she repeated the word and she seemed to be mocking me. 'I've never done that in my life. I've always drifted.'

At this point the husband came out. 'What are you two discussing so seriously?' he asked, taking a chair on the other side of the table. He was like the third point of a triangle. Only, there was none.

'Nothing,' she replied calmly. 'Just the reason for existence.'

'But why in the dark?' He switched on the light. I blinked. I was furious with him. And her.

'Actually,' I spoke deliberately, 'I was making love to your wife.'

He laughed. She gave him, and me too, an odd look I couldn't fathom. I went home nettled. This was almost the first time a woman had refused to play my game. And for no reason at all. It was like brushing off cobwebs. Her resistance added spice to the affair, though. I had to go on. What was she? An enigma? No, no woman is ever that. I was certain she would come to me. And then I would know again that strange mixture of anger, disappointment and contempt which is always for me the beginning of the end.

I was proved right. She strolled in one day. Casually, nonchalantly. I treated her the same way. The next move was up to her. I could see she had come prepared for something. There was a quality of stillness about her, different from her usual indolence. It was as if she was simmering behind that placid facade. And there was something else. A kind of rigidity that reminded me of a frightened child.

Then she spoke, 'Well?'

That was all. That and a queer smile. She had dark circles, I noticed, almost like bruises, around her eyes. But her mouth was soft and full like that of a young girl in her teens.

'Well?' I looked at her questioningly, determined not to help her.

'What next?' she said, as naive as a child.

And that was that! Her resistance had been inexplicable. Now her surrender was unexpected. But I had no desire to probe. Just to take what she offered me.

She let me do what I wanted with her. She seemed totally unconcerned and detached, as I went on. It annoyed me. I'm no connoisseur of female beauty. They all look good to me. So did this one. But her face puzzled me. It was so expressionless, it looked like the sketch of a face with the eyes left out. As if she wasn't there at all.

Is life lived only on the physical plane? Her own question came back to me. And suddenly I was filled with a savage fury. Why had she come if she was so disinterested?

And, all at once, she was not. Disinterested, I mean. There was a frantic quality about her that belied her usual indolence. There was nothing passive about her now. Nothing. It was much later, when the euphoria that had overcome me was passing away, that I said, 'So you decided to try the cliché, after all?'

She sat up abruptly in bed with a magnificent disregard of her nakedness. A kind of startled pain leapt to her eyes. It was like something filling a vacuum. For a second, I found myself submerged in that pain of hers. Then she lay back again, silent, refraining from saying what she had wanted to.

After a while she spoke in a normal tone. 'You were right.'

'Right?' I asked, drowsily drifting between sleeping and waking.

'Bodies . . . that's all we are. There's nothing else.'

'Did I say that?' I was idly incurious.

'Yes. But if that's true, why is this . . . all this . . . so meaningless? Where's the meaning, then?'

I was suddenly drowsy no more. I ignored the angry despair of her tone and concentrated only on her words. So the duel was still on, was it? And she would wallow in guilt, enjoying it, and expecting me to enjoy it too. But I had my own way of dealing with that kind of masochism.

'What kind of a meaning did you expect?'

And then I chuckled loudly.

'What's that for?'

'I was thinking of the wronged husband. I'm sure he'll tell you what this means.'

'Wronged husband?' The high note of interrogation expressed genuine surprise. Didn't she know whom I meant? I turned to her. She was lying unutterably still, hands folded on her chest, immovable as a corpse. And then, with a swift movement, she turned to me, propped her face on her fists and said, 'I haven't wronged anyone.'

And for the second time, there was a crack in the glazed surface. Emotion seeped through it. I refused to meet it. Or recognize it.

'Haven't you?' I asked, smiling lightly.

And now, I thought, she will tell me how unworthy he is, how unloving, how unreceptive . . . and I, I will agree, though I will now have, for this man, a strong affection. There will always be a strange intimacy between us, an intimacy he will never know.

But she only said, 'No.'

Nothing more. And silence again. I was wide awake now, and wished she would go away. It was like someone staying on after the party was over. I sat up in bed to give her a hint. She sat up too and said, 'And now, you'll write about me, won't you?' She was like a person insisting on being photographed. I wryly wondered whether she had been all the time posing for me. Not that it mattered.

'If you insist,' I said.

'Perhaps,' she went on, getting up at last and giving me a twisted smile, 'that may be my only justification for living.'

She dressed herself, and went her way. I felt released. And triumphant. She had come to me herself, and I had possessed her. That was enough for me. Now I could forget her.

But I couldn't. Not that I dreamt of her all night. But my first thought on waking the next day was of her. I had what

I can only call a visual obsession that was maddening. I kept on seeing her face. It was distinctly odd. I had never felt that way before. I found myself waiting impatiently for her to return. Women always do in my experience, if you leave them alone. Pique, curiosity—I don't know what—something drives them.

But she didn't come. And it was I who was piqued. Not that, I told myself, it makes any difference. There are always other women, other worlds. But there was a strong feeling in me that whatever it was that had happened between us was unfinished. I was as tantalized as a man waiting for the dénouement of a whodunnit. I can't remember now what kind of a final act I had envisaged. One thing is certain. What really happened was far removed from what I could have imagined even in my wildest moments.

It was, I remember, with a sense of defeat and shame that I found myself at her doorstep a few days later. I had never gone this way after a woman before. Why was I doing it then? Angrily I rang the bell and chimes echoed inside as if the house was empty. But no, there were footsteps. The door opened and a strange face stared at me.

After a small silence I asked for her. No, the woman said, with an odd look on her face, she wasn't there.

Her husband? I threw out the name hesitantly.

Don't mistake me, I was not apprehensive about meeting him. On the contrary, I wanted to meet him very much. But not then. I was all keyed up for something else. But at my question, the woman looked even more astonished.

'Don't you know,' she asked me.

'Know what?'

'He's dead.'

A moment of disbelief and then comprehension. The house today with its blank look. Like her face that day. The blood rushed to my head. My mouth opened, my chin sagged.

The woman's face registered enjoyment of my shock, while she went on, speaking fluently as if she'd said the words so many times before that, she knew them by heart.

'Not only him. The children too . . . it was terrible. It was an accident. They were coming home in the evening. It was a truck coming at full speed. It hit them head on. He, the children, they were all killed at once.'

'All?' I croaked out. 'And she?'

'She . . . that was strange. The door opened and she was thrown out. She escaped almost without a bruise.'

You come for a tryst with a woman and meet death. I was totally lost. I groped out of the fog with the vital question, 'When?'

'When? Ten days ago. Last Sunday.'

It hit me like a gloved fist. I had seen the blow coming, but I couldn't dodge it. I took it right on the jaw.

Five . . . six . . . seven . . . eight . . . no, I was not out. I came up reeling to find the door closed, and the footsteps retreating.

Last Sunday. And on Tuesday she had come to me. They were there in my hands now . . . all the pieces, all the clues. All the answers. Even the one I had come to find. Why had she come to me? And now I knew.

My first reaction was anger. I remembered her own words. *The only thing that occurs to me is that I've been cheated.*

Cheated! And the anger was so savage that if she had been there, I'd have squeezed her throat. Then there was bewilderment. And distaste. Bitterness. And finally there was in my mouth the taste of the flat apple I had eaten in her house that day.

I never saw her again. Nor did I have the least desire to.

That was for me the strangest end of a chase. One that ended, not in a blind alley, but in an abyss. No, I never want to look into that abyss again.

But, there's one thing I don't understand. How could she, a woman like that, lay the ghost of my dead mother. For that's what she did. Since then, my mother has slept in peace again, pure and undefiled once more. But what this has to do with that strange woman who gave herself to me under such strange circumstances, is something beyond me. All that I can do is, as I've said before, to write it down as it happened.

The Awakening

I opened my mouth to . . . what? Yell? Protest? Cry? Nothing seemed appropriate so I closed it again, while he went on unnoticing.

'You don't have to, you know. You can always refuse. But think it over first. You know all the facts, anyway.'

Yes, I do. A father who brought into this world more children than he can support on a small salary. A daughter to be married, a son stricken by polio, another daughter yet in school. And I, who will soon be passing my SSC. The conclusion is inescapable.

'I've had them dinned into me often enough,' I muttered.

'What?' he asked.

You had to shout to be heard in that room. The noises: the stove hissing loudy, the onions spluttering in the oil, Rekha's radio on at full blast as usual and Shirish and Shobha squabbling . . . also as usual. Hell!

'Nothing,' I shouted back. 'And why must we have so much noise? It's like a zoo. But even the animals live one in a cage.'

'Go and live there yourself,' Shirish retorted gleefully.

'To call your family animals! Mind your tongue, Alka.'

That was Mother. *God made mothers because he couldn't be everywhere himself.* What nonsense! There are mothers and mothers and mothers. Mine is a woman with a heavy, sullen face (but when she looks at Shirish) and a tongue like a serrated knife (but when she talks to Shirish).

'I don't know how you put up with her impudence!' She cast a venomous look at poor Baba. The man whose one aim in life is to avoid conflicts.

'Oh Baba is a saint,' I said lightly. 'He can put up with so many things. Like you, for example. Why not with my, impudence?'

A saint? Does being an unthinking, unfeeling walking zombie make you a saint? No, he's not a saint, but a fool. A blind fool. And it isn't optimism, but idiocy. If only he hadn't been so smugly content with what he is, with what he has, maybe we'd have got out of here. I can't forgive him for being what he is; I'll never forgive him.

'She should be thankful for what we've done for her. After all, Rekha left school after the ninth standard. She's finishing her SSC.'

She . . . doesn't my mother know my name?

'You know Rekha was different, Manda. She was never very interested in studies. But our Alka is a brainy girl . . .' he looked apologetically at me.

'What's the use of talking now? You know I can't go on. You know I have to give up studies and take the precious typist's job your precious Patkar has offered. You know you've ruined my life.'

'No one can ruin your life except yourself, Alka. Don't be so exaggerated.'

'Me? Exaggerated? That's the one thing I'm not.'

Where have I read the words . . . I am twenty-five unfulfilled dreams old? I am seventeen and feel a million unfulfilled dreams old.

'Oh, what's the use?' I threw down the book I was trying to read. 'What's the use of anything?'

The scene ended, as always, with my walking out of the house. House? One room. I stood in the gallery, my elbows on the faded, decaying wooden railings, my face propped on my palm. On either side of me people stood in identical poses. Watching . . . what? The same meaningless jumble of people milling around. With a gesture of impatience, I moved away. A boy walking past saw me, stopped. He smiled at me. I smiled back. You can't antagonize anyone in a place like this. Specially boys.

'When are your results?'

'Next week.'

'Going to get a first class, eh?'

His eyes roved over me as he spoke and finally settled where I knew they would. I felt myself getting hot as though he was touching me there with his hands instead of his eyes. But what can you expect when you live in a chawl?

I remembered how it had been when I had first come here from Nana's. I had thought . . . how will I live here? Six of us in one room. The sounds that came from beyond the curtain behind which Baba and Mother slept. The common toilets. The smell, as if the whole building was one vast sewer. And everyone looking as complacent and satisfied as if life could offer nothing better. If only I hadn't known anything better! If only Nana hadn't taken us away!

I had been three and Rekha six when we had gone to live with Nana in Poona. Nana had a chemist's shop and lived . . . Oh, it was heaven compared to this chawl. We had gone to a good school where we wore beautiful uniforms of white with coloured sashes and black shoes. Now it all seems a dream.

'How could you have married Baba and got into this mess?' I had asked Mother in one of our rare moments of cordiality. 'I mean, look at the way Nana lives and look at this!'

Mother's face had closed up even more than usual and she had said nothing. But my question had been purely rhetorical.

I had learnt the answer long back. Unlikely, improbable and fantastic though it now seemed, Baba, that dull man and Mother, that bitter, angry woman, had fallen in love and got married in spite of Nana's disapproval. There was one daughter. And then another. And Baba, who had started as a postal clerk continued to be a postal clerk. And then, when a third child, a son, was born, Nana had relented and taken Rekha and me away. But, of course, he had to die, and we had to come back to this hell. Where you open the door and everyone, anyone can look inside. Where nothing is private, not even your thoughts. Where the boys and girls, stupid, mindless robots, are interested in nothing but movies, clothes and each other's bodies. And God knows if we'll ever get out. And Rekha says, 'What's wrong?'

'You'll never get out, Rekha,' I had told her pityingly, confident I would get out myself. 'Look at the kind of husbands they're trying to get for you. All the same sort. All clerks. And you'll marry one of them and live in another chawl like this all your life and have three or four children. Like Mother. And one day, they'll become clerks too, by the grace of God. Oh God!'

And then Rekha, stupid, slow Rekha had said something that had shaken me. 'But Alka, why do you think of them as clerks? They're also people.'

And I had cried out, 'You don't understand. I don't mean they're no good because they're clerks. I mean their type. Look at them! How dull they are! How dull they look!'

It had been, a despairing cry, because I had known no one would understand. Surely there is something more to life than this? Something beyond and above this shoddy way of living?

'The trouble is,' Mother had said scornfully, 'you don't know what you want. You only know what you don't want.'

It's not true. I do know what I want. I want to go to college. Attend lectures and take down notes. And read and read. Pass exams with distinctions, go abroad for further studies. Come back and take up a job. Put up my hair and wear glasses and crisp ironed saris like the girl I see at the bus stop every day. Marry (what kind of a man? the face is a blur) and never quarrel with only a curtain between us and the children. And live in a house with a room of my own. A house that smells nice. And have my own clothes, not wear things out of a general pool . . .

All dreams. But more real than reality itself. Now . . . they were not even dreams. Only bubbles, like the ones children blow out of soapy water. Rainbow coloured, ethereally beautiful when they go up in the air. Then in a moment . . . nothing.

I looked back, not with regret, but with shame. I'd been childish. Dreaming of impossible things. I've got to be more realistic. Keep my feet on the ground. No, on the cracked cement floor of this dirty chawl. Where I belong. And where I'm trapped for ever and ever. I'll be a typist now. I'll never be like that girl at the bus stop.

In any case how could I have been like her? I, with my dark complexion, my long nose, my flat figure?

I often looked at myself in the mirror, in stealth of course, willing myself to look like the girl at the bus stop. But the face that looked back, sullen and dark, was Alka's and no one else's. Alka with better brains than all the family put together; Alka, who was to become a typist.

'I can't force you, Alka, I know that. But jobs like these are hard to get. It's Palkar's goodwill that has given us this chance. He knows how hard-pressed I am, specially since Shirish fell ill. I wish I could send you to college but . . .'

I could feel the pit yawning in front of me. Just a week more for my results. And then . . .

And then the world had shattered with a shocking impact. Breaking, not into pieces, but into dust. Into nothingness. The door opened. Two men, Baba's colleagues, entered awkwardly, with shocked faces. And then, pandemonium and hysteria.

How old was he? Only forty-five? Too young to die. It was the first heart attack. No, the second. It seems he had one before and never told anyone. Poor man, to go so fast. What about the family? Isn't there anything for them? So little? Three girls to get married? And the boy . . . how sad! How irresponsible to have a large family in such circumstances. Baba . . . what's happened to my Baba? Hush, Shobha, don't cry like that or you'll start Mother all over again. Shirish, let me do that for you. Thank God Alka's taking up a job. Imagine he was thinking of sending her to college!

A failure, I thought, a failure. He couldn't even struggle with death. Just went out meekly. He lived and he died a failure. What's left? Nothing. Only duties incompleted, responsibilities badly shouldered and empty tears. There was no pity in me for him. Only contempt. God, let me not live like that. Let me not die like that, having achieved nothing, having been nothing. Not even knowing that your life was nothing. Not once could I say, 'My Baba said this.' He said nothing that was not trivial, did nothing that had any meaning. I searched and searched the whole of his life for a meaning and didn't find it.

When all the noise died down, I realised what had happened. My last way of escape had been closed up. I would never get out of the trap now. I had to shoulder his burdens. I would go on doing it till I died. A huge anger filled me. He wronged me by dying. He continued to wrong me even after his death. There was no help for me. There are no fairy godmothers and rich uncles in real life. Not even a God. It makes me laugh when people talk of a God. How childish—a benign, bearded figure up there who looks after all of us. All nonsense, there's no God. Only us.

It was a month later that I came upon the battered briefcase I had seen him carry to work every day of his life. I had often wondered . . . what's there in it, Baba, for you? You go to work, come back, eat, sleep, wake and go to work again. Every single day.

Now I had to hide the briefcase from Mother. Even now, that stolid, sullen woman would break down into the most shaming, heartbreaking hysteria. I had never seen her smile at him, never heard her speak a soft word to him. And yet, I could hear her moaning into her pillow every night. I couldn't understand.

Stealthily I took the briefcase into a corner and opened it. His lunch box. All cleaned up. The newspaper, neatly folded. His glasses. The aspirins he carried around for his frequent headaches. A book to read on the train . . . a whodunnit. All so pitiful and small that for the first time a wave of pity broke over me. But the indifferent pity of a stranger for another stranger.

And then I saw the two letters. He must have written them that morning. One to his elder brother. Idly curious, I opened it. My own name leapt out.

'Alka will be starting her job next month. I still feel guilty about that. But what can I do? And then, I have this confidence in her . . . that she will make something of herself, in spite of us all. She has some guts, some spunk in her. If only one of my children achieves something in life, my own will have been worthwhile. Bhau, have you ever read *David Copperfield*? God knows how or why I began . . . I found it second-hand on the pavement one day . . . but now it has become my Bible. There's one line in it . . . 'In our children, my dear Copperfield, we live again!' How true that is, Bhau.'

'Alka! What are you crying for? Alka, stop it, please. Don't. If Mother sees you . . . Alka, don't be a baby.'

But they were not the tears of childhood. They were the first tears of adulthood, bitter, salty and painful.

Independence Day

THEY HAVE ALL gone leaving me alone here. This is how I had
wanted it; nevertheless, I am surprised that they went away so
easily. I had expected them to demur, to argue a little, to try
and make me change my mind. Perhaps they were being
tactful, leaving me to grieve over my father's death by myself.
But there's no grief; how can you sorrow for someone who
looked death steadily in the face, a person to whom it was but
the next step of a journey? I realize now that he'd been
preparing for this for some time. Each time I came home in
the last few years, I found the house denuded of a few more
things. I never asked him where they had gone; reticence has
always been part of our relationship, indeed, of his personality.
And living alone, in the years after my mother's death, he had
retreated even more into silence. It is his silence and solitude
that seem to enclose me now; they are both welcome and
comforting. And there are the memories. Is that why he cleared
the house so thoroughly—to make more room for memories?
I can feel them thronging around me, I can see my mother
at the sewing machine, her face lowered, her hand caressing
the wheel, her small bare feet going up and down on the
treadle. But how can this be *his* memory? No, it's my memory
that I am foisting on him. You can never get at another's
memories, can you?

The absolute quiet in the house makes me strangely restless, and it is a long time before I finally go to sleep. And wake up with a startling abruptness when I hear voices—the disjointed conversation of a group of people all talking together. It takes me a moment to realize it was a dream, a dream in which people were speaking a language I don't know. How strange! Are we not then the authors of our own dreams? Or were the voices real? I go to the window and look over the wall into the yard next door, as if I expect to see the people I'd heard talking there, sitting under the tree. But there is nothing, only the darkness and the emptiness of the night. Even the tree has gone. It was a dream, of course, a dream that came to me out of my past. I wonder what it is that had tugged these people out of my past to this time. Is it the emptiness of this house which reminds me of Padma's words *'they've lost everything'*? But nothing was *taken* from my father; it was he who voluntarily gave up everything. Whereas, those people Padma had been speaking of, the people who came back to me in my dream . . .

Refugees was the word for them, though it was a word never used in Padma's house, where they were spoken of as 'our family'. In any case, to us in the South, so far away from where the brutal division of the country was taking place, the steady stream of traffic that went through Padma's house those months before Independence and after, was only a curious phenomenon. The bloodshed and the tragedy were happening too far away to register with us. But the sight of the men and women sitting on the string beds under the neem tree in Padma's house was a spectacle to be gaped at. In a while I'd have lost interest in them, except for Padma's words which made them suddenly interesting and dramatic figures. 'They've lost everything,' Padma said to me dramatically repeating, I knew even then, words that were not her own. Recently, I saw a shot of the Partition refugees—miles and miles of hopeless trudging humanity moving in two opposite directions, two independent lines, each unaware, it seems, of the other. A rare picture, now that I think of it. It's as if we've stashed away all the ugliness—the uprooting, the killing, the raping—in some dusty forgotten archives, retaining only the sanitized pictures we are more comfortable with. Khadi-clad men and women moving forward in a non-violent surge. Gandhi lifting his fistful of salt at Dandi. The Congress leaders leaning against fat, overstuffed bolsters. It sometimes seems to me that we store our personal memories in old files, putting them away so that we can move on more easily. But memories are not records; they refuse to stay enclosed within covers. They choose their time and spring out at you. Like my own personal memory now does, rushing at me through the dark tunnel of the years. And I can see the woman I have not thought of for years, I can hear the indescribable sounds emerging from her open mouth, her hands flat on her thighs, rocking herself violently faster and faster . . .

'A flock of birds,' my father had said, speaking of the refugees once, in the early days. An unusual way for him to speak; he was not a fanciful man. Inaccurate word as well, for there was none of the joyousness of birds about the tired-looking, dishevelled, bewildered groups with their shabby bags and bundles. The first time we saw them, getting out of the tonga that stopped before Padma's house, we had stared in amazement at the hugging and sobbing that went on. But soon the sight became a familiar one and the people themselves were quickly absorbed in Padma's house, becoming part of it, like ordinary guests. Which is why, when Padma said to me, 'They've lost everything,' it conveyed no more than a kind of monumental carelessness. It was hard to associate tragedy with that house, bursting at the seams and so full of bustle and noise. And yet, my mother always referred to them as 'poor things'. Even my father, who so rarely spoke to any neighbours, got into conversation with Padma's father one day; such an unusual sight that I stood and stared. Padma's father, excited perhaps by my father's taking notice of him, kept respectfully addressing my father as 'Principalsaab', something my father would normally have corrected with an emphatic 'headmaster, not principal'. But that day he let it pass. And when he came home he said, 'A very generous man, our neighbour.' It was the first time in my memory that I had heard him speaking of someone else. Like his talking to Padma's father, this was such an extraordinary phenomenon that I knew something had shaken up my father's usual self. Do I give the impression of a cold and callous man when I speak of my father? But he was not that. Shy, I think; not easy with people. Distanced from most by his reputation as a learned man and a strict teacher. Often I had a feeling, specially when he was with my mother and me, that there was something he wanted to say but couldn't. Now, years later, I remember the way his fingers moved at such times, like a shadow artist creating shadow pictures on the wall.

But, yes, my father was right. Padma's father was a generous man, for, though he was only the owner of a sweetmeat shop, he took them in unhesitatingly, all the people who arrived with such regularity. Not everyone who came stayed on, though; many went away in a while, specially the young ones, and others took their place, so quickly that I forgot those that had gone. But I still remember a young pair, a sister and brother I think from their resemblance, who enchanted me with their beauty. With their fair complexions and sharp features, they had the chiselled look of marble statues. But now, when I think of them, it is not their beauty that I remember, but their eyes. Empty. As vacant as the eyes of a statue.

It was the older people who sat on the string beds under the neem tree, some in loud and animated discussion, one or two always lying on the beds, staring at the sky through the branches of the neem tree. And often, in the evenings, a group of them played cards. I had never seen adults playing cards before. To me, it was a game children played during their holidays. But the way these people played, with a desperation and a kind of silent passion, made it into something that was not a game at all. And, what seemed even more odd to me was that even the women joined in this game.

But everything about these people was odd to us, actually. Not just their language, but their clothes, for example; the women wore huge baggy salwars and kameezes, 'Punjabi dress' as we called it then, something we had never seen adult women wearing. Grown women, according to us, wore saris. It was the dress that made them 'Punjabis' to us, something that Padma energetically refuted and never tired of correcting. 'We're not Punjabis,' she would say. 'We're Sindhis.' I remember her exasperation in school when, one day, a girl again spoke of her family as Punjabis. 'We're not Punjabis, we're Sindhis,' Padma began, then suddenly stopped and grabbed the girl by her hand. 'Come,' she said, 'come, I'll show you.' I followed the two of them into the assembly hall which was a hive of activity that day. It was only a few days before the first Independence Day and the school was preparing to celebrate. The hall looked like a house a few days before a wedding, there was the same joyous buzz of excitement in it. A sense of chaos, yet each one knew what she was doing. Padma went straight to the group of girls who were drawing a map of India—a huge one—which would be the backdrop for the stage on the day. The girls had an old map by their side to look into. Compared to the old one, the new map seemed incomplete. As if someone had clipped its wings. And the proportions too, were, somehow, not quite right; it looked elongated, as if the whole country was standing on tiptoe. Padma stood with her victim firmly in her grasp before the map and said, 'I'll show you, I'll show you Sind . . . ' And then she stopped. Her hand hovered over the map, moved up and down searchingly and then fell to her side. She looked bewildered as if she had lost something. 'It's gone,' she said, turning to me, as if accusing me of having taken it away. 'It's not there.'

They've lost everything. Was this part of it? Was it possible to misplace a piece of land as well? Did I think of this then? I don't remember. But I can remember Padma's face as it was then, the look of total bewilderment on it. It meant nothing to me at that moment. After all, what did a blank space on a map mean at that time and in that place of joyous excitement?

Memories don't come in sequential order. I have to fit them together. And when I do this, it seems to me that it was the morning after Padma's futile search for her homeland that we heard the cry. There had been the usual sounds of arrival, the clip-clop of the horse's hooves as the tonga arrived, the jingle of bells round the horse's neck, all the sounds loud and clear in the silence of the early morning. Then the bustle of arrival with a jumble of voices speaking all at once. Doors banged, voices receded and the morning quiet enveloped us once more. Until it was shattered by a cry. A cry? It was a long-drawn-out mournful wail, like the howling of a dog in the night. It sent a shiver up my spine, the goosebumps came out on my arms and even my mother rushed out, a startled look on her face. But there was nothing after that cry. As if a spell had been cast on the house, its inhabitants remained cloaked in silence and invisibility.

But news, bad news specially, can never be sealed in. We soon heard what had happened. One of the women, she whom we called the 'fat aunt', had come to know that her only surviving daughter who had been missing all these months, was dead. Dead, it seemed, in some terrible way, from the manner in which the adults who spoke of it looked and whispered.

My mother went next door in the afternoon. And when she returned she wept aloud, so rare a thing that I was frightened. Even my father hovered around her as if he wanted to do something, to say something. I felt the weight of the woman's loss through my mother's weeping. Still, it was hard to connect the woman, who to us was a figure of fun because of her bulk, to this enormous tragedy. Tragedy receded anyway, put into the shade by my own moment of glory which now arrived. The two are connected in my memory by Padma's absence, for Padma was away from school the day I was chosen to be Bharat Mata in the finale of the Independence Day pageant. I was walking out of the schoolroom, I remember, when someone came and told me I was wanted in the assembly hall. There was a group of girls there gathered around the teacher, a group that parted to make way for me, so that I was facing Pushpa teacher, one of the youngest and the most popular among the teachers. She looked gravely at me for a moment when I stood before her and then suddenly smiled and said, 'You'll do.' And then, turning to the girls, 'She's right, isn't she?' The girls looking at me questioningly, doubtfully, as if assessing me and finding me wanting. Pushpa teacher then picked up my plait and said, 'Look at her hair, just look at that.' The girls were still silent, but as if that sealed the matter she let my plait drop and told me what it was: I was to be Bharat Mata on Independence Day.

I can see myself, bursting with pride, rushing home to tell my mother about it. But her response was not as I had expected it to be. Her face was doubting, questioning, almost like the girls', yet not quite.

'Why you?' she asked me, suspiciously I thought.

Because, I told her, the girl who was supposed to play the role had suddenly fallen ill.

'Yes, but why *you*? Is it because your father is the headmaster?'

'No.' I exclaimed indignantly. 'It's because of my long hair. Pushpa teacher said so.'

Not only did this not satisfy her, she seemed even more displeased. I heard her speaking to my father in the evening. I was terrified she would say something that would take my glory away from me. But I heard my father say, 'Nonsense!' And then, 'She knows what she is doing.' *She?* Did he mean me?

My mother's displeasure was even more obvious when Pushpa teacher came home the next day to choose a sari for me to wear on the day. Her face closed up, she brought out some saris of hers for Pushpa teacher's choosing. Pushpa teacher, unaffected by my mother's silence, went on talking and picked up the saris one by one. Finally, holding one against me, she said, 'This one, I think. Sir, don't you think so?'

Yes, my father was home that day. How strange it was to find him taking interest in any of my activities apart from my studies. He spoke little, was almost as silent as my mother, but Pushpa teacher included him in the discussion, calling him 'Sir' at the beginning of each sentence. I remember the enormous emphasis with which she said the word and even today, when I hear someone say the word, I think of her, I think of that day.

'Yes,' my father said, realizing some response was expected of him. 'Yes, it's good.'

Pushpa teacher wanted to try out the sari on me right away. I could sense my mother's reluctance, but she did it nevertheless, her fingers deftly making the pleats, tucking them in, arranging the edge over my shoulder. I felt a kind of anger in the roughness with which she did these things, but when it was done and I looked at her face I knew she was not angry. Not with me, anyway. She was amused. And no wonder. When I looked in the mirror, I thought I looked like a pincushion. But Pushpa teacher was not amused; she chewed her lip, looking worried. 'Well,' she said finally, 'I think you will have to cut the sari.'

'No,' my mother said. 'No! It's my wedding sari.'

And she held me close as if it was I who was being threatened.

I heard my parents arguing again that night and the next day I saw my mother sewing the cut edge of the sari, her head lowered over her sewing. Memory comes to me now spiked with insight and I know that she was concealing her face so that I should not see that her eyes were red. And I know too—now—that it was not always the wood-fire smoke that inflamed her eyes, as she said. And even then I knew that her moods had much to do with my father. I can see so clearly her curious under-her-lashes look following my father's retreating back. An only child, I was too close to the pulse of my parents' marriage, too linked to my mother's emotional being. There was something about the manner in which she got my dress ready that made me uneasy and subdued my joy.

It was Padma who restored it. Even the shadowy memory of that joy is stronger than any happiness I have known since. She listened silently, her eyes and mouth three 'ohs' of amazement when I told her I was to wear a sari, a grand Benaras sari, a crown, jewels, and yes, make-up too. No one had said this to me, but I knew that you never went on stage without lipstick and two spots of rouge high on the cheeks.

Padma was there, watching with awe when my mother made me try on the sari and blouse, she walked around me in silent admiration, like a devotee circumambulating in a temple. And then, stopped before me and exclaimed, 'Let's go and show my mother.'

I hesitated, I remember that, I drew back when we came to the yard, as I draw back now from the memory of what was waiting for me there. They were all there in the yard under the tree, but silent now, wordlessly working together. I must have noticed it then, though my mind was full of myself and of the effect I would have on them, for I seem to know now that they had two baskets in their midst, one piled with sweets, the other with some fried stuff. They were busy packing small paper bags with these—two sweets and a fistful of savoury in each bag. These were for us—I knew this when they were distributed to us in school the next day.

It was Padma's mother who saw us first. 'Look who's here,' she said with a smile. 'Bharat Mata herself.'

As if a breeze had rippled through them, there was sudden movement. Heads were raised, faces turned to me. Words flew about, incomprehensible yet familiar sounds to me by now and I knew I was being admired. And then suddenly, as if cut by a knife, the voices ceased. They turned away from me to the woman who'd made a queer sound. Somehow, I could no longer call her the 'fat aunt'.

'She wants you to go to her,' Padma's mother said. I had loved being the centre of attention, but this was not the same. Her blank fixed stare made me uneasy. Nobody spoke. And when, finally she did, her voice was hoarse as if it had been unused for a long time.

'Bharat Mata,' she said. And laughed, laughter that changed in an instant into a cry—the same cry we had heard that morning.

Padma's mother moved swiftly, she put her arms round the woman, saying, 'Padma, go away, both of you, go, just go.'

I could not move. Mouth open, I watched the woman still uttering that cry, her hands on her dough-like thighs, rocking herself, violently, faster and faster. And then she fell, face down, right there on those two baskets, spilling all the stuff out on the ground. I began to retreat at last, backwards, and my last sight was of her being lifted and dragged away, the huge breasts we had found so funny almost touching the ground.

I suppose everything happened on Independence Day as it should have—the flag hoisting, the games, the songs, the fireworks. But all that I can remember is the rain on my face as the tricolour went up and the quiver that went through me when I saw the packets of sweets, piled in those same baskets.

As for the evening, which should have been my time of glory, I remember that the sari was too heavy, the pedestal seemed to rock under me and the crown and armlets had been tied on so tight that the string cut cruelly into my skin. I had thought I would dazzle everyone when I stood there, but it was I who was dazzled by the spotlights. Standing against the truncated map edged by glittering little lights, when I looked down into the audience, I could see none of those I wanted to see. Instead, in the darkness I saw the woman lying face down among the baskets. And when, as the grand finale, the girls marched in singing *Jhenda ooncha rahe hamara*, I thought I heard above all the girls' voices, the woman's scarcely human cries, the sound of her keening.

The Day Bapu Died

HE WAS NEVER Gandhi, or Gandhiji, or even the Mahatma to us; we always spoke of him as Bapu. This was because my father had lived in Sabarmati Ashram for two years. Those two years, my father often said—not to me, no, he rarely spoke to me—were the best years of his life. I'd heard the story so often, I knew it well—of how he had run away from home, how Bapu had sent him back to get his parents' permission and what Bapu had said to them . . .

I don't need to say it now, do I, that my father was a Gandhian? That was the most important thing about us then. Not only did it set us apart from other ordinary people, everything in our life was shaped by that one fact. Even my father's job, as principal of the college, and the house we lived in, were part of it. These were given to him as a reward for having been in jail during the Quit India movement. Memory, for me, begins with that house.

We were proper Gandhians. Which meant simple living—that is, wearing khadi, eating plain food, no tea and no servants. And my father, in spite of being a college principal and possibly the next muncipal president, swept out the two front rooms himself. After which I could scarcely complain, could I, about having to do the rest of the house? Gandhians, I was told, did their work not only without complaining, but joyously. I did try; nevertheless I must confess I was happy when Tungi came to us and took over this chore from me. And it was all right, it seemed, for Tungi to do this, because she wasn't a servant, she was one of the family. She was the daughter of a distant cousin of my mother's who came to us from her village for her schooling. After failing her fifth standard—not once, but twice—she gave up and stayed at home to help my mother. This was what was said, though actually it was Tungi who did most of the work. My mother was so bulky—well fat really—and puffed and panted so much even when she just walked, that she couldn't do much except the cooking. She was good at that, though; I can still remember her sitting in the midst of all her cooking paraphernalia, her face absorbed, her hands flying about the pots and pans like little birds.

We did have a man to do all the outside work; perhaps he could be called a proper servant. But having Kalappa actually proved that my father was a real Gandhian, because Kalappa was a Harijan. That's the word my father used; Tungi used another word which sounded ruder—or maybe it was just the way she said it. My mother reprimanded her whenever she used that word, but I heard her say it herself once or twice too, though in an absent-minded kind of way. It didn't sound so rude then. Kalappa had a room at the back of our compound; this was called 'living with us' and much was made of it. I couldn't understand it and wondered why they spoke of Kalappa as living 'in' our house, since he never came into it at all. He kept his distance. It was his son Ashok who hovered around the house and I noticed it made my parents a little uncomfortable. Whenever they saw him, they invariably asked him, 'What is it? What do you want?'

Ashok was a friendly and cheerful boy, but I could sense that my parents, specially my father, didn't quite approve of him, though he never said this in so many words. Take his name, for example: it was not really Ashok, it was Basya. He'd adopted 'Ashok' himself. I don't know why this was wrong, but my father obviously thought so. He always mentioned him as 'that boy of Kalappa's', never Ashok. My mother, when she spoke to him, said 'you' or 'you boy'. Tungi went even further and called him all kinds of rude names. Tungi had an amazing vocabulary of foul words, but Ashok never seemed to mind what she said. He just grinned back at her. In a way, I think they were friends and I became a part of that friendship too that year—the year Bapu died.

How old was Ashok then? He must have been fourteen or fifteen; he was younger than Tungi certainly. But he seemed enormously experienced. He drank soda out of bottles, smoked cigarettes, played cards and that other game with stones which involved money and he saw films. I knew all these were vices. Tungi agreed, but she was not so sure about the films. After all, she said, he was working in Ganesh Talkies, so he couldn't help seeing the films, could he? He didn't spend money to see them, did he? The problem was that Tungi, after listening to the stories of films which Ashok narrated to her, had become an addict herself. These sessions took place in the backyard, with Tungi, an utterly fascinated listener, sitting on the steps that led down to the yard, and Ashok in the yard, acting out all the roles by himself. I stood in the doorway, to show, perhaps, that I was not really part of it, for somehow I sensed that my parents would think this activity wrong. Tungi tried to whitewash it: it wasn't like we were watching it in a theatre, she said. Look how your mother drinks coffee, she said—milky, sweet, cardamon-flavoured coffee—because she is not supposed to drink tea. This is the same kind of thing, she said. I wasn't entirely convinced, nor, I suspect, was she, for the storytelling took place in the afternoons when my father was in college and my mother sleeping. And for me, the sense of wrongdoing remained.

The stories Tungi loved were the ones in which lovers were parted—she had tears in her eyes at that—and, after many harrowing ordeals and in spite of everyone, were finally united. Tungi, you see, was a romantic. She was always speaking of her future husband, a mythical being whom she kept following in her mind almost every moment of the day.

'Where do you think *he* is now? What do you think *he* is doing? Do you think *he* knows where I am? Do you think *he* is thinking of me?' And so she went on and on.

At first, bewildered by her references, I had asked her, 'He? Who's that? Whom are you talking of?'

'HE, silly! HE. The man I will marry. The man my parents will find for me any day now.'

She listened with a rapt, ecstatic face to Ashok's stories and when he quoted lines from the film like 'my love for you is like this rose', I suppose it was that 'him' she imagined saying such words to her. She didn't like it when Ashok hurried over these bits, eager to go on to the climax, to the fighting and the hero defeating the villain. Tungi had to keep Ashok's excitability in check when he came to these bits, mindful of my mother sleeping in the next room. But once Ashok's enthusiasm carried him away and we were interrupted by my mother. Tungi got up guiltily in a flurry of movement, tripping over her sari, but Ashok gave my mother a cheeky smile, and to my surprise she smiled back. Sometimes I thought that she really liked Ashok and it was my father's unspoken disapproval of him that kept her from showing it.

'What are you all doing?' she asked me.

'Ashok was telling Tungi a story.'

I disassociated myself from it, you see, in case she got angry, but to my surprise, she wasn't annoyed at all. When she came out of the bathroom wiping her face with her sari, she asked, 'What picture was that?'

'I don't know.'

How did she know it was the story of a film? Had she been listening? I looked at her retreating figure and wondered—was she interested in films then? What would my father say if he knew?

And then my brother came home. He had been away all these years, staying with our uncle in Pune while he did his law. He had fallen ill with typhoid soon after his exams and had come home to recover. Things changed when he came home—to some extent, anyway. For one thing, my mother looked almost animated. She became more adventurous in her cooking too and when she cooked, it was almost like she was playing the *jaltarang*; the pots and pans made musical and happy tinkles, unlike the usual thuds and bangs. My father didn't like her making so many different dishes, I suspect, for he pointedly rejected all the special dishes. My mother's face would change and for a day or two she would restrain herself and then the house would be full of wonderful cooking smells once again.

I must admit that my brother's being home made little difference to me. There was no question of our being companions; there were eight years between us and we hadn't grown up together. He had lived with our uncle most of the time, because of our father being in jail and we were almost strangers to one another. I'm sure it was dull for him at home, for he went out a great deal. My mother was proud that he had many friends, though I never saw him with anyone. It was Tungi who told me about his friendship with Amanda.

Where did Tungi, who stayed home the whole day, get her news from? I don't know, but there she was, with all the information. I guessed even then that a good bit of it was made up. Now, I imagine that, to Tungi, this friendship of my brother's with a girl was somewhat like one of Ashok's stories—romantic and exciting. I could see that she was torn between the excitement of having a love affair going on right before our eyes, so to speak, and her disapproval of Amanda being a Christian girl. That's how she referred to her—'that Christian girl'. It was not just that she thought the name Amanda both unpronounceable and excruciatingly funny; this was her way of showing her dislike of her being a Christian.

'It doesn't matter to you people, of course; you Gandhi people don't care about these things. And if you can have Kalappa in the house, you won't mind a Christian girl. But I'm warning you, if your brother marries her, I won't stay here, I'll go back home.'

'Why, Tungi?'

'What do you mean why? What will *he* think if I stay in the same house as a Christian girl? Why, *he* may even . . .' and she paled at the thought, 'refuse to marry me. No, no, I can't stay here, I'll have to go home. But I feel sorry for your poor mother.'

I'd heard enough about love by then to understand that my brother was in love with Amanda. But there were still mysteries. What did they say to each other? Did they say things like 'my love for you is like this rose'? And did they do the *other things* as well? It was Tungi again who had told me of these *other things*, describing what males and females did to each other when they were in love. It disgusted me. One day I swore I'd tell my mother all that Tungi was talking about, but she only laughed and said, 'Go on, tell her. She does it too. How do you think you were born?'

I was only twelve then and hadn't yet 'grown up'. In fact, after listening to the gory details of this growing up from Tungi, I had no desire to do so. But my body was betraying me; things were happening to it, it was sending me messages to which I didn't seem to have the code. And though I hated this change, part of me wanted it too, for I knew it was the key to the world my brother and Amanda were in, the world Tungi herself was longing to inhabit.

I was even more confused when, one day, I saw my brother and Amanda together among the mango trees. The orchard was owned by a retired judge, whose wife, an uneducated woman, didn't suit him. And so he lived alone in solitary grandeur in the house he'd built for himself among the mango trees, while she lived in the family house in town. I can't remember why I was there that day. It was not a place we willingly went to, there was a kind of sinister feeling among the trees that frightened us. But there I was and I saw them together. I saw the parasol first, I remember, lying open on the ground as if she had been in too much of a hurry to close it. A pink parasol. Nobody carried parasols in those days; most people had those large black umbrellas which were brought out only when it rained. But I had seen Amanda one day with a pink parasol. So it was her. No, it was *them*, there were two people there. I stood rooted to the spot, afraid of being seen and yet unable to move away. As I watched the two figures lying on the ground, closely entwined together, strange shivers ran up and down my spine, my legs felt heavy and weak at the same time. It was a slight movement of the two bodies that brought me out of my stillness. I walked rapidly away from there as if someone was chasing me.

I didn't speak even to Tungi about this; somehow, I didn't want to hear her comments. Nevertheless, Tungi knew all about their meeting among the mango trees. And it was soon after this that she said, 'I suppose he'll bring her home now. She's begun wearing a sari, have you heard? Yes, you're going to have a Christian sister-in-law very soon.'

If I have made it seem that I had no other interests then but my brother's and Amanda's love story, I'm giving the wrong impression. My world of school, studies, friends and teachers was full and busy. And with the school annual concert approaching it became even more absorbing. I wasn't taking part in any of the dances and dramas, of course; my father being what he was, I couldn't have appeared on the stage. I knew this, but I have to admit that I had to struggle to subdue the self that longed to dress up and become someone else. It was even harder to be content with the job of selling tickets. What made it worse was that I was given more tickets than anyone else; as my father's daughter, I was made to understand, there was a greater chance of my being able to sell them.

Which is why I was knocking at the door of a family friend that evening, hoping to sell some of those hateful tickets. My heart fell when the woman, on opening the door, snapped at me, 'What are you doing here?' I thought it was disapproval, that I was doing something a Gandhian's daughter shouldn't. But no, she was not angry; her face looked as if she had been crying. 'Haven't you heard? Gandhiji is dead, he's been shot. Go home at once.'

Bapu shot? Bapu dead? There had been a bomb thrown at him a few days back, but he had escaped. I remembered my father saying then, 'What do they think? Do they think they can kill him?'

And now . . . ? Bapu dead?

I ran home as I'd never run before, a breathless, chest-hurting, guts-twisting race all the way back. The blood pounded in my ears as I ran, blocking out all thought, until I found myself at our gate. I stood there a moment, taking deep, painful breaths. The house was quiet; surely it meant nothing had happened?

What had I imagined? That the house would be full of mourners? That my father would be weeping and my mother beating her chest? It was nothing like that. There were only the three of them, my parents and my brother, standing like the three points of a triangle. It was like a tableau, the kind we would be having in our concert, the actors frozen in a pose. None of them saw me, they were so absorbed in what was happening between them. My father and brother were looking at each other—looking? no, glaring—and my father's hand was raised, while my brother was like someone offering himself to the blow. While my mother—her eyes staring, her mouth open, as if she wanted to say something—her arms were held out before her like she was warding off the blow meant for my brother. Even as I looked at her, in that very instant, her face changed. Her eyes turned blank, no, it was like her gaze turned inwards to something happening inside her. For a moment she stayed that way, her arms still held out before her. And then she collapsed, not slowly, but suddenly, falling sideways, her body hitting the ground with a pulpy thump. She was dead before she touched the ground.

I saw her every night for months after that, her face changing, her body sliding sideways, night after night I heard the sound as her body hit the ground. But there was no one I could talk to about it. My brother left as soon as the thirteen days of mourning were over, he went without a word to anyone. Tungi went away too, back to her village and then only my father and I were left at home, living in a silence that it seemed would never be broken. And when, sometimes, my father tried to speak to me, in a way he had never done before, almost humbly, I thought I preferred the silence.

Amanda disappeared, but a few months later she was seen, looking pale and ill and haunting the mango grove, they said. You know how rumours fly about in a small town. Which is why, when I heard the story that she had become the old judge's mistress, I thought it was just one more of these rumours. But a couple of years later, when she was found in the mango grove, hanging from the branch of a mango tree, it was the judge who claimed the body and dealt with everything, including her funeral. Her family stayed away, not one of them showed up, no, not even her mother.

Ashok told me all this when I came home for the vacation. I'd joined art school by then, thankful to get away from our gloomy home, hating the vacations when I had to come back. But my father's pleasure in my being home made me feel ashamed of my feelings and I tried not to show them. There was no need for me to be scared of talking to Ashok now, I knew my father would not interfere with anything I did. But old habits die hard and it was like one of our old storytelling sessions, Ashok in the yard and I standing in the doorway. Ashok told me about poor Amanda's death and when he came to her sad funeral he began to cry, such gut-wrenching sobs that I went down the steps to him and patted him on the back, futilely trying to comfort him, while sobbing uncontrollably myself.

All these things happened at different times, but for me it is as if it all happened the day Bapu died. That is a day I will never forget. Even today, when I hear Bapu's favourite bhajan, *Raghupati raghava raja ram*, it is my mother I remember and the way she died, it is Amanda I think of, walking daintily on her heeled sandals, her pink parasol casting a rosy glow on her face.

The Shadow

FOR A LONG time now she had known that she was different. The knowledge had seeped into her slowly, gradually, until she was full of it. It weighed on her like a burden, making her movements awkward and heavy. They had none of the unselfconscious freedom of a child. There was, something wraith-like about her too. When she moved, she was silent and grey like a shadow. She had lived in a silence and solitariness for so long that it seemed to be the only way of living. But now, the doubts within her had begun finding shape and form as questions which she flung at her mother; at her brother and sister, sometimes. But never at him . . . her father. And the question that recurred most often was the one she asked herself . . . *Why am I different?*

It was, she somehow knew, not only that she looked different from her brother and sister, that she was small and fine-boned and dark, while they were large and fair and healthy-looking like him. No, it was not just that. It was something else, something she could not get hold of.

'Why can't I go to the same school as them?' she asked her mother.

'It's too far away.'

'But they go by bus.'

'You'll get tired sitting in the bus for so long. You know you're much smaller than them.'

'I promise I won't be tired. I promise.'

As she persisted, the familiar look of bewildered grief appeared on her mother's face. Only, she could not identify it as grief. All that she knew was that the look was associated with her: that it was only she who could make her mother look that way. It made her feel ashamed of herself. And guilty. She almost relented. But she couldn't. She had to know. If she didn't persist, they would never tell her. She would ask again and again and yet again until they told her.

School . . . she dreamt of it often. Not her school which she knew was, in some way, inferior to the one the other two went to. Their uniforms, their shoes, the things they learnt and did, their brown-paper-covered books . . . all these carried an aura of superiority around them. She listened to stories of their school, their teachers, their lessons, the things they did with a greedy mind, absorbing everything like a sponge, so that she could pretend to herself. Dream of going to another such school. No, the same one. Of having a uniform like them. And a red leather satchel that she could carry on her back, instead of the cloth bag she carried slung over one shoulder. She dreamt of it all with such passion that it became more real to her than her own school, which receded and became insubstantial and shadowy like a dream.

There was the dancing class her sister went to. On class days she waited impatiently for her to return. The minute she was home, she would ask, 'Show me what you learnt today.'

'Oh, don't start the minute I come home. I'm tired.'

'Show me once. Only once.'

'No, I'm tired. Don't be a pest. Go away.'

It was no use being importunate. But sometimes, very rarely, if her sister was in a good mood, she would dance a few steps for her. And then she watched with a passionate intensity, absorbing the gestures into herself. The hands like this, the feet like that, the neck this way and the eyes that way. And when it was over, she called out impetuously, 'Oh, that was beautiful.'

And the sister, mellowed by such overwhelming praise, smiled and said, 'Come on, I'll show you how to do it.'

It was just once or twice, and it was just those few steps and gestures. But she did those movements over and over again as if by learning them she would move into the world her sister lived in; a world where you were free and welcome and loved.

One day, as she was practising secretly by herself, her mother entered.

'Oh!' she said. Just that 'oh' and no more.

And that look on her face. She knew that it had hurt her mother to see her dancing. She stopped abruptly, coming painfully out of a rapturous self-absorption.

'I'm sorry, Mother. I'm sorry.'

The dark shadow which the dancing had banished for a while, was back with her. The dark shadow of a nebulous wrongdoing. She did not even know whose wrong it was. Maybe hers, for otherwise why did she feel impelled to say to her mother so often 'I'm sorry'?

'I'm sorry,' she repeated.

Her mother stood there, rigid as a statue.

'I won't do it again. I promise you I won't.'

She wondered that her mother rushed out at that without a word. I have made her angry again, she thought in desolation. But no, it could not be so, for soon after, her mother called her into the kitchen and chatted with her as she worked and gave her tidbits to munch as she fried. That was happiness. But it wasn't real. Because, what did her mother matter? She knew it was he who mattered. And he . . .

That night she heard them again, her parents, talking. She had no room of her own. She slept in the small veranda of her parent's bedroom and through the window their voices came clearly. She woke out of her sleep yet again to the angry, incomprehensible sounds.

'It's cruel,' she heard her mother say. And a sound that frightened her. It sounded like a sob. 'You're cruel.'

'Cruel? I? I have forgiven you. How many men would do that?'

'Forgiven me?'

No, that could not have been a sob, because now her mother was laughing. But could you call that a laugh? It sounded very much like crying. There was very little difference between the two.

'You know whose fault it is,' the father said.

Whose fault? Whose?

'Not hers, anyway. Why punish her? Isn't it enough that you punish me?'

Punish her? Punish my mother? How does he do that?

'What about me?'

The father's words now somehow had the quality of fierce, clawing little animals.

'Isn't it a punishment for me to see her face? Each time I see it, I am reminded of my own dishonour.'

Dishonour. Fault. Punishment. Strange words loaded with impossible meanings. Trying to understand, to find the meaning, was like trying to visualize shapes and sounds she had never seen. She could connect them to nothing.

'If I have dishonoured you, why don't you kill me?'

No. No. No. She almost sprang out of bed, expecting to see him flourishing a sharp, shining knife, which he would push into her, her mother. But her father's voice, now cold and composed, stopped her. He did not even sound angry. Just bored.

'Don't be hysterical. You know you agreed to all this . . . for the sake of the children.'

'Yes, your children. What about her?'

What about her? That's me! But that means . . . that means . . .

'My children? Are they not yours as well?'

'Yes, mine too. But this child . . . she's innocent. And I . . . I could have lied to you, couldn't I?'

'Lied? How could you have? When she looks just like . . . No, don't make a virtue of that. And that's enough of this. Go to bed. I don't want to talk about it any more.'

Now his voice was angry. The puzzle became more intricate, the maze more complicated. Her mind couldn't find the way out of it. She was lost and, struggling to get out, she fell asleep.

But she was constantly on the watch now. She would listen, she would watch. And some time, someone would let it out. And she would know what was wrong and put it right. And then . . . she would become like the others.

She woke up light and buoyant—to a child each morning is a fresh beginning—and found her brother dressed.

'Where are you going?'

'Swimming.'

'Swimming?'

'Papa's going to teach us how to swim.'

'I'm coming too.'

She jumped up, frantic she would be left behind. Her brother, towel casually slung over his shoulder, stopped at the door and looked back.

'You!' he said, and there was something very like pity in his eyes. 'Catch Papa taking you!'

She watched the three of them setting out, her sister holding the father's hand, all of them talking with animation. Why am I always excluded? Why am I always left out? Why?

She went down to her mother in the kitchen.

'Why didn't they take me? Why can't I swim? I want to learn swimming too.'

'Oh, don't start that now,' her mother exclaimed irritably. 'You were sleeping, that's why.'

'Can I go next time? Can I? I'll wake up as early as you want. Can I?'

The mother's face had a trapped look.

'I don't know. We'll see.'

We'll see. That means nothing. And anyway, it doesn't depend on her. Nothing depends on her. She's not important. Child though she was, she knew her struggle was with him. That afternoon she took her courage in her hands and approached her father. It was a holiday and he sat relaxed in an armchair, reading the newspaper with concentration.

'Papa,' she said, standing before him resolutely.

He didn't reply.

'Papa,' she said again and loudly as if speaking to a deaf man.

He looked up in surprise.

'I want to go swimming.'

Her heart was thudding madly, her voice quavering, but her eyes were steady, her chin determined.

'You can't.' His eyes had gone back to his newspaper.

'Why can't I? Tell me why.'

It was as if all the whys that had been gathering inside her since her birth had exploded into a large one that could not be left unanswered.

A look of distaste crossed his face, but he replied, 'I can't manage three children.'

'I can manage myself.'

'No, you can't. Not till you learn swimming.'

'But how will I learn if you never teach me?'

'Don't try to talk smart.'

His face frightened her, but she stood her ground. She could not give up now.

'I want to learn,' she said and it surprised her that her voice came out so thin and quavery.

'That's enough. Stop that nonsense.'

His voice was cold. It was like having an ice cube pushed down the back of her dress. At any other time it would have scared her into a terrified, submissive silence. Now, it shattered all her composed resolution. She could do nothing. She could not move him. She would never be like the others.

'I want to go. I want to go. I want to go,' she began to scream, unable to control herself. She went on repeating the words in the midst of her tumultuous sobs, while the other two children stared at her aghast, astonished by her behaviour. The mother rushed in saying, 'What is it? What's the matter? What's going on?'

As she saw the man and the child confronting each other like two antagonists, there was a flash of gladness on her face, a brief flicker of joy that turned swiftly to dismay, then anger.

The father retreated behind his paper and said, dully and indifferently, 'Deal with her yourself. You can see she's hysterical.'

'What are you doing here?' the mother's voice was sharp and high. 'Weren't you told to keep out of the way? Go to your room.'

The child seemed to shrivel up at the words. She stared at her mother's face in consternation.

'Go, child. Go.'

Even then she could not move. And then the doorbell rang.

'Take her away,' said the voice from behind the paper. The mother whirled upon her with a look that terrified her. She held her by the shoulders and pushed her out of the room. Still, something in her resisted so that her mother had to drag her. They were both sweating when they reached her room.

'Don't do that again,' her mother said, putting her sari to her face. 'Don't ever do it again.' As the sari came away, the child saw that her mother's face was wet again. She was crying. It meant nothing to her. She was too full of her own terror to take in anything else. For long after that, the sound of the doorbell drove her to her bed where she lay whimpering, her face buried desperately in the pillow.

That night she heard her mother saying, 'I can't go on.'

'What do you want me to do? You made your bed. Now you have to lie on it.'

'I'll lie on a bed of nails all my life. But she. . . that child. I can't bear to see her. Have you no pity? What wrong has she done?'

'She was born, wasn't she?'

She was born. I was born. She said the words to herself, her lips moving in the dark. Why, when he said the words, did it sound as if she had done something terrible?

'Born? She didn't ask to be born, did she? The fault is mine. I admit it. But, oh God, haven't I paid for it? One moment of weakness and you want to punish me for it all my life? And an innocent child as well? Just because she was born?'

I don't understand, I can't understand, she thought in despair. I was born. How can that be a wrong? And how can I put it right?

And then one day, she thought she had found the way. Her brother had brought home his report card and stood in front of the father, doggedly silent, shamefaced, while his father went over it, subject by subject. After he had finished—and I wish he would scold me like that, he never does, he doesn't even look at my report card—he gave back the card saying, 'You've got to do better next time. I know you can do it. Try. Think of how much you'll please me by doing well.'

As she heard the words, her heart leapt with happiness. She had found the way. I will do well. He will be pleased with me. And then . . . we will go swimming, and I will hold his hand like my sister does. He will play cards with me. He will carry me pickaback. Take me with him on the motorbike.

She felt breathless and giddy with the excitement of her visions.

She worked hard now. There were no limits to her patience, to her desire to excel. She even wondered, hesitantly, whether she should pray to God. But, could she make demands on him? Perhaps, he too would say, 'That's enough now.' Maybe he would be as shocked by her prayers as her father had been by her importunities. No, safer to leave God out of it.

And then, she got her report. She ran home with it, holding it in her hand, her face overflowing with joy. 'Papa,' she screamed, calling out as she had never done before. 'Papa, I got my report. I came third. I came third.'

As she ran in, he raised his head and looked at her. She had the sensation of running against a blank wall. A wall of stones, not bricks. His face looked at her without expression. Her steps faltered. Her hand holding out the report card fell to her side. Her face became devoid of all expression, the joy flowing out of it, as if she was a mirror, reflecting the blank face of the man in front of her.

'What is it?' he asked her, after a dreadful pause.

'I came third.'

'Do you have to run wild because of that? And look at your hands. Filthy. Third?' He barely glanced at the report. 'That's very good. Now go and tell your mother. And don't behave in that stupid way again.'

She dragged herself into the house, feeling heavy and dull. She had a pain in her legs as if she had run too far, too fast.

'What is it?' her mother asked.

'My report.'

'Have you done well?'

'I came third.'

'Why, that's wonderful! Let me see.'

The expression she had longed to see, the response she had so desired, confronted her now. But it didn't matter any more. She was full of hatred and anger.

Her mother saw her face and asked, 'What is it, child? Aren't you pleased? Is anything wrong?'

Her lips moved. But no sound came out of them. It was to herself that she was saying . . . Whatever they say, I was born. And I am. I am.

For a moment, before desolation flowed back, the words filled her like a triumphant, resounding cry.

The Homecoming

PUSHING THE BUCKET of dirty water away with her foot in an unconscious imitation of her mother, she swiped the floor in a final wide arc and thought of her mother's words—*after you've mopped the floor, you should be able to see your face in it.* Can I, she wondered? No, there was nothing. That's just Ai's way of talking, she thought scornfully. And did she really want to see her own face? She remembered the day she had looked at herself in Anju's mirror—it was new then, Anju had just bought it with her first pay—and how startled she had been to see her face so clearly. This square face with the thick eyebrows and frizzy hair—is this me? She much preferred the grey ghost the old mirror gave back to her. Anju never had enough of looking at herself in the new mirror, though. She would turn it this way and that to get the maximum light from the small window set high in the wall. But then, Anju was pretty—her fair complexion, her dainty little nose . . .

'Finished, Suman?'

She turned round startled. Her face changed, it took on a look of utter devotion. How silvery Tai looked standing there in the morning sunshine that poured in through the window. Even her voice was silvery.

'Yes, Tai.'

'Had your tea?'

'No, Tai.'

'Go and have it then. Have a good breakfast, mind.'

'Yes, Tai.'

'You'll get a good breakfast before going to school,' Ai had said when she was trying to persuade Suman to work in Tai's house the two mornings a week she went to the temple.

'Yes, yes, teach her to become like you—to work like a dog and be grateful for the scraps they give you, for this pigsty they allow you to live in.'

'You be quiet! You don't want to work yourself and you don't want your sister to do it, either. What's wrong with her doing a little work and having something filling in her stomach before she goes to school? What can I give her anyway?'

But for Suman it was not the breakfast. It was Tai—the way she looked, so light and airy in her saris that seemed to float around her, her soft voice, her smile, the way she spoke to her, called her Suman . . .

'Baby?' Tai had smiled when Ai had said, 'Baby will do the morning work on Mondays and Fridays.' 'If she's big enough to work, she's too big to be called Baby. I'm going to call her Suman.'

That was the beginning of a happiness she could not speak of to anyone. She had kept it locked within herself, guarding it jealously. At night, she had lain awake, her eyes fixed on the light that came in through the window from the veranda outside Tai's bedroom. Looking at the square of light, she could imagine Tai reading. Or, listening to music, maybe. Sometimes, rarely, both of them sat outside on the veranda and she could hear their voices. One night, she had heard Tai laughing and suddenly a kind of sob had welled up in her, taking her unawares so that she had been unable to stifle it.

'Baby?' Ai's response had come immediately out of the darkness. She had remained rigidly silent. 'Anju? Anju?'

'What is it?'

'I thought I heard someone crying.'

'Crying? No, I'm not crying. But I feel like it. Can't I get a bit of sleep even at night?'

With the four of them sleeping in that tiny room, it was a tight fit. Suman had the worst of it, actually, sandwiched between Anju, who got into a rage if she as much as moved a finger and Barkya who wet himself every night.

'Why don't you let him sleep outside with Suresh?' Anju had complained. 'He's big enough, nearly six now.'

Ai had tried. But he invariably came back, clambering over their bodies until he found the soft mound that was his mother. And in a while, he would wet himself. That night, he had done it again. Suman, feeling the wetness seeping under her, had woken up to Anju's angry outburst, more vicious than usual.

'I'm going to get out of here. I've had enough.'

'No, you're not going anywhere. Not if I can stop you.'

It was then that Suman had come out of her dream world to realize the conflict raging between Ai and Anju. She had cowered in her blanket, trying to close her ears, to shut out the cruel, hurting things they were saying to each other.

'Marriage? You think it's a game? A child's game? You meet a boy you know nothing of—neither his caste, his home, nor his family. And you want to go and put a garland around his neck.'

'I know why you want to stop me. You don't want to lose my pay.'

There had been silence after that and the next morning Ai's face had the same defeated look it had had when Anju had said, 'I don't want to become like you—cleaning the dirt of other people's homes all my life.'

Ai stopped speaking to Anju after that night. And one day Anju just went away and got married. Ai wouldn't let them even mention her name. But when Anju came back, in all her newly married glory—green bangles, silver toe rings, black beads and a beautiful blue China silk sari—Ai had done all the things that were done to a newly married daughter, but her face had been stern and unsmiling, as if there was no pleasure for her in it at all. And when Anju had left, she had stayed inside their room. It was Suman who had stood in the doorway, watching Anju walking daintily down the mud path in her high-heeled slippers, as if she had never walked on it before, her sari tucked round her waist, accentuating its slimness, her hair clips glinting in her sleek dark hair. She had turned back when she reached the gate, waved casually to Suman and was gone. Suman, giving a faint sigh, came in to find Ai sobbing, a terrible rending kind of sobbing.

'Ai, what is it? What is the matter? What has happened?'

Ai had straightened up. 'Nothing,' she said and wiped her face of the tears with rough angry rubs. And when, some days back, Suman came home to find Anju at home, lying in a corner and she had asked, 'Anju? Ai? What's happened to her? Ai, why is she sleeping?' Ai's reply had been again the same word. 'Nothing.'

Nothing? How can Ai say that? How can she do nothing? Suman suddenly thought—why don't I speak to Tai? Why don't I tell her about Anju?

'Finished, Suman?' Tai was asking her.

'Yes, Tai.'

'All right, you can go. Tell your mother to come a little early today. I have to go out.'

As the girl hesitated, not making any move to go, Tai asked, 'No school today?'

'I'm not going. Anju . . .'

'Anju? Has she come home? Why hasn't she come to see me?'

Anju had visited Tai last time. Suman had followed Anju and she had wondered at Anju, talking so easily to Tai. Casually, as if she was just any person, not the daughter of Tai's servant. And Suman had also thought how Anju, who had seemed so beautifully dressed until then, had suddenly looked loud and gaudy. And her voice too—so shrill and loud when compared to Tai's soft one. Suman had been angry then—with Tai? With Anju? Or was it with herself? She didn't know.

'Tell her to come and see me before she goes back.' Seeing the girl's face, Tai asked, 'What is it, Suman?'

'Tai, Anju says she is not going back.'

'Why? Fighting with her husband already?' Seeing the girl's face, Tai's smile faded. 'Is anything wrong?'

'She doesn't say anything. She won't speak.'

Since her return three days back, she had said nothing, except, once, 'I'm not going back.' It was Suman who had seen the marks on her back. Anju had been sleeping on her side, leaving her back uncovered. And Suman, the moment her eyes had fallen on the sight, had called out in a strangled voice, 'Ai . . . Ai . . .'

'What is it?'

The girl had just pointed to Anju's bare back. Ai saw the scars then, some of them still raw, oozing blood and cried out so loudly that Anju had woken up with a start. She sat up, her hands held out before her, her eyes like a frightened animal's.

'What did he do to you, Anju? What did he do? Tell me.'

Awareness had come slowly into Anju's face. Eyes fixed on them, she had moved backwards on her haunches—like an animal, Suman had thought again, yes, she had even grunted like an animal—moving, until her back had touched the wall. As if she was protecting it from their eyes. She had not moved from the spot since then.

'Tai, help us. Tai, Ai says Anju must go back, she says she's married to him and she must . . . how can she say that? I saw her back. She's hurt, she's . . . she was bleeding . . .'

'Oh my God!'

'Tai, please come and talk to Ai.'

'All right,' Tai said finally. 'I'll come in the evening. I have a meeting at five. I'll come after that.'

'Please don't tell my mother I spoke to you,' Suman wanted to say, but lacking the courage, walked away silently.

'No, I don't want to speak to Tai, I will not speak to Tai,' Ai had said angrily when Suman had suggested it to her.

'But why, Ai?'

Ai had been squatting as she cleaned the vessels, her large feet firmly gripping the squelchy mud under them. The fetid smell of stale food came from the vessels.

'Tai knows what to do, she works in that place where they help women.'

'This is our business, we don't want anyone to interfere.'

'But Ai, Tai could do something. She can talk to Anju's husband—or—or—she can do something. Something at least.'

Ai had laughed at that. 'Something? No, no one can do anything. No one can help when it's her own husband. Move aside, don't just stand there. You can pour out the water for me while I wash. No,' she had gone on, throwing the clean vessels into the wicker basket with bad-tempered clangs, 'this is our business. Keep your mouth shut, don't talk to anyone.'

Suppose she comes to know what I've done, the girl thought fearfully now, imagining the weight of her mother's hard hand. But I know Tai will do something, she'll help Anju. And then Ai won't be angry with me any more.

As soon as Ai went out that afternoon, Suman began a frantic cleaning of the house. She pushed everything that was lying about into the large steel trunk. And then she looked at Anju, in her unwashed clothes and uncombed hair, still sitting against the wall. There was a dark spot on the wall where she had been resting her head. The room reeked of sweat—and of something else? What was it? Suman sniffed and then felt a little sick. It was Anju, her fastidious sister, stinking.

'Anju,' she said gently. 'Tai is coming. She'll help you.'

There was no reply. Anju's face was as blank as if she hadn't heard Suman. No, worse, as if Suman hadn't spoken, as if she wasn't in the room at all.

'Anju' she repeated. 'Tai is coming. Shall I comb your hair?'

Still no reply. The silence frightened Suman. Nevertheless,

she got out the comb and mirror, the old one Anju had despised so much, and gently removed one of the clips from the ugly tangle of Anju's hair. Immediately, like a puppet whose strings had been pulled, Anju began to twist about, moaning, 'No' over and over again. Suman watched her helplessly. The cries went on and on. Finally she got up, put the clip and comb away and went out. She picked all the washed clothes off the bushes, folded them, put them away and sat down from where she could see Tai's house.

Hasn't she come home as yet? She said after five. No, she said the meeting was at five.

In a while it became dark.

It's nearly seven now. Has she forgotten? No, she said she would come. She will come. I'll count up to hundred.

She counted a hundred, two hundred, three hundred—then gave up. She sat trailing a stick on the ground, drawing meaningless patterns in the dust, feeling a kind of pain begin inside her. Ai came in through the small gate, Barkya clinging to her as usual. She went straight in without looking at Suman. Soon Suman heard the Primus hissing. Suresh vaulted over the wall and went into the house calling out, 'I'm hungry.'

'Baby, Baby . . .' she could hear Ai's voice calling her.

She felt the pain grow inside her; she crouched, trying to find a position that would give her some comfort.

Oh, God, I can't bear this. I can't bear this. Why hasn't Tai come? She said she would come, she promised . . .

Ai came out. 'Baby, didn't you hear me? What's wrong with you?'

'I have a pain.'

'Where?' Ai's face was suddenly suspicious.

'Here.'

Suman pointed to her stomach.

'Is it . . . ? Get up, let me see . . . God knows I have enough to bear without having you too . . . Thank God, not yet. Come inside and get the plates. And stop crying. A big girl like you crying like a baby! We'll see about your pain after you've had your food.'

Suman went in and collected the plates. She picked up Anju's plate after Ai had served all of them and was about to take it to her when Ai said, 'No, leave it here. Let her come here and eat with us.'

Suman, plate still in hand, looked hesitantly at Ai.

'I said put it down. Anju, come and have your food. Anju, did you hear me? Anju come and have your food. Anju? Anju—look at me!'

The cry was so compelling that Anju looked straight into her mother's eyes. The mother and daughter stared at each other for what seemed to Suman a very long time. Then Anju's eyes went blank again. Ai began to cry, hitting herself on her forehead with her palm, the serving ladle still in her hand.

It seemed strange to Anju, when they went to bed, that it could be a night like any other, that the same sounds were going on outside. Everything as usual—the croaking of frogs in the garden pond, the howling of a dog and a snapping, barking reply from far away, footsteps and voices on the road, someone coughing. She lay watching the window. It was still dark. So, she still hasn't returned home. That's why she didn't come. Her heart jumped up and down in relief. Once she moved and felt a quick convulsive movement of Anju's body. 'Anju, it's me, it's Baby,' she said and Anju's body became still.

She woke up suddenly to a jumble of sounds—shouts, cries, thuds, a clatter of things falling. She felt a blow—there was someone, something on her. She felt a small, trembling hand. This was Barkya—what was he doing? And then it penetrated, a thin scream that seemed scarcely human. It was Anju, Anju screaming as if she had been saving up her voice all these days just for this. Suman got up, wrenching Barkya, clinging to her, off her. Now she could see the man holding

Anju with one hand, while with the other he was hitting her, anywhere, everywhere, banging her head against the wall at the same time. Each time he moved her head, she could see Anju's face in the squares of light on the wall, her eyes blank, mouth open. Suresh—yes, Suresh was in the room too, throwing himself at the man, trying to drag him off Anju. And Ai too was part of that melee, grunting, panting, saying something in a voice that was not Ai's. She joined them, she tried to get to Anju, to get past all those bodies. She felt blows on her body, blows she ignored, until she felt a hand—or was it a foot?—smash into her chest. She fell down, gasping with the pain, and then, trying to get back to her feet became aware what the square of light on the wall meant. Tai—it was Tai. She was back. She ran out of the door, down the mud path. For the first time in all their years there, she went to the front door, not to the back. She threw herself at the door, hammering on it, her body heaving. She could still hear the tumult she had left behind her, as if she had brought it here within herself. She realized, with surprise, that part of the noise was her own loud sobbing. She hammered again. The door opened. It was not Tai, it was him.

'Tai,' she gasped, 'I want Tai.'

'What is it? What's the matter?' he asked. The questions were echoed from inside by Tai and it was to her voice that she replied.

'Tai, please come, he's here, he's killing Anju, he'll kill her, Tai, please come, Tai . . .'

The sounds were louder now. She looked back and saw that he had brought Anju out and was dragging her along the path she had walked on so proudly, while Suresh and Ai followed him, trying to stop him, Suresh holding on to him like a limpet.

'Oh my God!' Tai gasped.

Suman didn't hear her, she didn't see the woman, her face terrified by the scene of utter violence she was witnessing, shrink back into the house and close the door. Suman ran, stumbling, sobbing, frantic to get to Anju. As she got to them, the man pushed Anju through the small gate, giving Suresh a final brutal blow that flung him against a wall. The boy fell down and lay still. Ai ran to him, crying out his name. He got up, looking dazed, his face bleeding.

'Suresh, are you all right? Suresh, let me see . . .'

'Leave me alone.'

He ran back to the house. They followed him, Barkya sobbing, sobs that seemed to be torn out of him, clinging so tightly to Ai that she could scarcely walk.

It was Suman who cleaned Suresh's face, though he kept pushing her away, brushing her hand off his face, saying, 'Leave me alone.' When she had finished, he turned his back on them and lay still, though occasionally his body gave small shudders as if he was crying. Barkya, still crying in hiccups, was lying with his head in Ai's lap. Ai's tattoed hand mechanically stroked his head, though she was scarcely conscious of him it seemed, her face was so blank. Suman looked around. The room looked like the scene of a battle.

'Ai, shall I clean the room?'

She waited a moment for a reply, then, when there was none, began cleaning the room methodically, while her mother watched her with lacklustre eyes. As she shook the sheets, something fell out with a dull clink.

'What is it?' her mother asked her, watching the girl pick up something from the floor and stare at it.

Instinctively her fingers closed on the thing she was holding. Then she opened her hand and showed it to Ai. It was Anju's clip, a hank of her hair entangled in it. Ai's face worked. For the first time the tears came.

'Ai, don't . . .'

'Throw it away,' Ai said suddenly, fiercely. As the girl hesitated, she repeated, 'Throw it out. She's gone, she won't come back, she'll never come back here.'

Suman stood staring at the pin in her hand.

'What is the matter? Are you hurt?'

Yes, she felt bruised all over, even inside her, but it was not that. It was the picture she saw as she looked at the clip—Anju walking, her head held high, the clips gleaming in her sleek dark hair. Instantly she made up her mind. Carefully she removed the torn bit of hair from the clip.

'What are you doing?'

'I'm keeping it.' She put the clip carefully back in the box with the other one she'd removed from Anju's hair in the afternoon. How long ago that seemed to be! Then she turned back to Ai.

'She'll come back. We won't let her stay with him. We'll bring her back Ai.'

'Bring her back? How? You're talking big. Big girl now, huh?'

Suman said nothing but looked back unflinchingly at her mother. It was her mother who spoke finally.

'All right, keep it,' she said, her body slumping. Her hands went back to their soothing patting of the child who was now quieter. After she'd done tidying the room, Suman lay down in her place. For the first time in months she did not notice the light streaming in through the window.

The Boy

MY GRANDFATHER WAS a great believer in keeping things in their right places. I can still remember him standing on the straight long path that led from the gate to the house, his very stance an accusing one, pointing with his cane to the few leaves that had fluttered down from the mango trees. One of the servants would then come scurrying with a basket and a broom, and, sweeping away the offending leaves, throw them behind the hedge under the mango trees. That, my grandfather's expression clearly said, was the right place for those leaves.

I imagine now that it was this sense of order that made it possible for so many of us to live together in our house. Not only were there grandfather's four sons—my father and three uncles—and their wives and children living in that house, but a number of distant relatives drifted in and out, some staying long enough to become part of the household. And there was always a married aunt who had come home with all her children, either to have another baby, or for a family occasion, or, as they said 'just for nothing'. Yet, the house never seemed overcrowded. Certainly it helped that there was a place for everyone. Each couple had a room, but only the youngest children slept with their parents. All of us boys slept and studied in the big hall, while the girls and the aunts went into the inside 'women's room'. The newborn babies and their mothers, of course, occupied the cradle room, a dark and mysterious place, suffused with a variety of smells, which, in spite of babies' piss being part of it, combined in some odd way into a not-unpleasant odour. When you sniffed, it gave you the same heady feeling that smelling your own body did. Our places were properly marked out in the dining room as well: Grandfather and the adult males sat along the wall with the boys right opposite them, while the girls sat in a row that linked the two rows of males. It was not really a very comfortable place, for they had no wall to lean on. We envied them, nevertheless, for not being right under Grandfather's eyes. His rule of absolute stillness and silence during meals made them times of torture for us, but the girls could get away with nudges, winks and gestures. Females were better at communicating without words anyway, I thought, for, from where I sat, I could see the women in the kitchen, waiting beside the vessels to serve us. And signals flew fast and furious between them.

The kitchen was Subbayya's domain. Subbayya was an Udipi Brahmin and had once been a cook at the Shri Krishna temple in Udipi. This was said in tones of great pride—in public, that is; within the family, nobody had a good word for him. He was a dictator; nobody could tell him what to do. He decided what he would give us to eat—and that was that! I imagine that they put up with him not only because he was a good cook, but because he could provide meals on time, something Grandfather was very particular about. Both mornings and evenings Grandfather would appear in the dining room on the stroke of the hour, announcing his arrival by a cough. By then, the plates would have been laid on the floor, the water jugs and glasses by their side, and the food all ready to be served, the vessels uncovered, to avoid the jangle of removing the lids and putting them down. For the same reason, to avoid noise, the women let the ladles and spoons into the vessels as gently as they put a sleeping baby back into the cradle.

This silence was an awesome demonstration of Grandfather's power, for, just a little earlier, the kitchen had been a scene of roaring chaos. The only light there was a solitary unshaded bulb, sooty cobwebs hanging in dispirited clumps along the wire, as if the spiders had given up on them. It was the wood fire in the fireplace that really lit up the room—the cooking corner of it, that is. There were three cooking stoves and it was a sight to see Subbayya working on all three simultaneously, his movements swift and purposeful. The noise was terrific—the clanging of lids and spoons, sounds of Subbayya thwacking the logs, blowing into the fire, the grating and grinding. Above all this clamour rose his voice, asking questions of his son who sat nearby, a slate in his hand, 'Seventeen times eight? Twelve times fourteen?' As the tempo of the cooking accelerated and the oil began to sizzle in the kadhai for the seasonings, the questions came faster, more frenzied. The boy's answers became almost inaudible, but obviously Subbayya could hear him, for suddenly there would be a pause, a loud, 'What did you say? Say that again,' from Subbayya. And then the sound of a blow. The boy's voice came hoarse and muffled after this as if he was choking on his own tears and the mucus that was always running down his nose.

As the cooking came closer to the end point, the sea of pots and pans advanced, gradually pushing the boy further away from his father. Finally, by the time we were having dinner, he would be near the door that led to the backyard. I could see him, his head sunk on his knees, only his cap, which came down to his ears, visible. The kitchen, with the silent standing women, the sleeping boy and Subbayya sitting on his haunches by the fading fire, was now a different world altogether. It was as if someone had cast a spell on them.

Subbayya's son was 'the boy' to everyone, to his father as well. We never knew his real name, never saw him outside the house. He must have gone to school and returned from it at some time of the day, but, except when he was in the kitchen in the evenings, he was invisible. We could hear his voice in his room at night though. And sometimes, during the holidays, we heard his voice loudly reciting lessons and chanting the multiplication tables. If it were not for his voice, we wouldn't have known he was there, for the door was bolted from the outside. I don't remember thinking it odd that a boy of our age was not allowed to play; we took the situation for granted. The adults must have noticed it, but they didn't interfere, either. I suppose they thought it was none of their business. And, of course, there was also the fact that everyone was a little frightened of Subbayya. It was not only that they were apprehensive of losing him, there was something intimidating about the man himself. None of us children, not even the naughtiest and the boldest, dared to cross this path. And the eldest aunt herself, so authoritative otherwise, had a different, an almost wheedling tone when she spoke to him.

But the youngest aunt once spoke to him about the way he treated his son. This aunt was always in the news, she was forever being discussed by the other women. All this women's talk filtered to us through the girls who repeated what the women were saying, using almost the same tones. Listening to them was like watching the shadow play of fingers on the wall. And so we knew that the youngest aunt 'didn't know her place' as they said. She'll soon learn, they had said, when she came home as a bride. But she didn't seem to change. She spoke to Grandfather even when he hadn't spoken to her—something none of the others, not even the men did—she barged into the room where the men sat by themselves, she called out to her husband in public. Oh, her blunderings gave the other women much amusement all right.

I was present when she spoke to Subbayya about the boy. I was in the passage, getting myself a glass of water, and as I drank, the sound of Subbayya's questions and the boy's choked answers fell on my ears. Then there was a pause, followed by the sound of a blow—this was routine. What was unexpected was the youngest aunt's voice asking Subbayya, 'Why do you hit that poor child, Subbayya? Let him go out and play with the other children. Why do you make him study all day?'

Curious, I went towards the kitchen. The youngest aunt was standing in the doorway, but it was the boy I noticed. Perhaps it was the first time that I saw his face so clearly—he looked like a moron with his gaping mouth and frightened eyes. But it was an angry bruise, showing up on his cheek, that caught my eyes more than anything else. My aunt was pointing to it. 'Look at that! And you're his father! How can you treat a poor motherless child—your own child—so cruelly?'

Subbayya had gone on with his work until then, ignoring my aunt as if she wasn't there at all. Now suddenly he straightened and looked her right in the face. Subbayya was a strong man; I'd seen him drawing water from the well, his arms moving effortlessly like two pistons. And when he hoisted the pot on his shoulders, as easily as if it weighed nothing, the muscles on his shoulders and arms rippled and bulged. Now, in that firelit corner, he seemed not only physically intimidating, he looked malevolent. I felt my aunt's hand clutch at my shoulder as if she felt the menace in him too. But she didn't give up. Oh no, she was not one to do that.

'You must stop this, Subbayya,' she said, 'or I'll have to do something about it.'

She was a brave woman. I write this now but I'd never have dared to say it aloud then. It was understood among the boys that females were cowards—and silly and ignorant as well. This knowledge was part of the code by which we lived our lives as males. I had my own doubts about it, though, and not just because of the youngest aunt. There was my sister, two years older than I was and smarter in her studies than all of us—the older cousins as well. It was she, not my father, who helped me with all my school work. She wasn't a coward, either, not by any means. And I don't mean by that that she wasn't frightened of the dark or of cockroaches and things like that. It was more; she was the only one who dared to stand up to Grandfather. I felt a traitor when I turned my back on her, when I joined the others in ridiculing girls. But it was a price I had to pay for the companionship of boys.

When I look back at those days, all the days seem to telescope into one chain of similar carefree days. Yet there is something that sets this time apart from all other times, for I reached the peaks of glory that year: I became the marbles champion both in school and in the neighbourhood. With my two heavy steel 'killers' I was invincible and captured so many marbles that my mother gave me a bag to keep them in. And then it was lost, the bag with all my booty. And, worst blow of all, my two steel 'killers' as well. I can still remember the rage that filled me. I was sure that one of my cousins had stolen it and not being certain who the culprit was, I got into so many fights that I didn't have a single whole shirt to wear.

Time and routine would have absorbed this sorrow anyway, but I forgot about it even sooner in the excitement of being allowed, for the first time, to join my older cousins who, in summer, slept on the small terrace that overlooked the backyard. Since the terrace had no parapet wall, it was considered dangerous for children. Which made it even more exciting to be allowed to be there. And there was the heady excitement of being in the company of older boys who treated me like one of themselves. Perhaps it was the darkness that erased differences and made democracy possible. Or the sky, maybe, heavy with innumerable stars, that flatted everyone to the same level. Lying under a blanket that smelled strange in the open air, I could hear the voices of the servants in the backyard and wondered whether they felt this removal of differences too; for there was Subbayya's voice among the other servant's voices. Normally he kept himself aloof from the others; as an Udipi Brahmin he considered himself superior. But there he was among them—and smoking with them? The striking of matches punctuated the murmurs and the smell of their bidis was wafted to us. I could hear old Fakeera's hollow smoker's cough. A little later, the wavering light of a lantern moved drunkenly up and down, there was the sound of the metal clasp falling down with a jangle, the creak as a door opened and then the bang of it closing. After this the conversation quickened and became easier. Yes. Subbayya had gone to his room, the others were more comfortable now.

I'd begun avoiding him more than ever. I would be entering high school that year and all my pleasure in this had been lost since Subbayya had caught hold of me and asked me, 'Will you teach my boy English?'

'I don't know it myself—how can I teach anyone?'

'You'll begin this year. You people are clever. You'll soon learn. As soon as you learn, you must teach my boy.'

Trying to smile, flattering, almost fawning on me, he seemed to me more fearful than ever. Helplessly I stammered, 'Yes, yes.' Anything to get away from him, but I was careful to avoid both him and the boy after that.

The day before school was to reopen the ultimate disaster happened. It was dinner time, Grandfather's cough announced his presence, but dinner wasn't ready. Subbayya hadn't come at his usual time and the women, after waiting for him, were struggling to cope. The explanation came later: 'the boy' was missing and Subbayya was out searching for him. Subbayya didn't turn up the next day, either. The women had to manage and roped in the girls to help. They enjoyed the sense of crisis. Besides, there was the additional pleasure of hearing the women talk and retailing all this gossip later. We pretended not to be interested, but we listened nevertheless. And so we learnt that 'the boy' had a mother—we had never thought of that!—who had run away some years back. And the youngest aunt was hoping 'the boy' would never be found. And when the girls, echoing the women, said, 'How can she say that!' my sister retorted, 'I don't want him to find "the boy" either. And I'm glad his wife ran away. He's a terrible man.'

As the days went by and 'the boy' stayed missing, Subbayya became even more fierce, almost savage. He wouldn't speak to anyone and came and went as he pleased, so that the women never knew whether he'd come to work or not. They complained and Grandfather said that if he didn't resume work, if he didn't come to work at the proper times, he'd have to go.

And then one day I saw 'the boy'. I was on my way to the pond some distance from our home and was crossing the open ground used for grazing cattle, when someone called out my name. It took me a few moments to realize that it was a boy sitting astride a buffalo who must have hailed me. There was no one else within sight—it had to be him. I was surprised and, I must admit, offended. How could a cattle-grazing boy talk to me! And call out my name with such familiarity! After all, I was—well, Grandfather had been the diwan of a small state once. And so I ignored him, but the boy jumped off the buffalo's back and came to me.

I didn't recognize him even then. To tell the truth, I had scarcely seen 'the boy's' face; I had always identified him by his large cap, his stunted body and that stifled voice. Now there was no cap and I could see that he'd made an attempt to chop off the tuft of hair he had always had. The hair around that tuft had begun growing; the short, fine down gave him the look of a newborn animal. The bruises I had so often seen on his face were no longer visible on his now darkened face. He smelt—he stank, rather, of animals, animal dung, of sweat and other unpleasant things. His mouth, which was open, showing me missing teeth in a moist pink interior, was foul, too. But he was smiling. No, he was grinning.

'What are you doing here?'

Yes, even his voice had changed. It seemed released—free of the tears and the mucus that had thickened it. And to hear him speak an ordinary sentence like this one, instead of lessons and tables, stunned me into silence.

'I've come to catch a frog,' I said when he repeated the question. And then I suddenly blurted out, 'Your father's looking for you.'

His face changed.

'He says he's going to find you, however long it takes.'

Instantly he turned, poised for flight, as if his father was already in sight.

'Go away from here, run, go quickly,' I urged him.

On the point of flight he paused, then came back to me. 'I took your marbles,' he said. 'I found the bag outside and took them. They're in the room,' he said and told me where.

I never spoke to anyone about having seen the boy—no, not even the cousins. I knew the women were at the end of their tether—the eldest aunt had been hysterical that evening. I heard my parents quarrelling and the women arguing. I knew if I spoke, Subbayya would be back at work, the boy in his place in the kitchen, meals would be on time, Grandfather would be pleased and everyone would be happy. Ten, twenty, a hundred times I opened my mouth to speak. But I didn't. Why didn't I?

Perhaps—and this thought comes to me now, years later— there was something of my Grandfather in me and I liked things to be in their place. And, child though I was, I knew, specially after seeing him astride the buffalo, that the boy's place was not in our kitchen.

Subbayya never found the boy. He went away a few days later, alone, the servants said; no one knew where he had gone. I ventured into his room after he had gone and found my bag of marbles exactly where the boy had told me he had hidden them. I quietly threw them away; I don't know why I did that, either.

A number of cooks came and went after that until the family split up, but I can't remember any of them.

Waste Lands

IT IS WHEN we pass through the third locked gate that the reality of what a prison is hits me. The high walls and the huge door outside are only the beginning. This deadly claustrophobic maze inside, these enclosures within enclosures, the metallic sounds of gates screeching apart and together, the clang of keys against locks, jingling of keys against one another—how do they live with this? It is a kind of relief when we finally come to an ordinary wooden door that leads into a courtyard and a peaceful domestic scene of women cleaning grains. But the illusion of cosy domesticity is soon dispelled when the wardress leads me into a room. It's utterly bare, nothing in it but a table and two chairs. The low roof catches the heat and spreads it over us like a warm blanket. I am wiping the tiny beads of perspiration on my face when the women file in at the wardress's command and stare at me with an apathetic curiosity.

'You have to answer this madam's questions,' she says, settling herself in the other chair. 'Go on, now, one by one. You first, Shantamma. She's a lifer. She killed her husband,' the woman says to me as casually as if she's speaking of a petty bad habit.

'No, Amma, I didn't do it, God promise I didn't do it. May their tongues rot, all those who say I did.'

'Stop that now. We've heard that story before. Now, forget that and just tell madam the truth.'

'I didn't do it, I swear I didn't do it,' she repeats. And so it goes on, a terrible story of ill treatment—I think so, though the jailor sits back with a smile as if she's heard this so often it means nothing to her. A story that's interrupted every few minutes with the same denial with which she began, 'But I didn't kill him, Amma, I can swear on any god that it was not I who killed him.'

Later, back home, I look at the pile of notes on my table in despair. How am I going to make an article out of this? What do I focus on? The prison conditions? The women's crushed state? The poor conditions in which they have to live? Their drab ordinariness, a total contrast to the crimes they have committed? Their own versions of the crimes and their protestations of innocence?

It was not just Shantamma who said it, Shakila who had killed her child, Gangubai the thief, Rekha the prostitute—they all said the same thing, 'I didn't do it, Amma, I swear I didn't.'

'They're liars, madam, they all say the same thing. It means nothing.'

The jailor's knowing look, putting us both on the same side, on the other side of the fence from the women, had sickened me. I didn't want to be on her side. But she must be right. They're convicted prisoners, after all. They can't all be innocent. And why protest their innocence now? Why say it after it's all over? They are liars. It means nothing.

We need to invent our own truths. How else can we live with ourselves?

Who said that?

Abruptly I get out of my chair. I can't do this, not today, not now. I'm too tired. And anyway, the deadline is two days away. I'll be able to tackle this better after a good night's sleep.

But sleep eludes me. And suddenly the child springs out at me out of the dark, the child who was playing in the courtyard. I could see him through the open door, pushing a toy, a wooden animal, from one point to another. Over and over again—to the same point and back again. As if, living in prison as he was, space was to him forever circumscribed. Clackety-clackety the uneven wheels went as he pushed, his face concentrated and joyless. Why did he have to be there? Did he have to share his mother's punishment? Perhaps I could begin my article with this child, the child who looked as if he could scarcely hold up his large, shaven head on the pathetically skinny neck . . .

Shaven head? The child – did he have a shaven head? No, what am I thinking of? I'm confusing him with another child, that child I had seen on the railway station. I can see him in his father's arms, listless, the shaven head drooping on a thin neck, unnaturally still and quiet. He didn't get out of his father's arms, not once, I remember, in all the time they were there, no, not even when his mother got into the train. In fact, the three of them were like statues in the midst of the milling crowd on the platform. Man, woman and child. The Holy Family, I'd thought and guiltily suppressed the thought. My mother would have been horrified if I'd said it aloud. We didn't make jokes like that in our family. My mother took religion very seriously, specially since one of her sons became a priest.

You couldn't really joke about those three, anyway; there was a kind of bleak hopelessness about them. Looking at them, specially at the woman who was to be my companion on this journey, I had a sudden moment of regret at having joined the trip. It was not just her, it was the others, too. We were such a motley crowd, all of them older than me, nothing in common between us—how would I spend a fortnight with them? But there was Tushar—I saw him approaching through the crowd and all my regrets vanished. It was hard to believe that we'd known each other for only six months, meeting twice a week in the classroom of our part-time journalism course. It seemed as if we had known each other for years. And now, I thought with pleasure, we would be together for a fortnight.

It doesn't take long for alliances to form within groups. Tushar and I inevitably became a pair. We created a world of our own with its allusions, signs, language and silences that kept the others out. We soon had our names for the others. The two men, always together with their card games and their crude jokes, became the Gemini. The older woman was Auntie. It was the younger one, whose husband and child had come to see her off, who stymied us; it was impossible to name her.

At first Auntie, a good-natured, if rather loud and gregarious woman, tried to make a companion of her. It should have worked out, for, even if she was younger than Auntie, they were both married women. That's how I saw them. But somehow it didn't work out that way. She didn't want Auntie, she wanted to cling to us, to Tushar and me. The other three found it a constant source of humour, both Tushar's and my constant togetherness and her efforts to break in. But she was oblivious of everything—of their jokes and not-very-subtle hints, as well as of our embarrassment and annoyance. (My annoyance, really, for Tushar didn't feel about it the way I did—not exactly, anyway.) What was even more astonishing was that she made no attempt to hide the fact that it was Tushar she wanted to be with. I was flabbergasted by the openness with which she displayed her feelings. And yes, I confess, disgusted as well.

'For God's sake. She's a married woman with a husband and child.'

'Which means, of course, that she shouldn't look, no, not even want to look at another man.'

'Of course. Why are you laughing?'

'What a kid you are! You have a lot to learn, child.'

'Child!'

Sensing my displeasure, Tushar changed the subject. 'But, listen, I've found a name for her finally.'

'What?'

'She's *the third who always walks with us.*'

And then he had to tell me about the words, where he had got them from and all the rest of it. He even had a copy of the book, *The Waste Land*, with him. He said he loved it so he always had it with him. He opened the pages and read it out to me, the part where the words 'the third who always walks with us' were. And then of course he had to go on reading a little more. By the time we had done all this, all was well between us again. She was only an insubstantial shadow who had no place between us.

Finally the working part of our tour was over and we decided to spend the two days left in visiting a famous temple some fifty miles away.

'Are you sure you'd like to go?' Tushar asked me.

'Because it's a temple, you mean? I'm not a bigot, you know. I've visited temples before.'

'No, not because of that. I meant because it's a—it's got a lot of very erotic carvings, you know.'

'I'm not a Puritan, either. And in case you haven't noticed it, I'm an adult as well.'

But when I saw the carvings, I realized what Tushar had been trying to tell me. I was totally unprepared for what I was seeing. Erotic! It was mind-blowing, mind-boggling. It was like going on a roller-coaster ride—you went up the heights one moment when you saw the sheer beauty of some carving and then you went plummeting down with a sick-in-your-stomach feeling at the crude schoolboyish bawdiness of another. How absurd the whole thing is, my mind said, how unnatural and crude. And yet, my body responded involuntarily to the absolutely primal male-female link that I saw on the stone. For the first time, I was glad she was with us. I could not have gone through it alone with Tushar. I have to smile when I think of it now, but I was scarcely twenty then. And those were the pre-MTV days; such explicit images formed no part of my world of imagination.

We were walking in silence when a sound from her startled us. At first, I thought she was laughing; it sounded like a snort of laughter escaping after long suppression. But when I turned to her, I saw she was crying—ugly, painful sobs that would not stop. I tried to soothe her, I tried to hold her contorting body, but she kept pushing me away, as if she could not bear my touch. And suddenly she broke out of my grasp, ran to a tree and was violently sick. I waited by her until Tushar came with some water, then helped her wash her face. She calmed down after that. She sat down under the tree, her body limp, her still-wet face passive and expressionless. The silence went on while Tushar and I stood, shuffling about restlessly.

'Don't you want to go on?' I asked her finally. She shook her head. 'All right, I'll stay with you. Tushar, you go on.'

She jerked her head up at that. A swift movement, her eyes flying to Tushar's face. 'No, *you* stay,' she said to him. Just that. Looking straight into his face, her neck elongated as she gazed up. Even I could feel the power of that look; it was as if she was claiming him.

'All right.' It seemed hours before the words came from Tushar. 'I'll stay.'

I should have argued then. I should have said something, insisted that we could all three of us be together. Something. Anything. But I said nothing. I just walked away from them. I went dutifully around the temple, but I can remember nothing of what I saw after that. It's a total blank.

I kept away from them all day. Tushar tried to join me, he tried to induce me to join them, but I could only think of her face as she looked at Tushar, at her '*you* stay' and Tushar's 'all right'. Somehow, these things seemed inextricably linked to the carvings, the things they said, the world they hinted at.

'What's wrong with you?' Tushar asked me when he finally found me after dinner. 'Can't you see how pathetic she is? How could I say no to her?'

'Can't you see how ridiculous she's making you look? She's a married woman with a child, for God's sake!'

'I have no intentions of marrying her. I only feel sorry for her. That's all!'

'And I feel sorry for you. That's all!'

I stayed by myself the next day until it was time for us to go to the station. If it wasn't for the fact that I was sick of the place and longing to be home, I'd have stayed back to avoid travelling with them. I knew that in the train we would be forced into a closeness I couldn't escape. I hated the thought. As if he had guessed my feelings, Tushar kept away. He was never in his seat. I didn't know where he was—in the corridor, perhaps, smoking—and I was glad of it. She, however, kept looking for him all the while, an unlovely desperation showing on her face. He came to his seat just before the dinner halt, though he didn't sit down.

'Have you ordered your dinner?'

'Yes, I've ordered yours too.'

He had spoken to me, not to her, but it was she who replied. As if he hadn't heard her, he kept looking at me, waiting for my reply.

'No,' I said finally, realizing he wouldn't go away until I had given him an answer. 'I don't want any dinner.'

'Can I get you something?'

'No.'

He went away. The train swayed to a halt and the compartment was filled with the smell of railway meals. Tushar didn't return. She kept his plate for him, arguing with the boy when he came to take away the plates, but the boy was adamant. The train rocked a little, a sign that it was ready to leave. She got up then.

'Where is he? Did he get out of the train? Has anyone seen him? Why hasn't he got in?'

She wove her way through the crowded aisle, her head whirling on her neck like a top, but it was I who saw him first. His eyes met mine across all the people between us and he smiled at me, a smile that leaped over the crowd and took us back immediately into the world the two of us had created between us. At that moment, as if some awareness of his presence had penetrated into her, she turned round and saw him too.

'Thank God!' she said and she was panting as if she had run miles. 'I was so frightened, I was sure you'd been left behind . . .'

'Why would I let that happen? Here,' he gave me a packet. 'I've got this for you. Let's share.'

He came and sat by me as if nothing had happened and by the time we'd finished eating we had gone back to our earlier pattern—the two of us together and the Gemini with their interminable card games. No, that's not right, there was a difference, for they were together now as they should have been earlier, Auntie and she. The two of them chatting about their homes, their families and kids, a kind of cosy domestic chatter. I was astonished that she left Tushar severely alone; in fact, she didn't even look at him, or at me, either. When we went to bed, Tushar in the next cubicle and I in the berth above the two women, I could hear them still talking. I fell asleep, lulled by the rocking of the train, the soothing drone of the two voices below me.

I woke up sometime during the night, conscious of something missing, of an absence. Of course, it was the silence that had woken me up. The train had halted and there was the kind of deathly silence that envelops a train waiting at a small station in the night. There was something else missing too—what was it? I looked down and saw that the berth below mine was vacant. Was it . . . no, Auntie was there all right, sprawled all over her narrow berth in splendid abandon. Where had she gone? Must have gone to the toilet, I told myself and tried to go back to sleep. But when she hadn't returned a little later, I got down, and slightly ashamed of myself, looked into the next cubicle. Yes, there was Tushar, fast asleep. There was no hiding from myself the relief I felt at that. The train began to move. I went to the toilet and found both of them unoccupied. When I returned I noticed for the first time that her blanket was folded, the sheet unrumpled as if she hadn't slept on her bed at all. Or, as if she'd tidied it before she . . . before she *what*? No, she must be somewhere. But where? I stood for a moment, holding on to the railing while the train rushed and rocked under me. I had an impulse to wake up Auntie, to tell her what had happened. But *what* had happened? What *could* have happened?

I got back on to my berth and tried to go to sleep. A child woke up somewhere, whimpering. I could hear the mother's voice, hoarse with sleep, murmuring something. The baby's cries died away. Silence again. Except for the sound of the train.

She must be somewhere, she must be somewhere—the wheels seemed to be repeating the words endlessly. They went on and on, a maddening, exhausting refrain in my head. I covered my ears with my hands to keep out the sound, I put my blanket over my face to shut out the words, but they wouldn't stop. *She must be somewhere, she must be somewhere.*

When I woke up in the morning, her berth was still empty. We got off at our destination with her luggage and without her. We were standing in a silent huddle when a railway official came to us with the news that they had found a body on the tracks—it was just before the station I had woken up at—and perhaps the body was hers?

It was.

'Different religions—you'll have problems,' my mother warned me when I told her that Tushar and I were getting married.

Different religions? I've now read Tushar's beloved *The Waste Land* which gave me the words 'Damyata, Datta, Dayadhvam'. Self-control, charity, compassion—all religions say that, don't they? No, it's not religion that's our problem. It's this thing between us—what do I call it? What's the word for nothing? Of course, a wasteland. It's this wasteland between us. Since the morning we got off the train, it's been there between us.

Yet we stay together, for there's still a world we share. A world in which we sometimes cry out—whether to ourselves or to the other I don't know: *I am blameless, none of it was my fault, it was all hers, she was neurotic, unhappily married.* We need each other for this, there's no one else we can say this to.

We need to invent our own truths. How else can we live with ourselves?

Tushar's words. Now I remember, it was he who said them once. But he's wrong. Lies are no good, you never believe in them, anyway. You only despise yourself for being a liar.

My Beloved Charioteer

I SMILE AS I hear them at last, the sounds I am waiting for. A rush of footsteps, the slam of the bathroom door and then, bare feet running towards me.

'You shouldn't bang doors that way,' I say reproachfully. 'You might wake Mummy.'

She sits opposite me, cross-legged, on the low wooden stool, hair tousled, cheeks flushed. 'Oh, she won't wake up for hours yet,' she says cheerfully. 'Have you had your tea, Ajji?'

This is part of our daily routine. I can never confess to her that I have had a cup an hour earlier. This is her joy, that I wait for her.

'No, I've been waiting for you. Have you brushed your teeth?'

She makes a face. 'I'll do it later,' she says, trying to be brusque and casual.

'You'll do no such thing. Go and brush them at once.'

'Only today, Ajji. From tomorrow, I promise I'll brush them first,' she pleads.

'Nothing doing,' I try hard to be firm but I can't fool her. She knows I am on her side. She lowers her voice to a conspiratorial whisper, 'Mummy won't know, she's sleeping.'

Now, of course, she leaves me no choice. I have to insist. She goes reluctantly and is back so fast, I have to ask, 'Did you really brush? Properly? Show me.'

'Look.'

I have to smile at the grinning, impish face.

'Now, tea for me.'

'No, tea for me, milk for you.'

Ultimately, as always, we compromise and her tea is a pale brown. I switch off the Primus and without the hissing sound, our voices seem loud and clear. We look at each other guiltily, thinking of the sleeper and try to speak in lower tones. Happiness can mean different things to different people. For me, it is this—the beginning of a new day with this child. We talk of many things; but too soon it is time for her to go to school. Bathed and fresh, she sets off.

When she is gone, silence settles on the house. A silence that will not lift till she returns. I had got used to this silence in the last seven years. It had never seemed terrible to me. It was a friendly silence, filled with the ghosts of so many voices in my life. They came back to keep me company when I was alone—my younger brother, my aunt who loved me when I was a child, my two infant sons who never grew up, and even the child Aarti who seems to have no connection with this thin, bitter woman who now shares the silence with me. Since she came, the friendly ghosts have all gone.

It is late when she wakes. I have had my bath, finished my puja and am halfway through cooking lunch when I hear her stirring. I take down the dal from the fire and put on the tea. By the time tea is ready, she comes into the kitchen. Wordlessly she takes a cup from me, drinks the tea in hungry gulps as if she has been thirsting for hours, then thrusts the cup back at me. I pour out some more. I too say nothing. Earlier I used to ask, 'Slept well?' And one day, she had put the cup down with a trembling hand and said, 'Slept well? No, I never do that. I haven't slept well since Madhav died. I'll never sleep well again all my life. I have to take something every night so that I can close my eyes for a few hours. Now never ask me again if I slept well.'

Nine months I carried this daughter of mine in my body. I had felt every beat of her heart, every movement of her limbs within me. But—and my doctor had told me this then— my pains and shocks could never penetrate to her, she was insulated against them. Even now, she is protected from my pains, even now, I have no protection against her pains. I suffer with her but, like all my other emotions, it is a futile suffering. For I cannot help her. I can only fumble and blunder and make things worse.

'Why didn't you let me know earlier?' she had asked me angrily when she had come home after her father's death. 'Why didn't you send for me earlier?'

'Don't tell Aarti yet,' he had said. 'I don't want to frighten her, not now, especially.'

Habits of obedience die harder than any others. I had not dared to inform Aarti. And the next day he had another attack and died instantly. Three months later Priti had been born. She never saw her grandfather.

'Who is that, Ajji?' she had asked me once, pointing to his photograph.

'Your grandfather, Priti.'

'My grandfather?' She had pondered over it. And then asked, 'And what was he of yours?'

What was he of mine? The innocent question had released a flood of feelings within me. 'My husband,' I had said bluntly at last. As I settle down to cooking lunch, I wonder whether today Aarti will like what I'm cooking, whether she will enjoy her food and eat well. I know she will not, but the hope is always in me. Just as I hope that one day she will talk and laugh again. But the day she had laughed, her laughter—loud laughter that shattered the tenuous peace of the house—had frightened me.

'What is it?' I had asked nervously, wondering whether to smile, laugh, to respond in some way to her.

She had looked at me in surprise, as if she hadn't expected to find me there with her, she had hesitated just a moment, then said, 'I always used to think I was very different from you. And look at us now, both of us alike. A pair of widows.'

She didn't mean to be cruel to me, I know that. Nor was I hurt by her words. What pained me was her calling herself a widow. My mother had been widowed when I was a girl and I can only remember her as one, her head shaven, wearing coarse red saris and shorn of all ornaments. While Aarti, after neglecting herself for days, suddenly dresses up, makes up her face and does up her hair. But it is her face that has the arid look of a desert; no smile, no happiness ever blooms there. Life has been cruel to her. It was her father whom she had loved and he died, while I live. It was her husband she had loved even more than the child, and he died, while Priti is left to her.

Children are more sensitive than we think. They understand so much we think they don't. Otherwise why would Priti have said to me one day, 'Ajji, can I sleep in your room at night?'

I am old and grey and have lost most of what I have loved in life except these two persons; but at her words, my heart had leapt with happiness. Yet, I had restrained my joy and asked her, 'Why, Priti?'

'I'd like to. You can tell me stories at night. And there are so many things I suddenly remember at night and want to tell you. And . . .'

'But Mummy is with you.'

The child's face had fallen. 'But, Ajji, if I try to talk to her, she says, "Go to sleep, Priti, don't bother me." And she never sleeps at all, she just reads and smokes. And I don't like that smell.'

The child has a high and clear voice and I had hushed her in sudden fear that she might be overheard. But it's true, she smokes incessantly now. At first, she had tried to hide it from me; but not for long. When I was a child, it had been considered wrong even for a man to smoke in my father's house. But today, I would of my own accord let my daughter smoke if I thought it brought her happiness. It doesn't. She puffs out smoke as if she is emitting bitterness. There is an infinity of bitterness in her. And I cannot help her. I can only try to look after her body. Such a small thing, but even in that I fail. She is thin and brittle. Most of the time, she never dresses up, just goes around in an old gown, her hair confined by a rubber band. Priti, looking at an old photograph, had wistfully said once, 'My Mummy was so pretty, wasn't she, Ajji?'

The child's pride in her mother had roused in me a rage against Aarti. She seems to me like a child, sulking because she does not have what she wants, wilfully ignoring the things she has. Has anyone promised us happiness for a lifetime, I want to ask her.

'Why don't you go out?' I had asked her once.

'Where?'

I had mumbled something she had not heard. She had gone on, 'There is nowhere I want to go. Everywhere I see couples. I can't bear to see them. I could murder them when I see them talking and laughing.'

This kind of talk amazes me. I cannot understand her. My niece had once told me of something she had read in an American magazine. Of young children who stab and throttle and rape and gouge out eyes, often for no reason at all. And I had wondered—what kind of parents can they be who give birth to such monsters? Now I know better. The accident of birth can be cruelly deceiving. We fool ourselves that our children are our own, that we know them. But often, they are as alien to us as baby cuckoos born in a crow's nest. And yet we cannot escape the burden of parentage. If my daughter is so empty that she can hate people who are happy, the fault is, to some extent, mine.

These bitter thoughts do not often occupy me. I have my work. The quiet routine of my day is like balm to my soul. Daily chores are not monotonous but soothing. Now that the child is with me, the day is full of meaning. I wait, eager as a child myself, for her to return from school. When she has a holiday, I don't know who is happier, she or I; if it is an unexpected holiday, we are equally full of glee. But when she, my daughter and her mother, comes to us, we feel guilty and hide our happiness.

'Do you remember your Papa?' Aarti had asked her one day with a sudden harshness.

'Papa?' There had been a moment's hesitation. Then she had replied, 'Yes, I remember.'

'No, you don't. Don't lie to me.'

The child had stared at her with a frightened face, feeling she had done something wrong, though she didn't know what it was. When Aarti had left us, she had burst into sobs, clinging to me. And I had been full of pity, more for Aarti who could turn happiness into a wrong. But I can say nothing to her. She has never shared anything with me and now she hides her sorrow like a dog its bone. She guards it jealously and will not let me approach. And I have kept my distance, too. It was only in my imagination that I cuddled her as a child, only in my imagination that I shared her happiness and confidences when she was a girl. And now I assuage her grief in the same way. 'Look,' I tell myself I will say to her, pouring some water into my cupped palms. 'Look,' I will say as the water seeps through, leaving nothing. 'You cannot hold on. You will have to let go.'

But I know I am fooling myself. I have no courage to speak. I am only a foolish, middle-aged woman who has never known how to win anyone's love. Priti's affection—that is a gift from heaven, the ray of sunshine God sends even to the darkest corners.

For Aarti, it was always her father. Even now, she spends the whole afternoon prowling in what was his room. It is seven years since he died, but the room is unchanged. I have kept everything as it was. I dust and sweep it meticulously myself; but strangely, in spite of this, it has a neglected look, like Priti has at times. Priti is well fed and well dressed, she has her tonics and vitamins and all the other things they give children these days. And yet, a neglected child peeps out of her eyes sometimes, filling me with sadness.

Now I can hear Aarti moving in his room. Even after his death, he can give her something I can't. The thought hurts. Hurts? It's like having salt rubbed into a raw wound. Suddenly it is unbearable and I go and open the door of his room. She is sitting on his chair, her feet on the table, smoking and staring at nothing. Her feet are the feet of a young woman, but I see with a sense of shock that her face is that of an old woman. She hears me and turns round, startled, the movement knocking down his photograph which stands on the table. It lies on the floor, face down and when she picks it up we see that the glass has cracked. Long splinters of glass lie on the floor. The photograph seems somehow naked and pathetic. She looks up at me, something showing through the deliberate blankness.

'I'm sorry, Mother, I'm sorry.'

I stare down at the photograph and say nothing.

'I'm sorry,' she repeats. 'Don't look like that.' She passes her hand over the photograph, uncaring of the bits of glass. 'I'll get it fixed tomorrow, I promise I'll do it.'

'No, don't!' My words are so harsh and abrupt that she looks at me in surprise. 'I don't care if it's broken. I don't want to see it here. I never want to see it again.'

She seems stunned, frightened. 'What's wrong with you? What's happened to you?'

'Nothing. I'm all right. But I don't want it. Let it go.'

'What are you saying?'

'Let it go, let it go,' I repeat. We are speaking in sibilant, strangled whispers, as if he is here, as if he can hear us. Can he hear us? Can he hear me?

'I don't understand you. Let what go? He is my father.' She is still crouching on the floor, holding the photograph in her two hands.

'Yes, your father, but what was he to me? The day he died, I let him go. Like this.' Now I make the gesture I had imagined—cupping my palms together and then separating them. She stares at my hands in fascination. 'And there was nothing left. Nothing.'

'But I—I'm his daughter. And yours. Am I nothing? Am I?' She is panting, her eyes hot and angry.

'What are you then?' I ask her. 'You are just smoke and a bit of ash, like those cigarettes you smoke. Like my married life.'

Pain lays its talons on her face, her eyes are anguished. But I force myself to go on. What have I to lose? Only the child's love. And I know this cannot destroy that. On the contrary, I have a feeling that she is with me now, giving me strength for the battle, urging me on. My beloved charioteer.

'He was your father, but what was he of mine? I lived with him for twenty-five years. I know he didn't like unstringed beans and hated grit in his rice, I know he liked his tea boiling hot and his bathwater lukewarm. And he hated tears. And so, when your baby brothers died, I wept alone and in secret. I combed my hair before he woke up because he didn't like to see women with untidy, loosened hair. And I went into the backyard even then because it made him furious to find stray hairs anywhere. And once a year he bought me two saris, always colours I hated; he never asked me what I liked and I never told him. And at night . . .'

She is still crouching, her hair falling about her face. She whimpers like a hurt puppy. 'Don't,' she says, 'don't tell me, don't.' With each negative, she bangs the photograph she still holds in her hands and the glass splinters again and again. Now he is totally exposed to us, but there is no pity in me. It is not the dead who need our compassion, it is the living; not the dead who crave loyalty, but the living.

'I don't want to hear,' she says.

How innocent she is in spite of her age, her education, her marriage and her child, if knowledge can hurt her. It reminds me of the day she had grown up and I had tried to explain. And she had cried out in the same way, 'Don't tell me, don't!' This is another kind of growing up, when you see your parents as people. 'At night,' I go on relentlessly, 'I scarcely dared to breathe, I was so terrified of disturbing him. And once, when I asked whether I could sleep in another room—I don't know how I had the courage—he said nothing. But the next day, his mother, your grandmother, told me bluntly about a wife's duties. I must always be available, she said. So I slept there, afraid to get up for a glass of water, scared even to cough. When he wanted me, he said, "Come here." And I went. And when he finished, if I didn't get out of his bed fast enough, he said, "You can go." And I got out.'

I know these things should not be said to her, his daughter and mine. But I am like a river in the monsoon, nothing can control me now.

'And one day, when you were here, you and Madhav, I heard you both talking and laughing in your room. And I stood outside and wondered—what could you be talking about? I felt like I did when I looked at a book as a child before I learned to read. Until then, I had hoped that one day he would say he was pleased with me. That day I knew it would never happen. I would always be outside the room, I would never know what went on inside. And that day I envied you, my own daughter. You hear me, Aarti? I envied you. And when he died I felt like Priti does when school is over and the bell rings. You understand, Aarti? You understand what I'm saying?'

Why am I also crying? We look at each other and she is looking at me as if she has never seen me before. Then, with a sudden movement, she springs up and glares at me. I have made her look at me. But what, my heart shrivels at the thought, if she does not like what she sees? And then, moving backwards from me, her eyes still on my face, she goes out of the room. In a moment I hear her running feet. My legs can no longer support me. I collapse in a chair. As I sit there, my mind a blank, I hear the cry, 'Ajji, I'm home, where are you?'

I sit up and look about me. 'Ajji,' the voice is peremptory. For a moment I can't speak. Then I call back, loudly, 'Here, Priti, I'm here.'

My cry rings through the house like hers had done.

The Valley in Shadow

GREEN FORESTS COVERED the slopes of the two hills, leaving indentical bare crowns on top. At the base too the lush growth gave way with a shocking abruptness, so that the valley in between was stony and arid, as if a giant hand had scooped all the greenery out of it. I had thought it a beautiful view on the first morning. Now, as I stood alone on the veranda of our room for the fourth day in succession, the view was already stale, tainted, as it were, by my vision. I avoided it and looked instead at the garden that lay before me, the usual hotel garden with potted bougainvilleas and cemented walks bordered by wilting flowers. There were all the appurtenances of a holiday spot in it . . . swings, sandpits, and at this time of the day, the men who made their living out of the hotel guests. The man who sold curios and picture postcards was moving purposefully from room to room, while the one with ponies squatted, patiently waiting for the children to come out and claim their ponies. The monkey man had settled down with his rattle, and the monkey, off duty as yet, gazed around in a kind of bewilderment. Sounds and sights already as familiar to me as the cries of hawkers on the road outside our home. Now the children gathered around the monkey and the man's voice rose, speaking to the monkey in a peculiar sing-song tone, a tone that never varied in volume even by a decibel.

And then, everything else receded. For a moment, the world narrowed to a pair of hands. The hands that now appeared on the wooden railing of the veranda of the next room. 'Hi,' the voice greeted me, 'and how are you this morning?' I smiled, then realized he couldn't see my smile. The thin partition wall was between us. He could see me only if I leaned forward, as he was doing, with my elbows resting on the railing, my face propped on my hands. Stealthily I felt my elbows. Roughened. It was reassuring, like a symbol of our intimacy. Rub cream gently into your elbows each night, the beauty tips advised. Never again for me, I thought. I will never do that.

'Family out?'

'Yes.'

I moved my gaze once again to the valley which the sun resolutely refused to brighten. All day it remained untouched by the sunshine, while the peaks on either side glowed triumphantly.

Family out?—that was what he had said the very first morning. 'Family out?'

'Yes.'

'Cute little fellow you have.'

'Yes.'

'You haven't gone with them?'

'No.'

'Oh good,' he had said, 'you do know another word apart from "yes".'

He had laughed. I had already noticed that his voice was deep and resonant, but the laughter, however, had been high-pitched. I had laughed too, but hesitantly, nervously. My uneasiness encompassing the question . . . why was he talking to me? For me, communication with a man is like exploring foreign territory. A woman's responses I can guess, her mind I can follow, whichever way it goes. But with a man it is always a groping in the dark. As we stood there and talked,

I had looked at our hands resting on the wooden railling in front of us and they had emphasized the difference between us. Was that why, I had wondered, he was talking to me?

Now I could see he had just had his bath, for his wet towel lay on the railing, a bright orange-and-black striped one. The whiff of soap and aftershave lotion came to me from him. Suddenly I wished I was bathed and dressed and . . . no, that wish I had abandoned long back.

'Don't you ever go out?' he asked me.

'No.'

'You don't like to walk?'

'No, I don't.'

It was not a lie. And yet it was not the whole truth, either. The truth, the whole truth and nothing but the truth, so help me God. But this was not a courtroom, and I was not a criminal or a witness. And we would soon part, this man and I, going our different ways, and he would never know that I had not told him the whole truth. Why then, did it matter so much? Why did I feel ashamed to keep the truth from him?

'The thing is,' I blurted out now, awkwardly and shamefacedly, my speech and words, I thought bitterly, as awkward as my walk, 'I can't really walk very much. I had polio when I was a child. I'm crippled.'

I used the worst possible word. The word I hated above all, a word which seemed to have nothing to do with the real me. Now he would be silent, uncomfortable; he would say a word or two to me from that height on which he stood as a normal human being. And I would continue to sit here, watching the sunshine take over everything, leaving only the valley in darkness until I saw them returning, my husband and child. My child would run to me, laughing, clamouring for my attention, wanting me to share his excitement with him, and I would forget what I was for a while. But he would soon run away from me and I could not follow him, and the thought of what I was would be forced on me once again. It's my fault, I thought. I should not have agreed to come here. What would I do on a holiday . . . I, who could neither walk, run, nor enjoy myself like the others?

I carried my inability to enjoy with me wherever I went.

Even as a child I had noticed how people looked at my legs first and then, very perfunctorily, at the rest of me.

'Who will marry her?' my mother had moaned as I grew up. But my father had gone on doggedly with his proposals to young men, never hiding my disability, so that each time the matter ended there. When one young man had consented to meet me I had thought perhaps he will see me and not my legs. When he agreed to marry me I had thought, he *has* seen me.

'Well, if you can't walk, why don't you ride then?'

This man spoke in a voice so matter-of-fact, so devoid of any awkwardness, sympathy or condescension that I was startled. I leaned forwards and looked at him. He was looking at me too. It gave me a strange feeling as if I was flooded with sunshine. I thought of the valley and of how, if the sunshine ever illuminated it, its ugliness and aridity would be emphasized. And for some reason my thoughts went back to that night, six months after the birth of my son.

Six months now, I had wondered, and still he avoids me. I had not known how to tell him that there was nothing to keep us apart any longer. Each night I had rehearsed the words in which I would say this to him and each night shame and some kind of a fear had held the words back.

That night I had gone to him and tried to tell him without using words. Gently, and yet very firmly, he had put me away from him and said, 'It's better we don't.'

'Why?' I had asked him stupidly.

And he had said, 'After all, we have a son.'

And all at once I had known that the sight of me was distasteful to him. He had put up with me because of his desire for a son. But why, I had thought in a last spurt of anger, had he married me at all? But I had known the answer to that one as well. I had known it from the first few days of our marriage. He had married me for the usual reason—money. Not just the money my father gave us, but the money I earned each month. And even if I was earning more than he did, the fact of my being crippled levelled out the difference between us, so that he did not have to feel humiliated as he would have with any other woman. That night I had shut out forever all hopes of any human contact.

And yet, now, the morning after my confession, I had my bath early. I dressed myself in a soft cotton sari, one that I knew I liked. I went out and seeing the two towels hanging there—the child's gay and colourful and my husband's, a sober grey—I savagely whisked them off the railing and took them in, telling myself they were dry anyway. When I came out I noticed that his feet were on the railings now, two feet, clean, naked and, somehow vulnerable. As I sat down the feet disappeared and the hands appeared. I put my own in front of me.

'Hi, you smell nice today,' he said.

'Sandal soap,' I said boldly and despised myself for being unable to accept anything gracefully.

The monkey man now came up to us, started his rattling and said to the monkey, '*Saab ko salaam karo.*' The monkey obeyed and the spectators tittered appreciatively. I felt sick. '*Memsaab ko salaam karo,*' he now said and I uttered a strangled protest.

'Would memsaab like the poor little monkey to go away?' the voice said to me across the wall and over the monkey man's rattle.

'Yes,' I said emphatically and immediately he called the man over. I saw some money pass from hand to hand and the man went away leading the monkey which walked with a sort of hideous coquetry emphasized by the skirt it wore.

'OK?' the voice said.

'Fine,' I replied and even to me my voice sounded different.

'Memsaab seems to be enjoying her holiday at last,' the voice went on. And I wondered . . . had I got away at last from the bitter woman who dragged her resentment with her like the monkey its skirt? I imagined how the monkey would look without that skirt, leaping agilely from branch to branch . . . but I was no monkey, was I? I laughed suddenly and he said, 'What's the joke?'

'I was thinking of those scientists who work on monkeys, guinea pigs and rabbits and apply the results to humans.'

'I know. Give a monkey coffee to drink and when it gets some kind of carcinoma, they tell you, "Drink too much coffee and you'll get carcinoma too."'

We laughed and I said, 'Imagine, I didn't want to come here for a holiday.'

'Where did you want to go?'

'I don't know. Nowhere. I just wanted to go on working, I suppose.'

'Absorbing work?'

'What! Working in a government office?'

Now the feet came up again. I heard the sound of a match scraping. The smell of a cigarette. 'You make me feel an idler.' The smoke drifted languidly towards me and in an instant was nothing. 'I must have a few days off each year. I can't go on if I don't.'

'And where will you go next year?' I waited with painful eagerness for his reply. A small pause. Then he said, 'Depends. It's something I don't plan too early. And you?'

'I don't know, either. I don't dare to look beyond today. Sometimes it frightens me, the thought that I have to keep going. I don't know where, or what for. So I stop thinking about it and just drift.'

Silence. It doesn't do to be too serious. People aren't interested in your miseries. *How are you? Fine, thank you.* What if you say, 'I'm wretched, I'm absolutely miserable'? Nobody will ever ask you that question again.

The feet disappeared again. I heard his voice say, 'Shall I come over there? We've had enough of this Pyramus-Thisbe stuff, I think. Though that doesn't really apply here, does it? All right by you if I come over?'

I panicked. 'No,' I said. 'Please don't.'

I heard him settle back in his chair. I cursed myself for my cowardice. Why did it matter so much that he would see me, see how clumsy and graceless I was?

'You make too much of it, you know,' the voice came to me remote, all expression carefully kept out of it. 'It doesn't matter all that much really.'

Doesn't matter? To whom? To you? A group of youngsters ran out into the garden. A boy playfully pulled at a girl's arm and she shrieked, shrieks that turned into laughter. I smiled. I could have laughed. And then I saw the valley again, dark, brooding and barren. I shivered.

'Can I come out with you?' I asked my husband the next morning.

'What, for a walk?' The disbelief could have been insulting, but somehow wasn't.

'We could ride.'

'You couldn't.'

'No, I couldn't.'

'Of course, if you're bored with being alone, we'll stay here with you.'

'Daddy, let's go, I want to go.'

'No, you go on, both of you. I'm all right.'

'Do you have something to read?'

'Yes.'

'Sure you don't mind?'

'No, you go.'

Go, please go. At last they went. And I sat in the room telling myself . . . I won't go out, no. I won't. And yet, each time there was a knock at the door, I was aflame with hope. Once it was the dhobi to take away our dirty clothes. Once the boy who came to polish shoes. And I wondered whether I would be able to identify his steps if he came. Maybe I would. And then there would be the knock at the door, my gruff, 'Come in.'

'Are you all right?' he would ask.

'Fine,' I would reply.

'You didn't come out today.'

'No.'

'I was a little worried. I thought . . .'

My heart would be pounding . . . surely he would hear it . . . my hands trembling. He would see them and say, 'What's the matter? Why are you so scared?' He would hold both my hands in his and . . .

I came out of it with a start and stared stupidly about me. The fantasy had been so strong I could almost feel the taste of his lips on mine, the smell of his cigarette in my nostrils. For a moment, revulsion against my own self filled me; until the thought came . . . what the hell is wrong with me, a thirty-year-old woman with a responsible job that I should behave like a hysterical adolescent? The words steadied me somewhat, giving me a kind of spurious courage that pushed me out of the room. I went and stood at my usual place, staring ahead of me. There were clouds in the sky today, so that one of the hills was dark and shadowy, while the other gleamed brightly. The valley in shadow, as usual, as always.

And then I saw the hands. Hands on the railing beside me. Hands like mine. A woman's hands, but the nails shaped and painted so that the hands had an edge of sophistication. I stared at them as they lay on the orange-and-black towel in a kind of caressing intimacy. And then I heard the voice from inside, 'Mamata . . .'

'What?'

'What are you doing out there? Come on in.'

I went in myself and lay rigid on the bed. I imagined the voices next door. I imagined even more and was engulfed

with shame to think of the fantasies I had woven round him.
Me with my crippled body.

I was still lying there when they came back . . . my husband
and the child. The child was whining and came running
towards me. I thought he was tired and cradled him, soothing
him with soft words, but when I touched him, I found his
body hot.

'He has fever,' I said accusingly. 'You shouldn't have taken
him out.'

'I wish to God I hadn't,' he said moodily, throwing himself
into a chair.

'Let's go back,' I said suddenly. 'Let's go home.'

'Yes, let's,' he agreed instantly to my astonishment. 'I'm
tired of this place.'

You too? I wondered, but I didn't want to know anything
more. Since the day he had turned his back on me I had
closed my mind to him. And yet, now, as I looked at him,
compassion flowed into me. And, momentarily, it was as if
the shadows had lifted. So that, somehow, it suddenly seemed
possible to talk to him. And perhaps in the evening, I would
meet the other man as well. 'Hi,' he would say, as friendly as
always, 'come and meet Mamata.' And I would get up and
walk towards them smiling, uncaring of how I looked.

And now, I had a feeling that if the valley was in shadow
no longer, if the sunshine fell on it, perhaps even its bareness
and aridity would look beautiful.

The Intrusion

WE LOOKED BLATANTLY out of place there. Tiny houses, almost miniature ones, but spick and span. A little path, so narrow, that if we stretched our arms we could touch the houses on both sides. Why had we come here? I walked stiffly, self-consciously, trying hard to seem unaware of the stares, the curious eyes that followed us. I wished I could turn around and stare back with the same frank curiosity, but all I could do was to peep covertly through the corners of my eyes. Men in checked lungis sitting at fishing nets, drying fish laid out in rows on poles, women with bold faces and gold ornaments . . . all the signs of a fishing village. But, I thought, if this is a fishing village, where is the sea? And then we reached the end of the lane, turned right, and there, suddenly, enchantingly, was the sea in front of us, immense and fascinating. And again rows and rows of fish hung up to dry, looking at us and at the blue of the sky with sightless, accusing eyes.

I stopped and stared. He stopped too, and looked at me with a slight, a very slight impatience which aroused the faintest wisp of annoyance in me. Then he beckoned to me with a friendly smile and I hurried on. Now we were walking on the sand, squelchy, oozing, almost black. The sea must have been here not long back, during the high tide. I found it difficult walking in my high heels, with my heavy sari squashing damply round my ankles. I was conscious of an unreasonable pang of irritation against him. As though sensing my discomfort, he held my arm to help me, but awkwardly, too tight, and I wanted to protest, to release my arm from his constricting grip. The sea had left innumerable shells on the shore which crunched under our feet and I bent down to pick up one— any excuse to loosen his hold on my arm. But horrors! There was something alive, something crawling in the shell and I threw it away in disgust and hurried on after him.

Now, thankfully, we were out of the sand and back in the village, but a village that looked so different that it was difficult to believe it was the same. The paths were broader and went steeply uphill. There were scarcely any signs of the sea—no fishing nets, no dried fish. Instead, there was the familiar lacy foliage of the drumstick tree outlined sharply against the sky, the drumsticks hanging limply and peacefully from the branches. I had no time to look around. The man, loaded with our new, expensive suitcases, was already at the top of the hill and I had to hurry, to stumble on uphill, panting, wishing now for the support I had earlier spurned.

'We're almost there,' he said encouragingly and yes, we had left all the huts behind us. We went up a steep, rocky path, lined by big boulders, and suddenly we were at the top. A square, squat building stared at us blankly. My hair blew anyhow and my sari began billowing into odd, ugly shapes. Someone came forward to receive us and opened one of the rooms for us. I sank gratefully into a chair, easing my tired feet out of my slippers, too exhausted even to look around.

'Isn't this nice?' he asked me beaming, pleased with himself, all signs of nervousness and irritation gone now that we had arrived.

'Yes,' I said.

It had the usual dullness and impersonality of any room where people stay for a short time and go away, leaving no impress of themselves behind. Just a jumble of stale smells. Even, I sniffed surreptitiously, a smell of bedbugs. The man flung open the windows and the breeze rushed in at us, destroying, at one stroke, all the smells.

'Do you want anything?' he asked.

'Yes, some tea. Is that all right?'

I nodded and the man went out. Though when he was in the room I had looked away from him, painfully aware of a secret smile, a smirk on his face that showed an awareness of what we had come here for, suddenly I wished he had not gone. He left behind him a painful silence, an embarrassment that occurs between two people who scarcely know each other and I wondered wildly, desperately, what we could talk about. As if the silence made him uneasy too, he began to move about the room whistling tunelessly. Then he suddenly burst into speech, telling me how fortunate he was to get this place for our honeymoon. What luck, he said, that one of the top executives, who was to have come here, had cancelled his visit at the last minute, so that we were here all by ourselves. 'Complete privacy,' he smiled, emphasizing the words and I felt suddenly, completely sickened. He went on, unaware of my feelings, telling me it was only the lucky few who could get this place to stay.

And then I began to wonder about these few, and did they come here with their families? Somehow it didn't seem like a place where children had ever played and shouted, with mothers hovering around, anxious and nagging. There was something furtive about the place, something deadpan about the servant's face, which made me feel that the men who came here did so with 'other women'—girls, perhaps, bold-faced and experienced, who would laugh and chat with the men, not go through what I was enduring now. Fears. Tremors. The way I averted my face from the beds. The sheets looked grubby and the pillow covers disgustingly greasy. 'Tell the man to change the covers and sheets,' I wanted to say, but couldn't. I imagined the man giving me meaningful looks when I said it, and later, perhaps, he would discuss us with the other servants. And all of them would make bawdy jokes and laugh aloud.

He went inside—I could hear sounds of him vigorously washing his face. I lay back in the chair, full of lassitude, too tired even to examine all my emotions, only one thought penetrating through the haze—I wish I was back home. The tea arrived. It smelt of kerosene, so did the bread and butter. I was suddenly very hungry and had a sharp pang of longing for the sweets my mother had packed for me. 'I've put some sweets in your bag,' she had said, turning her tired face to mine. 'Ridiculous!' I would have snapped, even a day earlier. 'You can't go on a honeymoon with sweets in your suitcase.' But something forlorn in her face and eyes had restrained me and I had silently acquiesced. Now I knew that my hunger for her sweets had something to do with the look on her face as well. Yet I felt shy, unwilling to open my suitcase and devour the sweets before him like a greedy schoolgirl.

'We are looking for a girl, simple but sophisticated,' his mother had said. 'My son is working in a foreign company. His wife must be able to entertain and mix with foreigners.' She had made the word foreigners sound like 'Martians'. Simple and sophisticated—was I that, I wondered? It had seemed I was, for my mother had joyfully told me that they had agreed to our proposal. No one had asked me if I had agreed; it had been taken for granted. I had taken it for granted myself, when suddenly, a few days before the wedding, I had gone to my father, stricken by doubts. 'Why?' he had asked me, again and again. And, 'What will you do then?' In a panic I had asked myself, 'What will I do?' And I had thought of a thousand answers, but none to the question, 'What's wrong with him?' I had nothing to say, either, when my father said quietly, 'I have two more daughters to be married.'

'Why are you so silent?' he asked, breaking into my thoughts.

'I'm tired. Just a little.' I smiled as I said it, a painful, awkward smile, the smile one gives a distant acquaintance. What if I had said, 'Now that I've had my tea, can I go home?'

He came closer, looking concerned, and put his arm around me, but awkwardly, stiffly, so that we looked like two marionettes sitting side by side. I tried to move but his hold was firm. He smelt of sweat. Through his glasses, his eyes had a sardonic gleam that frightened me.

'It's a bit stuffy here, isn't it?' I got up, trying to sound casual. 'Let's go out to the veranda. I want to see the sea.'

Unwillingly he let me go and followed me out. The sea was far away. There was only the breeze and a strong smell of dried fish. The cliff on which the building stood jutted out into the sea, giving the beach below us a private, secluded and inviting look. The sand gleamed orange in the light of the setting sun and even as we stood there in silence, the sun went down, swiftly and suddenly, taking us by surprise. I was conscious of a slight headache, a faint nausea. I had a great longing to go down, to scuff my bare toes in the sand, to pick up shells and sit on the rocks, letting the friendly waves climb up my bare legs. He would swim, I thought, and call out to me in a lazy and friendly way and I would respond with a wave and a smile. But all this was in the future, possibly, if at all. And at present we were not friends, not acquaintances even, but only a husband and wife. And the slightly glazed look in his eyes as he hummed a popular tune told me how unaware he was of everything but of what was to happen between us, making us truly husband and wife. When we were, I thought again, not even acquainted with each other. A month back we had not even heard of each other.

'Let's go down to the sea,' I said suddenly.

'Now?' He seemed surprised. 'Let's go in the morning.'

Yes, but before the morning there's the night—I quailed at the thought. He saw the look on my face and smiled at me.

'It's going to be dark soon. Look at the way.'

A little path went zig-zagging crazily down the cliff.

He put his arm round my waist. 'You don't really want to go down, do you?' It was said in my ear, almost a whisper, and it sickened me, like those furtive touches and glances from faceless, nameless men in crowds. My mind shied like a frightened horse from the words, from the thought.

'Come on in.' He pulled at my arms. 'It's getting chilly.'

So it was. And dark as well; we had to switch on the lights in the room. Someone had removed the tea things and made the beds. I thought with a wistful pang of my own narrow bed at home and of how I would lie on it, curled into a comfortable ball, reading into the late hours of the night. I felt a constriction in my throat, a longing for all the things I had left behind me forever: a melancholy that always assails one when away from home at this time, neither day nor night.

He seemed unaffected by the atmosphere or any melancholy and noisily opening his suitcase, took out some clothes and went in to change. I sat quietly for a minute, then flew to the veranda, unwilling to admit, even to myself, that I didn't want to hear the intimate sounds that were seeping through the thin walls and flimsy door. I stood there, leaning against the wooden railings, tugging savagely at my hair, wishing I were anywhere but here, with a strange man in a strange room. Wishing that I could project myself into the future, gulf this intervening time and become all at once an experienced, mature woman; one who would not turn a hair at anything. Just then he called out my name, using it so familiarly, with such a proprietorial air that I was startled. A little angry, too. Reluctantly I went in.

'Why don't you change?' he asked and it seemed to me that there was something insinuating in his tone, something eager and excited about him that put me off.

I changed, thankful that my nightdress was modest. His eyes slid over me briefly and he was once again a nameless stranger. Then they slipped away from me. I opened the door to the veranda.

'Where are you going?'

'Nowhere. Just out here.'

'Come here.'

'Let's stand out for a few minutes.' I was pleading now.

'No. Come here.'

Unwillingly I turned and went to him, my legs as heavy as lead. And suddenly his arms were round me, his face close to mine, his rough chin scraping, hurting my cheek. His embrace was too sudden, too rough, and I wanted to scream, to cry out. But somehow I knew that this was just between the two of us. I turned my face away from him, trying to escape, so that the kiss he intended for my lips landed in the air. He let me go abruptly. There was a foolish, angry look on his face. His glasses had fallen down in the struggle. Mutely I picked them up and gave them to him. He was silent while he wiped them and put them on. When he finally spoke, his voice was shrill, almost with a note of hysteria in it. 'What's this? Why are you behaving like this?'

'Like what?' I tried to keep my own tone level, innocent.

'Avoiding me. Don't think I haven't noticed it. Ever since we came here you've been . . . been . . . avoiding me,' he ended lamely.

'No, I have not, I'm not . . .' It was the reflex denial of a child.

'Do you think I enjoy feeling that I'm forcing myself on you? What's the problem? Why are you acting so strange?'

I felt contrite at the sight of his bewildered face. But I had nothing to say.

'You're not an innocent little girl, are you? You know . . .'

Yes, I did. No, I was not innocent. In fact, just before the wedding, I'd read a book. Not furtively, hiding in dark corners, but openly. And it was my mother who had blushed like a girl on seeing it. As I'd read it, strange shivers had gone over me:

finally I had thrown the book away in disgust. What things, I had thought, one has to do just to propagate the human race!

I stood silent. Angry, hurt, crestfallen, he waited for my answer. 'We . . . we scarcely know each other,' I stammered at last.

He seemed flabbergasted. 'Know each other? What has that to do with it? Aren't we married now? And how will we start getting to know each other if you put on such a touch-me-not air?'

I want to know all about you, I wanted to say. What you think, what you feel and why you agreed to marry me? And what did you think of as we went through all those ceremonies together, and do you like the things I do and will we laugh together at the same jokes, enjoy the same books? And there were all those fears crouching in me—would his breath smell, and were his feet huge and dirty with uncut toenails, and did he chew his food noisily and belch after meals? I wanted to tell him how shy and frightened I was about exposing the mysteries of my body to him and how homesick I was for my mother's face, my father's laughter and my sisters' chatter.

But I could say none of these things to him. Even if I did, I thought, looking at his face, he would not hear me. He was all keyed up for a different experience and for him other things would come later. While I wished to talk now, sitting up the whole night, so that in the morning we could smile at each other like old friends. I stammered as I tried to explain, I flushed, I almost burst into tears looking at his angry face. The eager look in his eyes died as I spoke, and finally he turned away from me, violently flung himself on a bed and lay there still. I felt as if I had committed a crime, yet there was a light-hearted sense of escape, too. Quietly I went to my bed and lay down, trying to sleep, while countless erotic images came out of the pages of the book I had read and tortured my distracted mind. I lay wondering if I was that thing I had read about, a frigid woman, incapable of love. And what we would do if it were so. I imagined myself returning to my parents' home, shamed and rejected, and the consternation and grief it would cause there, my sisters' marriages held up forever, my parents disgraced—all because of me.

Simple and sophisticated, I told myself, choking myself with my blanket to prevent my gurgle of laughter from being heard. But how can I, with a man I scarcely know? It's not fair, I thought angrily. It's indecent. He should have given me some time. What a way to spend our honeymoon, I thought, imagining him sulking the whole time, and I, moving around with a load of guilt, shame and fear. What will we tell the others when we go back?

I must have drifted off into sleep at some time because I woke to the dull, booming sound of the sea coming in. There was scarcely any pause, I noted drowsily, in the thundering noise. I did not wake up all at once, but drifted for some time between sleeping and waking, struggling out of a confused dream that I was lying there on the beach, where I had so longed to go and that the waves were pounding me.

And then I woke up to realize that the sound of the sea was real, but I was on a bed, not on the beach. And it was not the sea that was pounding my body but he, my husband, who was forcing his body on mine. I was too frightened to speak, my voice was strangled in my throat. I put my hands on his chest to push him away, but it was like trying to move a rock; I could do nothing. He put his hands, his lips on mine and this time I could not move away. There was no talk, no word between us—just this relentless pounding. His movements had the same rhythm, the same violence as the movements of the sea; yet, I could have borne the battering of the sea better, for that would hurt, but not humiliate like this.

At last, mercifully, it was over, my body having helped him by some strange instinct beyond and outside me. And the cry

I gave was not for the physical pain, but for the intrusion into my privacy, the violation of my right to myself. I drew the sheets over myself and lay quietly, afraid to move, thinking of nothing, my mind an absolute blank. When sensation and feeling came back with a surge, my first thought was that I could not hear even the sea now. I wondered why, till I realized that there was another sound drowning it. I looked at him. He was lying on his back, legs flung apart, snoring loudly and steadily.

The Eternal Theme

THEY HAD ALWAYS told me the carvings were beautiful. Now, watching his profile sharply etched against the unending frieze of the dark, stony figures, I realized for the first time how beautiful they were. He stood there alone. It suited him. I thought, to be alone.

'Coming?' they asked me.

'We're just taking a small stroll. Plenty of time before the bus leaves.'

'No,' I said. 'I won't come. I'll stay here.'

I stood there, alone like him, trying not to look at him. Trying to admire the azure blue of the sky melting into the greenish-blue of the sea. Or to stare at the white-edged waves crawling lazily, deliberately, on to the gleaming sand. But it was no use. All that was only the setting against which he stood. Everything else faded away into the background. Rapture flowed out of me and an air of well-being and languor filled me. I closed my eyes and leaned back against the rocks which had gathered the heat of the sun the whole day. Warmth seeped into me. I thought of the warmth of the human body and of the man who stood there, so unaware of me, and I trembled as if I was cold. But the rocks were still warm against my body. I felt a shadow come across my eyes. I opened them and he stood there.

There was no surprise, no wonder in me that he was there. It was natural, inevitable.

This is why all this beauty has been created . . . so that you can stand against it and dazzle my eyes.

'All by yourself?'

Yesterday I saw you for the first time. Since then, nothing has existed for me but your face. And now I feel I have known it since the day I was born.

I could not speak. Something had come into my throat, stifling me, not letting me speak.

'What's the matter?' He smiled and ripples, as gently undulating as the waves, passed over my body. 'Your mother told you not to talk to strange men?'

They told me so many things. But they never told me I would meet you. They never told me you could do this to me by just standing there . . . that you could take me out of myself, leaving behind a hollow, vibrating shell.

Now the something in my throat slipped and went down. My voice was free.

'No. You startled me. I didn't think . . . I didn't imagine . . . I didn't expect . . .'

You were only a dream, a figment of my imagination. Now you come to me and I see you are a man, more beautiful than any dream.

'I saw you yesterday during the sessions. I saw you staring at me intently when I was speaking. You frightened me.'

He smiled at this and I smiled too.

I am a reflection, an echo. You are the reality and I am the shadow.

'I thought you were waiting for me to make a mistake, to fumble.'

But you never did. You spoke fluently, your hands as expressive as your eyes, your mouth firm and controlled, your bearing erect. I had not understood your words, but I had understood you. I asked someone, 'Who is he?' And the answer had been the right one. 'He is a poet.'

'No? Then what were you thinking of?'

'I thought,' I said carefully, 'that you looked like a poet.'

And I thought you looked beautiful. And all the strange stirrings, all the fearful desires that had hovered over me since I stopped being a child converged on me, filling me with shame and ecstasy. But the mists lifted, the uncertainties disappeared, and there was only one certainty—you.

'But, I could not understand what you said.'

He smiled again and I felt as if the waves of the sea, warm and playful and strong, were eddying over me.

'You don't know my language? But, sometimes I think it is good not to understand.'

But not to understand you?

'I see you don't agree. Well, what do you do?'

I told him.

'Ah! A student of literature. And is that why you are here . . . at this conference . . . hoping to serve literature by serving aging writers coffee?'

Aging? But you are not old. Your voice is young and strong. Your laughter . . . when you laugh as you are doing now . . . is like a boy's. But your eyes have a shadow in them. Fleeting, like the shadows cast by the scurrying white clouds on the sea. It comes over me, like a monstrous wave of sorrow, that I know nothing of your grief, of your joys. I know nothing.

'No? We never seem to agree.'

I am a reflection, an echo.

'Well, tell me why you are here.'

This is why I came. So that I could meet you here.

'Oh, just a jaunt.'

'That's what it is for all of us. And now you've seen what writers are. Ordinary human beings. Talking some sense and a lot of nonsense.'

I must say it now. If I don't . . . only this one chance. I will never have it again. And even now. I can see them standing there, debating whether to go on or return. Soon they will return and the present will be the past, and this episode a memory.

'I want you recite it to me now. One of your own poems.'

'Now? Here?' His eyebrows shot up like startled birds. If I could put my fingers there . . . and feel those birds gently alight on them!

'Yes.'

'You won't understand.'

'I can listen. And feel.'

I had never imagined that a man could have a voice like a musical instrument. That it could climb up like a bird soaring in the sky and then come down and stroke you like a caressing hand, so that the whole of you was one quiver. And now I know . . . that this is why I was born. So that I could stand here and listen to your voice rise against the murmur of the sea and the rustle of the palms.

I listened with an intensity that was like a taut string drawn between us. I willed him not to stop, not to let go the string. But he did. And the string did not break. Fiercely I blinked back tears.

'Did you understand? Shall I tell you the meaning?'

'No,' I said hurriedly.

There is only one meaning to everything that is being said now, to everything that is happening now. I need to know nothing more.

'Only tell me what it was about.'

'What do poets write of?'

'Death,' I said. 'And disappointment. And sorrow.'

He laughed and the wind flung his laughter in all directions. When, I thought jealously, I could have gathered it all to myself.

'Poets,' he said, 'take the whole of life. All its beauty and all its ugliness. All its meaning and all its futility. So do I.'

'And I cannot understand you,' I cried in bitter disappointment.

'Which is why the best poems are these. Which all can understand.'

He laid his hands lightly, caressingly, on the stone carving.

I have never noticed a man's hands before. Now . . . I wonder that the dumb stone creatures do not exclaim in rapture when you touch them like that.

'Songs sung in stone. And the eternal theme . . . a man and a woman.'

I looked at the carvings with a new consciousness. And I saw repeated again and again in the stone a man and a woman. The couples intertwined. The woman clinging to the man, unashamed and passionate. Suddenly my whole body began to throb with the realization of his nearness. I moved away and saw his eyes on me. I averted my eyes from the figures, ashamed of myself.

'The ancient Hindus,' he spoke softly, almost to himself, 'enjoyed the whole of life. They rejoiced in all of it, rejecting nothing. Creation to them was a wonder and a joy, not a shame and a secret. We have lost that childlike joy in ourselves. We can no more sing such songs of delight. We only whine and moan and make ugly sounds. Look at that woman.'

I looked. And I wondered how the man who had carved her had so understood a woman's desire to cling, to become part of her lover. Was she his beloved? Or, was she pure fantasy, the creation of a disappointed man's frenzied imagination? Whoever she was, she was I.

'It could be you,' he said, still speaking softly, putting his hands gently on my shoulders.

Now you are whispering to me with your hands, but I cannot reply. I am tongue-tied. I cannot speak this language either. Teach me, oh, teach me.

'You are very young,' he said abruptly, letting his hands drop from me.

Why do you say it like that? When I am near you, I am neither young nor old. I am ageless. I am a woman. And you are a man. And perhaps the man who carved these, centuries ago, saw us in a dream and put us here. For we are one of these couples too. We are a dream as well as a reality.

'I can still see the child in your face.'

Can you not see the woman?

'And I . . .'

Why do you say it like that? There is strength in your face and your hands and your body. And looking at you, I know for the first time that I am a woman And I want to prove it to you in the sight of these couples staring stonily at us. My body is eager for you. And fearful.

'How many years between us?'

I look down at your feet and mine. So close. But the distances between us are vast. Your hands can touch me, but my thoughts can never touch you. For you I am a child with whom you are passing an idle moment. While to me . . . ?

'What is your name?'

I told him and he repeated it gently. And suddenly the distances between us dissolved and I knew why my parents had given me this name. So that this man could say it to me this way.

'A name as beautiful as you are.'

I felt as if I was carrying happiness in my bare hands. I had to be careful or it would seep through like water, leaving nothing behind, not even a fragrance.

'When I think of this conference, I will remember this . . .' he looked around him, 'and you.'

This was farewell. But there was no sorrow in me. Instead, happiness surged into me like the waves now rushing heedlessly on to the sand.

'But you will forget. The young forget soon enough.'

I thought of the men who had carved these figures, chipping away patiently at the hard rocks, creating for eternity images that had existed only in their minds. And you . . . you do not know it, but you are like them, creating, within me, an image of yourself. An image neither the sun nor wind nor sea can harm.

'You shake your head, but you will forget. That's how it is.'

I will never see a man again but I will set him against you and find him wanting. You have spoilt me for all men forever.

'I will never forget.'

Why do you look at me like that, forgetting to take away your eyes from my face? I cannot endure that look for long. It raises a tumult within me that frightens me.

Suddenly he straightened, took his eyes away from my face and held out his hand. 'This is for you . . . to remember me by.'

And he was gone. Once I had gone up in a giant wheel and there had been that moment of exquisite terror and happiness when I had been poised on top, on top of the world. I felt the same now as I clutched the flower in my hands. I felt weighed down by too much happiness and sat down on the sand, my hands clasping my knees, my head laid on them. The tumult had died down. There was a perfect stillness within and without. I held the whole world at bay and lived those few minutes over again.

But it could not last. Steps and voices intruded into my world. They were back. So short a time, I marvelled, just enough for them to take a little stroll. But for me it had been a whole lifetime. Spaces, greater than the sea, lay between me and that moment when I had stood here and gazed at him. I wanted desperately to be alone. If they speak to me, I thought with horror, I will burst into tears. But I could not run away. Clutching the flower convulsively in my hand I tried to compose myself.

'Not feeling well?'

'I'm all right.'

'You seem to be brooding.'

'Just lazing.'

'Oh! I thought perhaps the old man said something to upset you.'

Old man? I looked up.

'I saw him talking to you,' the voice went on.

'That one? Isn't he too old to be dangerous?' the speaker giggled.

'Too old?' What scorn in the voice. 'Don't you know his reputation? He has a daughter my age. But he's always after girls. Yesterday . . .' a sudden giggle. How foolish she looks.

'What happened? Come on, tell us.'

'He came to me in the coffee break. And, so fatherly and poetic, wanted to know all about me. And after some time, he began . . . you know.'

'What? Tell us.'

'Patting me . . . oh, very fatherly. But . . . my God! He was talking very innocently all right. But his hands! Anyway, I got out fast.'

Laughter. And more laughter. My hand with the flower in it dug deeper and deeper into the sand.

'Well, let's go. I can see the bus waiting. Aren't you coming? Going to sit there the whole day?'

'No, I'm coming.'

I brought my hand out of the sand. Empty. We walked away. We had gone a long way when I looked back. An hour, I thought. Or even less than that. And the sea will have buried that spot. And no one will know a song is buried there.